SPELLS IN REVENGE

Michaela L Cane

A HellBound Books Publishing LLC Book
Austin TX

**A HellBound Books LLC
Publication**
Copyright © 2022 by HellBound Books Publishing LLC
All Rights Reserved

Cover and art design by
HellBound Books Publishing LLC

www.hellboundbookspublishing.com

Printed in the United States of America

Michaela Cane

Michaela Cane

SPELLS
IN
REVENGE

Chapter 1

When the ambulance doors slammed shut, it took Adrienne another few seconds to look away from their small windows. Those expressions on the faces of Josh and David, which the doors had just shut out—she only wished she had a lover or family who'd focus on her like that. Her Raul had stood by jealously, sure enough, but only out of annoyance that she'd offered to accompany Lauren to the hospital.

The impulse wasn't entirely selfless, no matter how appreciative David and his partner had been. This was an easy way to escape her husband while also supporting the woman who'd helped get them out of this mess. It gave her an out, and the hospital would offer enough chaos that, with any luck, Raul wouldn't have a chance of tracking her down before she'd already disappeared. Where to, she'd figure out later, but the fact that Christopher and Lauren had both signaled they'd help was enough to give her the confidence that it would happen.

After everything that had happened at this center, it was almost hard to believe they were finally leaving—not to mention how this whole thing had unraveled. The fact that David and Lauren had been plants working for the government? She'd been stunned, and she couldn't claim to understand half of the conversations she'd been hearing since their team had stormed in. Just that morning, she'd been sitting in yet another useless therapy session, and now, hours later... fuck, but it might be days before she processed it all.

Settling back into her pull-down seat, she buckled her seatbelt and watched the paramedic fussing over her friend. The pain medication they'd offered for Lauren's burns had knocked her out again, but she looked to be resting easy. Her hands were still curled up loosely, as if she might stretch out her arms for a piano and play, and she was pale as could be, but they'd been assured that her vitals were good. Lauren might be burned—oddly, truly oddly since Adrienne still couldn't figure out how the burns might have happened outside of the girl pressing her hands to a hot stove—and she was certainly dehydrated, but she'd be fine in short order. It was good that she was sleeping, too; Josh had warned her that Lauren was deathly afraid of hospitals, promising he and David would be there as soon as possible. The paramedic had herself promised that the pain medication would take the edge off, but Adrienne had seen the guarded look on Josh's face. She guessed Lauren's phobia was more serious than the average case of nerves.

The young paramedic adjusted the IV hanging beside Lauren and then leaned back in her own seat, her eyes already coming up to meet Adrienne's. "You want something to slow your heart rate down?"

What an odd way to say that. Adrienne stared at her for a moment, but finally shook her head. After everything she'd been through, the last thing she needed was drugs. And wouldn't Raul love that—to come to the hospital and be able to play savior if he found her as out of it as Lauren was now. No, there wasn't a chance in hell she'd allow for that to happen. "I'm fine. It's just been a wild morning."

The woman sitting across from her quirked an eyebrow, inviting the story, but Adrienne remained silent. She didn't really know what had happened herself. No way was she going to try to explain it to a nosy woman who she'd never see again, soon enough.

"Water?" the paramedic offered. "My name is Evie, by the way. Adrienne, was it?"

"A bottle of water would be great if you've got one," she admitted.

The other woman finished pulling her curls into a loose bun at the back of her neck and then leaned sideways to rummage in a small cooler.

Taking a water bottle from her, Adrienne nodded in thanks and gave the woman a more careful look. She appeared young—really young, now that she had her hair tied back. "How long have you been a paramedic?" Adrienne asked before she took a deep swig of the water.

The girl smirked. "I look awful young, don't I?"

Tension broken, Adrienne laughed aloud and relaxed another beat or two down from the adrenaline she'd been running on. "No offense," Adrienne told her, sipping down more of the water.

"None taken. You want to make sure your friend's in good hands. And you're right—I've only been doing this six months, but I know what I'm doing."

As if to call her own words into question, though, the woman just sat there. She didn't attempt to examine Lauren's burns, keep tabs on her vitals, or even communicate with the driver. Between them, Lauren's breath came slow and steady, but the injuries spoke for themselves, and it couldn't be a short car ride to the nearest hospital, given how long it had taken them to bus out to the center. What was the woman waiting for?

Adrienne reached out and brushed Lauren's stringy black hair from her face, noticing that it was still damp with sweat. Her skin was clammy, too, and Adrienne had to stop herself from bringing her palm to the younger woman's forehead. They were in an ambulance on the way to the hospital, and Lauren was so warm that there wasn't much doubt she had a fever. Adrienne raised her eyebrows at the paramedic, but the woman didn't seem to be taking the cue. She watched her observing Lauren for a few seconds more, sipped at her water again, and finally asked, "You're not going to do anything about her burns? Her fever? Do you guys keep cold compresses, maybe, or is there something else we can do for her?"

Instead of answering, the young woman only caught Adrienne's gaze and sat there as if waiting. Unnerved, Adrienne gulped down what was left of her water and then looked back to her unconscious friend, whose breath seemed slower than before, but still even. And then she shook herself away from the thought. The center and Shea's sessions had truly made her paranoid, she realized. Of course, this paramedic knew what she was doing. The hospital had put her in an ambulance and sent her off to an emergency scene, hadn't it?

Adrienne's vision blurred, then doubled, and her stomach lurched so that she had to grip the seat beneath her for purchase. When that didn't help, she reached one hand out to Lauren's gurney and clutched at the cool metal. But that seemed to be as shifty as her own seat, and she felt bile rising in her throat.

She blinked. Motion sickness? She never got motion sick. Never.

"I think," she began, stumbling for words, "I think maybe… I'm in shock?" she asked. "Is that it?"

She closed her eyes, attempting to remember what Josh had asked her earlier, in trying to determine if she'd been in shock then—that was what he'd been worried about, right? She'd been distracted by that scar on his cheek, and how its roughness hadn't at all matched the concern in his voice. Or maybe he'd been asking David questions….

Adrienne leaned forward and put her head in her hands, her elbows on her knees. "I feel sick," she muttered. With her eyes closed against the sensations she felt running through her, she sensed more than saw the paramedic shuffling around to her side of Lauren's gurney, but couldn't bring herself to look up. Maybe the woman would get her a cool cloth—that was what she wanted. And then, perhaps, she could lay down when they got to the hospital. They'd be there soon, she told herself, but she couldn't seem to remember how long they'd been on the road. When she did open her eyes, she saw six grey ballet flats where there should only have been her two.

"You've had some shocks, Adrienne," the paramedic told her, some new and more formal tone having come to her voice. "But I'll take care of you."

Adrienne thought to say thank you, but her tongue was too thick. She tried glancing sideways, and saw six hands preparing three blurry hypodermics. I don't want anything. But the words weren't coming to her lips. Vaguely, she heard a mumble, and couldn't be sure whether it was herself or Lauren making the sound.

A haze of panic slipped through her, building, and she fumbled for her phone before remembering that she hadn't carried a phone in weeks, not since she and Raul had landed at the center to begin with. Her head got heavier with the thought, her breath becoming labored, and she looked back down to her multiplying feet and closed her eyes.

By the time Evie rolled her sleeve up and the injection found her skin, Adrienne was almost thankful for the excuse to pass out.

***

Nell pulled the ambulance into the big-box shopping center on the edge of the city, two full hours having passed since she and Evie had collected Lauren and Adrienne. That was nearly an hour's time behind the schedule they'd hoped to keep, but what they'd gained was well worth the delay.

The ambulance hadn't just been wiped clean. Once she and Evie had finished with the back, they'd felt sure it was cleaner than it had been right off the assembly line. Fredricks and Devlin might well suspect she'd been involved in the kidnapping, but they'd have no way to prove it, and that would split their resources. Particularly with this friend of Lauren's involved, they'd be forced to consider that angle, as well. Nell parked toward the middle of the lot and did one last visual sweep of the front seat after she wiped it down. They were leaving nothing behind, and the security camera recording the inside of the vehicle had long since been disabled. As soon as she slammed shut the driver's side door, Nell dropped the keys by the front wheel and headed toward Evie's SUV, which sat idling at the end of the row. Already, Nell was peeling the latex gloves from her fingers, and she stuffed them in a pocket before opening the passenger door to Evie's Kia Soul.

A glance backward confirmed that Lauren and her friend remained out cold.

"All good?"

"All good," Nell confirmed. "Let's go."

While Evie drove, Nell wriggled out of the paramedic's get-up and wig she'd worn all day, thankful for the tinted windows on the vehicle. Using her heel to cram the discarded costume into the space beneath the glove compartment, she squirmed into the jeans and t-shirt she'd left waiting on the floorboards and allowed herself a breath of relief that the morning chores were done. The danger, at this point, was well past. And while this vehicle might be smaller than was strictly convenient, the tinted windows and the unsuspicious size weren't a bad trade-off for the lack of storage.

When she'd finger-brushed her red hair and gotten her boots back on, she eyed Evie. The younger witch had done well, all things considered, and her absurdly young appearance had probably worked to their advantage in the end, staving off any potential suspicion of threat when it had come to their commandeering the ambulance. Her perkiness wore on Nell's nerves at times, but youth could be convenient. It was a reminder to her that she needed to re-dye her own hair sooner than later, and get rid of the grey creeping in if she wanted to stand up in appearance to the younger witches. "You good to drive for a while if I get some beauty sleep?"

"Hundred percent. I'm so high on adrenaline, I could get us all the way there."

Nell nodded, but waited until Evie was coming up on the highway on-ramp before giving herself real permission for the break in awareness. "Wake me up if you see anything out of place or either of them gets antsy."

"Fat chance of that, Nell. They've got enough tranq in 'em to keep 'em asleep for the duration. And those agents? They didn't suspect a thing. You ask me, we're in the clear."

Considering how things had gone, Nell agreed, and a smile tilted her lips as she let the seat back and closed her eyes. "Perfect, then. Drive on, dear girl."

Chapter 2

Josh Devlin didn't know what thick-headed agent had given Raul Rivers his number at the scene, but he planned to find them and give them an ear-full as soon as time permitted. He was hanging up on the blowhard for a third time when he finally managed to wave down the nurse he'd spoken to earlier.

When she saw him, though, her face went red and she did an about-face on her heels. He stood stunned for a full second before hurrying to catch up with her.

Reaching the nurse's station midway down the ER's hall of exam rooms, he found her talking a mile a minute to a scowling doctor who immediately looked his way. Josh didn't bother holding out his badge—it was clear enough they were talking about him.

"Sir. Uh, Agent Devlin," the doctor said, speaking over the nurse and stepping around her as he gave a quick glance to the clipboard in his hand. "I understand you're inquiring about Ambulance 568. We believe they must have diverted to another hospital, but we're working on—"

"Why?" Josh cut him off, looking between the doctor and the nurses at the nearby station, all of whom seemed to be doing their best to not appear to be listening, but clearly were.

"I'm sorry?"

Josh fought the urge to raise his voice. "We were told they'd be coming here. Why would they have been diverted?"

The doctor looked annoyed, then embarrassed. "I'm sure I don't know, and they don't seem to be answering their radio, but we'll have an answer as soon as possible. These things happen more than you'd think; someone could have requested the change or they might have expected us to be busier here than we were. Now, I'm guessing they're on break, considering how long it's been since your friend was picked up. If you'll go back to your partner, we'll be sure to tell you what we can when we can. But I'm afraid you'll have to be patient."

The doctor was gone before Josh could decide to argue, let alone explain that telling someone to be calm was the last thing which would help calm prevail. Instead, Josh caught the eye of one of the few nurses he hadn't yet spoken to as she passed by. "What's the other hospital nearest to Goodreau?"

"Main Street Mercy," she answered without stopping.

He'd just pulled up the number when he noticed three agents moving through the admit doors. They'd been at the scene when he'd left, though he couldn't recall their names.

"Agent Devlin!" one of them called, speeding up slightly.

Josh gave his phone a glance, and then pocketed it.

"What do you need?" he asked, meeting the agents halfway. Up close, he noticed that the youngest of them was wide-eyed and nervous, the other two somber. Like they were carrying some news they'd rather have avoided. "What is it?" he repeated as they ushered him sideways into an empty exam room.

"We found the paramedics on the side of Lane's Highway—about five miles from the center, near the freeway. They were the ones assigned to the first ambulance that left the scene; the one carrying your undercover agent, as we understand it."

Josh glanced between them. "Are you saying there was an accident? Is Lauren okay? And the woman who was with her—uh, Adrienne Rivers?"

The senior agent among them coughed, and then he shrugged. "That's just it. There was no accident as far as we can tell. The paramedics were tied up, two of them stripped down to their underwear—someone took their uniforms and their rig, and we believe it must have happened before they ever came for the pick-up, but they claim not to remember anything. We're proceeding on the assumption that we're dealing with a kidnapping; we've got another agent outside alerting your supervisor since there's an agent involved, but we need to know everything you can tell us about the two women you put in that ambulance today."

Josh stared, praying for a punchline to a bad joke, but the agents were stoic and blank-faced now, waiting on him to react.

"Gimme five minutes," he muttered, pushing between them and out the door. He barely registered the protests sounding behind him as he sprinted down the hall and crashed fists-first into David's room. A nurse was busy wrapping his partner's ribs and batting her eyelashes.

"We need the room," he announced, gripping her by the arm and all but shoving her out into the hall. When they were alone, he turned his back to the door and stared at his partner, trying to convince himself there'd been a mistake and that there was no need for this conversation. The faces of the agents he'd just spoken to had said otherwise, though, and the fact that the ambulance hadn't arrived at the hospital couldn't be chalked up to a simple annoyance at this point. The women hadn't checked out before he and David had arrived, as Josh had first guessed, and they weren't here. They probably weren't at the hospital he'd been about to phone, either.

David was on his feet now, finishing up with the remaining bandages.

"Tell me you didn't let her use her magic," Josh said quietly, mindful that anyone could be walking by the room, which only had a curtain for a door.

His partner froze, then looked up. The expression on his face was answer enough. "We didn't have any choice—that's how we got out, I told you," David answered. "I never would have been able to make that call to you, otherwise. What's wrong?"

Josh looked away from his partner's face and fell into a chair by the door, going over the morning in his mind. But the timeline didn't fit. Between Lauren growing those vines and the paramedics getting to the center, there was no way the remains of the coven would have had time to mobilize and get there if she'd just used magic that morning. It wasn't possible. The place was virtually in the middle of nowhere. He looked back up, still going over the timeline and telling himself there could have been some mistake. "Before this morning?" he pressed. "She didn't use it before this morning?"

David had come closer, and stood looking down at him with a frown on his face. "I'm not sure. I don't think she was using it…but it was being drawn out of her. I don't know for how long, exactly, but that's what they were doing there. Adrias catch wind of it? That she's still got some juice left?"

Josh looked from his partner down to the floor, doing his best to slow his breathing and think through next steps. The first of them being how he'd break it to David that the coven hadn't just caught up to them, but had managed to take Lauren right out of their hands.

He and his partner had even waved her goodbye.

***

The rig stank of antiseptic and bleach, and Josh knew before he stepped inside that there'd be no evidence worth collecting. They'd look, but he couldn't imagine they'd find any DNA or prints belonging to anyone but Lauren and Adrienne. He shone his light along the gurney and the seat that Adrienne had occupied when they'd left the center. Pristine. No blood or fluids, which was something.

DNA or not, you know who took her.

The voice in his head was on repeat as he played his light around and popped open various drawers before moving to the front seat and searching there. Supplies had been cleaned out entirely, and there wasn't even any trash to be found. He was surprised they hadn't taken the fucking gurney.

"We already took what prints there were!" an agent called from behind him.

Josh nodded, and then got out of the rig and went around to the front, where he leaned in to peer under the front seat. Nothing.

"Dash cam was disabled, like I said, but we've got an agent scanning this parking lot's cameras in case they caught anything. One at the entrance was taken out, so whoever dropped the ambulance here planned ahead, but they could have missed one and passed too close."

Nodding absently, Josh stepped back and eyed the rig. He should have known not to bother coming out here, but what else was he supposed to be doing? This was the only lead. "And the last upload from the ambulance's camera?" he asked.

"Only the inside camera was on—the one that should have showed us the road hadn't been working for a while, it turns out. Dumb luck. What we've got shows the rig stopping on the road where we found the paramedics. Something must have been staged. They stopped fast. Visual only, but it looks like something they saw on the road cut them off mid-conversation. All three got out—against protocol for an unscheduled stop, but you know how it is for those medical first responders. They don't have a cop's training for safety, so it's instinct over anything. After they got out, there was a minute or so of empty seats before the film cut out." The guy paused, and he coughed awkwardly before he continued, "Sorry we don't have more. I hear the missing agent's a friend of yours."

Josh waved off the sympathies and headed back to his car. Hearing others reference Lauren being an agent was getting to him. Only he, David, Barry, and Adrias knew the truth—or who might have been behind this—and there was no point in giving any of that knowledge away unless they had to. Nell and Johanna were wholly off the grid and already on the Most Wanted List since killing the agents who'd accompanied David to the farmhouse, back on the raid where he'd been captured by the coven. It wasn't like adding a kidnapping to the list of murders would up the urgency of the search.

In the privacy of his car, he ignored notifications of missed calls from Raul and Claudia, and he called David instead. Later, he'd owe Claudia a million apologies and a few dozen roses for missing their date that night, but he'd have to figure out what to tell her about Lauren before he could get to that point. She'd been disgusted with the fact that he and David had allowed Lauren to go undercover at all, and although he himself hadn't fought the plan, it was clear she'd been right.

"Anything in the rig?" David asked upon picking up.

"Nada. What's Barry got?"

Josh heard a thud—his partner hitting something, he guessed, and that predicted the answer.

"Nothing yet. It's not like they were tracking her non-stop—why would they, when she was with me all along, right?" A dark laugh sounded over the line, and Josh winced. He'd hoped it would take longer for David to turn the blame on himself. "So, we gotta go through the whole fucking tracking process all over again," his partner continued. "Just like before. And since they've been focusing resources on expanding the system and getting more tattoos in place for our undercovers, it hasn't gotten faster. Barry says it might be another week before we get a hit."

There was noise in the background, and Josh heard his partner muttering to someone. Barry, he guessed. When David announced he was back on the line, Josh had to force his own voice to begin working again. "We found you guys through her tattoo before. We'll find Lauren again," he promised, his eyes going unfocused on the team that was locking up the rig and packing up their gear.

The line clicked, and Josh realized his partner had hung up on him. It appeared they'd both had enough of empty promises and apologies.

Chapter 3

It took her two hours.

Two hours to explain who she was, who David was, who Nell and Johanna were, and how it was that things had ended up where they were. Two hours to sum it all up, answer Adrienne's confused questions, and apologize—over and over again—for getting the other woman entangled in whatever Nell and Johanna had planned. Two hours to explain that witches and magic were indeed real, along with the monsters they'd met at the center and whatever else Adrienne could probably imagine might be, and to tell Adrienne what she could without actually panicking either of them. Because it was Nell who was behind their kidnapping, if there'd have been any doubt.

Lauren had seen her upon awakening in this little room, opening her eyes and catching a glimpse just as Nell and the so-called paramedic they'd met had been heading out the door. How much time had passed since they'd left the center, she didn't know, but the ache in her stomach suggested that some real time had passed. Her stomach felt like she hadn't eaten in days, in fact, and she wondered if that was true.

There were no windows in this room. There was a bunkbed with a double bed on the bottom level and a twin on the top, a dresser, and a basket of bottled water. On top of the dresser sat burn salve, bandages, and safety pins for fastening them. Adrienne had spent the beginning of Lauren's story treating and then wrapping her palms and wrists, making use of all of the supplies they'd been left. Now, she was retching in the bathroom attached to the room, and Lauren didn't blame her. She wanted to throw up, as well.

"So…" Adrienne began, coming back and leaning against the doorframe of the bathroom. "You're not married. And not FBI—"

"David's not FBI, either," Lauren corrected her softly. "But he works for the government."

"Right. He's with some shadowy government organization you don't know the name of."

Lauren shrugged in embarrassment. Not that it really mattered, but why hadn't she ever asked?

"And you're a witch. An actual witch with magic—at least when you're around David, because of some spell that connects the two of you even though he and his secret government buddies tried to steal your magic—and magic is how you got those burns on your hands and got to the roof."

Lauren nodded, watching the other woman as she crossed the room to retrieve a bottle of water and then began pacing as she unscrewed the cap and took a sip. Lauren had drunk some earlier, explaining that she saw no reason for the witches to have drugged this water like they had what had been in the ambulance, and apparently Adrienne had come to agree with her. As if they had many options about what to drink at this point.

"And the therapists at the center were… not human?" Adrienne tried.

Another nod, which was all Lauren could offer since she wasn't exactly sure what they'd been. When it came to supernatural beings that weren't witches, she guessed David knew more than she did. Hell, he might know more about witches than she did, considering how much she'd separated herself from her mother and the coven over the years. She'd correct all that if she ever got the chance, which now seemed doubtful.

Adrienne sat cross-legged on the floor and leaned up against the dresser, closing her eyes and taking a deep breath. Lauren only watched, expecting more questions. The other woman was taking it surprisingly well, but she guessed they were both still processing the drugs out of their systems, operating in something of a fog. Adrienne's pretty brown eyes had a heaviness to them, and Lauren assumed her own eyes showed the same fatigue. She leaned sideways on the bed, half-reclining on the pillow beside her.

"And your tattoo is magic, and David can trace it, somehow?"

Lauren traced her bandaged hand along what showed of the vinework, the ink on her forearm being one of the few things she felt confidence in at the moment. "Not magic. It's got a rare metal in the ink—David's office developed the technology, and they can trace it. It'll just maybe take time." She wondered again if Nell and Johanna would have bugged the room, but didn't see how the knowledge would help them now if they hadn't already been prepared. And besides that, it was too late; she'd mentioned the tattoo's properties before the possibility of a bug had occurred to her, so she might as well rationalize the slip. One more pretty lie to make herself feel better, however slightly. Especially considering that she was almost sure Nell and Johanna must know about the tracking system.

She pushed the thought away, drinking down some water and trying to ignore the pangs of hunger in her stomach.

Adrienne looked at the ink doubtfully, and then met Lauren's gaze. "How long?"

"I don't know. A week? Two? It took close to two when… when they tested it," Lauren said carefully. No way was she admitting that she'd been kidnapped by these women before, as that would only make Adrienne question what had happened then. Lauren wasn't going there. "But that was a while ago. It's possible they've improved the tracking software since then. I just don't know."

Adrienne pressed the mouth of the water bottle to her lips as she thought. Her eyes came back to Lauren's. "But the witches here… they knew about the tattoo before?"

The lump in her throat had gotten bigger, but Lauren did her best to swallow it. She knew what Adrienne was thinking because she'd been thinking the same. If they knew about the tattoo and its tracking—which, deep down, she supposed they must, even if she couldn't quite know how that was possible—then they wouldn't have picked her up unless they had some way around it. Or unless their plans would be completed and done before time allowed for the tracking to happen. That was her more likely guess.

"I don't know. We thought…" Lauren broke off, trying to think of what she could say, and then decided she owed the other woman the whole truth on this, at least. "I didn't tell you everything. Before we were at the center, I was in protective custody at David's home because of what had already happened. When David and Josh were on a raid to try to track down the rest of the coven, the witches killed some agents and took David hostage. They wanted a trade-off—me for him, but they didn't let him go after they had me. I don't even know what their plan was because Josh found us before... before they did whatever they were planning to do. But since Josh and that team found us, tracked us, Nell and Johanna have to know that that happened somehow. They have to know tracking was involved, and they would have found any tech. So, I mean, I don't know if they connected the team finding us to the tattoo, but... well, it seems like they would have, yeah."

Adrienne had gone silent and still. Her hand reached out and swept down Lauren's tattoo as if making sure it was real before she commented, "Jesus, you guys have been through a lot. What the fuck do these bitches want?"

Lauren's mind went back to the letter she'd received at her old apartment. It seemed like a lifetime ago. And even when she'd seen the witches last, she'd gotten the impression that things had changed. Now, with Johanna and Nell the only ones remaining, she couldn't imagine they'd want anything but revenge, but she couldn't tell Adrienne that.

She shrugged for what felt like the millionth time. "Maybe they'll tell us when they come back. I'm still hoping for dinner," she added—meaning the words to come out as a joke, although they didn't.

Adrienne glanced to the clock, which read ten o'clock. "Well, it's either way too early for dinner or a bit too late. I think I'm going to get a shower and pass out. You look like you need more rest, too."

Falling all the way back into the pillow, Lauren grunted agreement. "The drugs must still be in our systems. I know we slept, but I'm still exhausted."

"Yeah. You want the bathroom first, before I shower?"

Lauren yawned and waved the other woman off. Her eyes were closed even before the shower turned on, her thoughts on David and what he must be thinking. She hoped, if nothing else, that he was with Josh, and that the witches hadn't somehow gotten to him, as well.

***

Lauren woke to the sound of nothing.

She'd expected to be woken up by Nell or Johanna coming in, or for that other woman who'd posed as a paramedic to make an appearance, but she'd slept soundly all night. She'd only woken briefly when Adrienne had come out of the bathroom and climbed up to the top bunk, the two of them having decided before that Lauren would take the bottom bunk so that she could avoid using her hands to climb. She'd thought, surely, that they'd be woken in the middle of the night, but a glance at the clock on the nightstand, dimly lit by the lamp they'd left burning there, suggested that ten hours had passed without interruption.

Mid-morning, or maybe night. At least twenty-four hours since we left the center. What are they waiting for?

"Adrienne?" she asked softly.

The mattress above squeaked with her friend's shifting, and Lauren breathed out a small sigh. Sorry as she was to have gotten the other woman dragged into this, she felt glad she wasn't alone.

Sitting up, she used her teeth to test the edge of the bandage on her left hand. There was still a dull ache to her palm, but no redness showed from around the edges of the bandage anymore, and she didn't feel any real sting in the skin that her teeth made contact with. So, she was healing already. That was a good sign, at least.

Her eyes made their way around the room, hoping for some package of food that might have been dropped off overnight, but everything appeared to be just as they'd left it the night before—until her eyes landed on the floor by the door.

A sheet of paper had been slid underneath and escaped her notice in the dim light.

She crossed the room and crouched down in the span of a heartbeat, but the handwriting was undecipherable without more light. She flicked the main light switch with her elbow, barely aware of the grunt of protest Adrienne let out behind her.

The note was face-up, and she didn't even have to crouch down to read it.

> *We need to talk.*
> *Plan for a friendly dinner and talk of a truce.*
> *Do keep an open mind, and we'll see you at 5.*

"Is the door still locked?"

Lauren jumped at the sound of Adrienne's voice. She hadn't noticed the other woman climbing down and coming up behind her. Now, she glanced at the doorknob and shrugged. She hadn't tried it.

Adrienne did, and then cursed under her breath when it wouldn't turn. "Some truce if they're keeping us locked up and starving."

Lauren's eyes went back to the note. "If they don't feed us till then, they know we'll cooperate just for a meal."

"How are your hands, hon?"

"Better. You mind helping me undo the bandages so we can take a look?"

Adrienne leaned back on the wall with Lauren in front of her, unhooking the safety pins and then unwinding the bandages. True to Lauren's guess, the angry burns had faded overnight. Some red remained, but they'd healed unnaturally fast already.

Adrienne drew her over to the bedside lamp and angled her palms up beneath it. "Impressive. Magic?"

"Enh… kind of, but not really," Lauren replied, trying not to think of how much energy her body would have used up for this bit of healing. No matter how little energy it had been, it had been energy she and Adrienne might have put to better use. "It was my magic that burned me, which means I was faster to heal. If someone else had burned me, it wouldn't have been this simple." Lauren stretched her hands, curling and uncurling her fingers. She could feel the burn, and the soreness ran deep, but it was nothing compared to what she'd felt the night before. Just like a slight sunburn, if anything. "I might ask you to help me with more salve after I use the bathroom and grab a shower?"

"Sure thing. Nothing else to do."

In the bathroom, though, another surprise greeted Lauren. Fresh clothes for her and Adrienne both, along with still-wrapped toothbrushes, hairbrushes, and a plastic bag full of assorted soaps and shampoos. Lauren fingered the clothes. They were soft—designer-expensive, she was willing to bet.

Without question, the witches were playing nice. Lauren just couldn't imagine why.

Chapter 4

The witch who'd played a paramedic for their benefit was the one who came to the door to escort them to dinner. She looked no older than twenty, but out of the uniform she'd worn before, there was a presence to her that reminded Lauren of Nell's. Deceptively friendly and playful, but in a fashion that suggested hyenas more so than kittens. The girl stood back in the hall, flipped her shiny blond hair, and introduced herself as Evie. Then, she turned, clearly expecting them to follow.

Adrienne had her lips pressed shut—to keep from cursing at the woman, Lauren guessed—but didn't argue when Lauren took the lead in following after her. Both of them were starving, and short of going on a hunger strike, there was no real choice here. The hallway they followed was utilitarian, and although Lauren had half-expected they'd find themselves in a warehouse like the one she and David had been held in, this place had the feel of an office building. Built of cheap carpet and glaringly white walls and ceilings. Pocket lighting and no decorations to speak of made it feel like a new-build without either character or warmth.

They'd seen no windows or exit signs when Evie opened up a glass door and gestured them inside. Lauren stopped in the doorway, her blood stalling in her veins for a moment now that she was being confronted with the witches who'd been haunting her nightmares for months. Both Johanna and Nell were dressed in expensive-looking casual wear, seated at a table for four. They looked like spoiled, waspish housewives, the room around them decorated and set up like a fancy dining room for their leisure. Nell's red hair nearly glowed in the lighting, and her plum lipstick gave her the look of a vamp out to seduce a rich and very married man. Beside her, Johanna's dark hair was long and curled; nearly as dark as Adrienne's black hair, it blended into the woman's black sweater. Unlike Nell, she wore no make-up, and her eyes were slitted as thin as her mouth as she gave them a once-over.

When Johanna nodded expectantly at the empty seats in front of them, Lauren forced herself forward, thankful for the sound of Adrienne's footsteps just behind her.

Nell's green eyes shone at them. "Sit down, Lauren, and… Adrienne, Evie said?"

Adrienne nodded, sitting down beside the witch as Lauren took the seat beside Johanna. "And you're Nell and Johanna, I'm guessing. Kidnappers extraordinaire."

Johanna reached to the middle of the table and uncovered a dish. "Adrienne, I like you. Here, hold out your plate."

Adrienne did as instructed, and Johanna began dishing up lasagna as Nell portioned salad out into bowls. Johanna took that as her cue to start rambling on about the recipe being a family affair as Evie re-entered to pour wine and water into glasses set before all of the place settings. Lauren traded a glance with Adrienne, trying to assure herself this was real.

Nell took a sip of wine first, gesturing for Lauren to follow suit. "Eat up, girls, and drink, too. It's not poisoned. You must be starving."

Lauren cut into the lasagna, which smelled amazing. Johanna and Nell were already lifting their forks to their mouths. "What about Evie?"

"Evie—and our other new coven member, Sarah—you'll meet at length later on. I thought just the four of us could get on the same page tonight. But let's eat before we delve into the details of the future, shall we?" Nell offered a surprisingly genuine-looking smile, and then began eating her salad.

Accepting Nell's words for what they were, Lauren focused on her food. Johanna and Nell exchanged comments about some movie they'd watched and recipes as if this were all a casual get-together between friends, and Lauren shut out the unreality of it, enjoying the meal. It was better than anything she'd had since last enjoying Josh's cooking at the ranch house, and since they'd all been served from the same dishes, she harbored no worry that there was some secret poison waiting to work on their blood. When Adrienne served both of them another helping of salad and pasta, Lauren poured the two of them more wine, as well. Whatever was coming, the alcohol wouldn't hurt. Adrienne raised her eyebrows as if to ask, but Lauren shook her head in an attempt to communicate that it just didn't matter. The women they were sitting with had an abundance of spells at their disposal; fighting or running wasn't an option, so Lauren saw no reason to stay on her toes for the potential of either.

Almost immediately upon entering the room, she'd decided she'd rather be comfortably numb.

As the meal wound down, Lauren wondered what David would have said, seeing the scene. It looked so domestic, so easy. Beside her, Adrienne had adopted an uneasy smile that was plastered to her lips; not unlike the smile that she'd so often held in place for her horrid husband, Lauren thought.

Johanna took the last sip of her wine and then looked around the table. "Everyone done? Good, then. Lauren, Adrienne, if you would?"

This time, Adrienne took the lead in heading out the door after Johanna, and Lauren followed behind her with Nell on their heels. Out in the hall, they entered a simple stairwell and headed downward, passing white wall after white wall in what felt like a fire escape. At the bottom of the stairwell, Johanna held the door and ushered them forward. On the other side, they found themselves in a large, dimly lit space that might have been meant to serve as a lobby area, if Lauren's guess of this being an office building had been correct. Instead, wall sconces offered an easy light, and a casting circle was set up in one corner, with floor mats and pillows surrounding a central arrangement of bowls and stones. The different walls were in some cases tiled white and in others painted in dark shades that did odd things to the space. On the other side of the room was a large sectional, which Johanna gestured them toward. No other options in sight, Lauren and Adrienne sat together along one L of the couch. The fabric was some expensive velveteen, a deep purple not too far off from the color of Nell's lipstick, and the wall behind it was painted a deep slate gray so that the area seemed to fade into the corners of the large space.

Lauren looked up and met Nell's eyes as the woman passed her a wine glass. "Sparkling grape juice to sip on," the witch offered. "Non-alcoholic while we talk business."

With Nell and Johanna lounging across from her and Adrienne, Lauren could almost imagine that was all this was, but the pretense was impossible to keep up. "The first business should be you letting Adrienne go," Lauren made herself tell them, ignoring the shift in cushions beneath her that told her Adrienne had just tensed in surprise. "She's got nothing to do with any of this."

Johanna's eyes didn't smile with her lips. "But she's your friend. You don't want a friend here?"

Nell kicked out her foot so that it knocked lightly into Johanna's shin. "Stop it, Jo." She set her eyes on Lauren, and then glanced over to Adrienne. Lauren's eyes followed her. The other woman looked on edge, but not like she wanted to flee, which was impressive enough. "Adrienne, let's put it to you. You felt the need to go with Lauren to the hospital, and you're an attractive woman who ought to be independent, surrounded by other attractive, independent women. Like us. What I've found online tells me your husband is a rich bastard and that you've got nothing holding you elsewhere. You went with him to that idiotic center, and I'm betting that means any real money or resources are in his name. We're about to invite Lauren to join our coven. What about you?"

Lauren's thoughts were frozen, working to catch up. At the same time as Adrienne asked what she meant, Lauren spoke up to remind them, "Your coven? Have you forgotten everything that's happened?"

Nell leaned forward toward them, and Lauren couldn't read the look on her face. "Lauren, what happened before was all because of Melania, and then the men you took up with. The spell Phillippa cast left you some power, and I've figured out how you can use it without staying tied to that agent's side. After he killed your mother—" Nell paused, reacting with a satisfied smirk to Adrienne's gasp. "Oh, you didn't know? That's right, he killed her mother, and other witches in our coven, along with his partner's help. And he tried to steal our girl Lauren's magic, but didn't quite manage it. Due to some red tape, you might say." Nell's eyes came back to Lauren's, and she reached out to clink glasses with the one resting in Lauren's hand untouched, though Lauren in no way moved to help with the gesture. "Jo and I are in as equal leaders. We've got Sarah and Evie, and other prospects we're considering to get us up to eight. But you and Adrienne are invited."

Beside her, Adrienne let out a strangled noise. "Invited? What are.... I'm not a… I'm not a witch, Nell. I didn't know they—you—existed until this week."

Johanna shrugged, taking over for Nell. "No matter. Everyone has some residual power. We can help you find it. In our old coven, we chose to work only with blood witches like Lauren and her mother. But now? Well, now, starting over, there's less reason or need to be quite so snobby as all that. You're Lauren's friend, and as a gesture of goodwill to her—peace-keeping and truce-making, shall we say—you're invited."

Lauren could feel Adrienne's shock vibrating in the air, it was so strong. But while this hadn't been what she herself had expected, it occurred to her that she shouldn't be surprised. Yes, Nell and Johanna would be focused on revenge, but on who? They'd see David and Josh as being at fault for the coven's fall. And now that they knew she had some remainder of magic, however slight—well, it was hard to find witches without covens. They'd want her for their new start, and what better revenge than to take her from David?

And maybe that meant she and Adrienne could get out of this, after all.

"Adrienne?" she asked. "What are you thinking?" She looked sideways to see the shock on her friend's face.

The woman shook her head, opening and then closing her mouth without saying anything. When she did, she stumbled over her words. "I… I'm not going back to my husband. Beyond that, I don't know what the hell I'm thinking. But leaving you alone now doesn't seem right, I know that. And then, this, witchcraft. Lauren—"

Jo stood abruptly, and held out her hand to Adrienne. "Walk with me. Give these two some time to talk over burying old wounds, and I'll tell you what you might be signing up for. Then, the two of you can go back to your room—for now, and we'll talk over nicer accommodations once things are more settled and we know your minds without doubt, of course—and there you can sleep on your decision. Come on, it's fine."

Adrienne stood, slowly, and Lauren shrugged at her. She didn't know what to think, beyond the fact that this perhaps gave them more time for the agents to come find them. But she couldn't exactly say that right now.

"And what if I don't?" Adrienne asked. "Don't want to join this… coven?"

Jo smiled, finally, but Lauren couldn't read what the expression meant. "Then that's your decision, my love. And you can stay here for a bit with Lauren or we'll take you back to where you came from."

Belatedly, Adrienne nodded, and then she bent down to give Lauren a quick hug before following Jo off toward another corner of the room, where Lauren could see a hallway leading off of the main space. When the other women had disappeared, Lauren looked back to Nell, who wore the satisfied smirk of a lioness just finished her hunting.

"What does she know of you and David? Your magic?" Nell asked.

"Less than you," Lauren admitted. She took a sip of the sparkling wine, and tasted only the crisp fruitiness of a carbonated juice. No alcohol, as the witch had said. "She knows David tried to take it away, and that it's still there when I'm around him. Some." Lauren forced herself to meet Nell's gaze. "And you know he's where it comes from—the connection I have with him keeps it going, to the extent that it does. So, what is this? Is he hidden in some room upstairs?"

"You'd like that, wouldn't you?" Nell replied, the smile leaving her lips.

Blushing, Lauren tried to still her blood, and her thoughts. She didn't want him there in the hands of Nell and Johanna, no, but she did want him. The idea of staying with their new coven, and not seeing him again, was unthinkable. "That's not the point," she said simply. "Without him, I'm no use to a coven. Less use than Adrienne or anyone else who'd be learning magic from scratch."

Nell waved her glass dismissively. "I told you, we have a way of getting around that. And you came from your mother's blood. You at a fifth of your natural power, or even less, is still more than what plenty of women would gain with training. You just need help to harness what you've got left."

Lauren heard Adrienne laugh from the other room, and wondered for a moment if her friend had forgotten they'd been kidnapped. Would the idea of having independence and magic be enough for her to forgive that? She didn't know. She was glad she hadn't fled yet, though. For a moment, she let herself think of whether or not being a part of a coven was something she could ever consider, let alone with Nell and Johanna. The thought of it turned her stomach now, just like it always had—more so when she thought of David and Josh, and all that had happened since she'd met them. Meeting Nell's eyes, she felt herself shake her head, frowning. "You wouldn't let David and Josh go. Not that easily, not after what they did."

"I don't want to," Nell admitted, reclining back into the sofa. "You're right about that. But a witch with pure blood is valuable to a new coven—even if they're not at full strength. A woman who values magic is important, and I like this friend you've picked up, but you have your mother's lineage. Your mother's blood. A portion of her power. You were always powerful, always hiding what you could do and pretending it wasn't in your path, but it was. Have you entirely forgotten your value?" she asked.

Lauren looked away, trying to ignore Nell and get her thoughts in order, but the witch kept talking.

"If we could kill David without harming your power, we would. I would. In a second. But we can't. Him being alive, out there and looking for you and suffering because of it, is a small price to pay for having you in our circle. And what of you? Would you rather hide in his home forever, and hide your magic, having to worry that he'll one day change his mind and try to take it from you for good, or have a life? You're either with us or against us, Lauren," Nell added. "Melania made the unilateral decision to have you against us, but I and Johanna are giving you the choice. No life but his walls, or a life of magic with us."

Lauren's fingers clenched on the wine glass in her hand, and she brought it to her lips. The liquid tasted suddenly stale, but it felt good going down her throat. Her eyes fell to the tattoo, without her meaning it to happen, and she heard Nell laugh shrilly.

"Still thinking about him riding in on a white horse, to the rescue, right. Hold on."

The woman put her glass on the floor and walked over toward the casting circle in the corner. From one of the mats, she picked up what looked like a bundle of shiny fabric and brought it back over toward Lauren, spreading it out in her hands as she got closer and angling it beneath the pocket lights so that Lauren could better see it.

It was a coppery bronze in color, and the fabric looked to be some sort of fine-mesh chainmail, shiny and delicate in appearance. More like a metallic fold of fabric to go around flowers or a wreath than actual chainmail, but with that appearance, nonetheless. It was fashioned into a long-sleeved shrug.

"Pretty, hmm?" Nell asked, admiring it. "It's made of the same metal in your tattoo. We've got the room you and Adrienne are in covered, but from here on out, you'll wear this when you're outside of that room. It'll disrupt the shape of that tattoo so that your agent friends' precious tracking software will overlook it entirely. Until we can do something about that tattoo, there's no way around it even if you're on our side, I'm afraid. For me and Jo's safety, you understand," Nell added, a falsely saccharine note in her voice. "I think you should put it on now, don't you? For Adrienne's sake?" Nell's eyes went toward the corner around which Adrienne and Johanna had disappeared, and with a stab in her gut, Lauren understood the implication. Whatever happened later, Adrienne's safety tonight depended on Lauren's cooperation.

Obediently, she put her glass down and stood up, and she held out her arms when prompted. Nell pulled away the soft sweater that Lauren had donned over the sleeveless blouse she wore, and then Lauren cooperated as Nell slipped the metallic garment up her arms and onto her shoulders. It wasn't as uncomfortable as it looked. It had the weight of a heavy windbreaker, and was oddly rough against her skin, but the fabric had been intended for wearable use.

Nell's hand ducked into her pocket and came out with some tiny padlocks that were no bigger than the fake wedding ring Lauren still wore. One of them went through two tiny openings at her neck, as if it were a button, and Nell clinked it shut. The opening, Lauren noticed, would be too small to allow her to pull the shrug over her head now. Nell tugged at the end of the sleeve on her right hand, fitting her thumb through a tiny hole that Lauren realized must have been there for just that purpose, and then the next lock went to connecting tiny holes slotted beneath her wrist, taking up any slack by cinching the sleeve tighter before it expanded over her hand. There was no way for her to roll the sleeve up now, or snake her arm out of it—that lock around the slack of her wrist and the thumb hole would never allow it, the garment was so fitted to her height and had so little give in it. Nell went through the same process with her other hand, explaining as she did that she and Johanna didn't want to accidentally safeguard the wrong hand at some point, so it was better to just keep both locked.

Nell stood back from her when she was done, a pleased smile coming to her lips. "There, now. Those boys won't find that tattoo in a year of searching."

Lauren felt herself sitting back down on the sofa, sinking into it beneath the weight of the carefully woven shrug. She could feel the metal in it, and the little locks at her neck and her wrists, especially where they and the fabric bit slightly into her still burned palms. The garment had no stretch in it, and was tight around her arms and her shoulders. This wasn't normal fabric she could tear off, and if it wasn't needed in the room, it was a fair bet anyway that the other witches would be with her when she wore it, giving her no opportunity to attempt slipping out of its embrace.

She swallowed, and felt the tightness of tears in her throat. Before they could take her, she asked what she had to. "You said you found a work-around, for me to keep my power without him. What did you mean?"

Chapter 5

David knocked again on the penthouse door, losing his patience for the man who'd already yelled out twice that he was coming. He wasn't coming fast enough. Beside him, Josh rolled his eyes as the man bellowed again that he was on his way.

"This is a waste of time," David told his partner. "The guy's a waste of air. You should have heard him talk about his wife while we were in there. He's got a fucked-up view of marriage, but he's not looking to get rid of Adrienne or let anyone else near her. He wouldn't have her kidnapped, and if he knew who had her, he'd tell us."

Josh tended to agree, but the fact remained that Adrienne was missing along with Lauren. "He seemed anxious when she drove off with Lauren. Maybe you're right and it was garden-variety possessiveness, or maybe not. If he's involved, we need to cover the bases and know what we're dealing with. If he's not—"

"He's not," David interrupted.

"If he's not, then we owe him the visit because his wife is missing. It can't hurt."

David scowled, though he knew his partner was right. They had no leads at the moment, and Raul had called repeatedly to demand answers. Until Barry made some progress, there was nowhere else they really needed to be more.

Raul slammed open the door with enough force that the drink in his hand sloshed over the edge, wetting his hand and the tile floor. He sneered in greeting, and then backed up to allow them entrance.

The opulence of the fancy hotel's penthouse had been undermined in nearly every way. Empty glasses and delivery containers were scattered across the central table, and various garments lay discarded over chairs and couches. The stench of stale cigar smoke hung in the air, despite the 'no smoking' sign propped on an end table.

"You've made yourself at home in, what… two days?"

"I'll be suing the pants off the center and making up for this expense. Take a seat. Can I get you a drink?" the man replied.

Josh held out his hand. "Mr. Rivers, we didn't formally meet yesterday. My name's Josh Devlin."

"Right, we met when you and Mr. Undercover let mobsters run off with Adrienne and his girl. I oughtta sue you, too."

David raised an eyebrow at his partner. Mobsters? The witch he remembered had looked more like a sorority girl, and she'd been convincing enough as a paramedic. Not only was Raul a jerk, but he was drunk off his ass at two in the afternoon, some bare forty-eight hours after his wife had gone missing. "Raul, we're here as a courtesy. Lauren's missing, too, and we're following up on all leads. Do you know anyone who'd have it out for you and Adrienne?"

Raul took a gulp from his glass—he was drinking rum, David thought, from how dark it was—and let his eyes rove between them. He was getting drunker with every sip. True to the form David had seen him in previously. "No," he answered after another minute. "I don't, and I don't appreciate you trying to pin this on me when it's clearly those crackpots from the center who took them. Who else would fuckin' have access to an ambulance?"

David sat back in the couch, letting his partner do the talking. This was a waste of time.

"Mr. Rivers, we're not trying to pin this on you. We don't believe the people behind the center had anything to do with this, though. So, anything you can tell us would be useful."

The man dug his hand into his inside jacket pocket and came up with a photograph that he stared at for a few seconds before tossing it at Josh. "Take that. Maybe you'll take this serious. I want my wife back. That's all I can tell ya."

David glanced sideways to see his partner look at the photo and then turn it over as fast as he'd seen it. His face had begun turning red, flushing instantly with the sight of whatever was in the shot, and David reached for it. Josh pressed it to his leg as if to burn its face into the fabric of his pants and shook his head, a grimace on his face. He coughed as if to clear smoke from his lungs, and then shot an angry glare at David before turning back to the now snickering man across from them. David leaned back to watch whatever this was unfold; he'd seen his partner like this, and he'd seen him deck people moments after.

"Mr. Rivers," Josh started, and then coughed again before continuing. "Are you in the habit of handing strange men pictures of your half-naked wife?"

The words hung in the air, and David reached out and took the glass of rum from Raul's hand. He set it hard on the table, out of the man's reach, and watched him. He didn't know what that picture showed, exactly, or what the man was playing at, but he was done being patient. "What the fuck is wrong with you?"

"You government types leave cold cases and missing women missing all the time," Raul sneered back at them.

He eyed his stolen glass, and then looked at the agents' faces and changed his mind. He rose from the sofa and walked over to a side table where a collection of mini-bottles could be seen. "You see her like that, maybe you won't forget about her so quick. Maybe you'll give a shit. But you bring her back to me, you understand? Whatever ideas your girl's putting in her head, they don't belong there. So, you find her, and you fucking bring her to this penthouse. My taxes pay your fucking salary."

David closed his eyes for a moment and then took a deep breath. This joker was a misogynist and a disrespectful ass, but he had nothing to do with the kidnapping and he knew nothing of where Lauren was. "We're wasting our time," he told Josh, already standing up.

"That's right, you are! Get out of here and do your jobs." Raul raised a mini-bottle of tequila as if in a jeering toast, and then downed it in a gulp. "Bring me my fuckin' wife and I'll give you a tip, too. Money speaks if her ass don't, right?"

Josh was already halfway out the door, the picture crumpled in his hand. Apparently, he'd decided he ought to dispose of it elsewhere rather than leaving it with the theoretically loving husband. David paused at the door, Josh waiting for him in the hall. "It'll be Adrienne's choice whether or not to come back to you, but because we will do our jobs, I'll tell you she's safe when we find her."

Raul eyed him, and drew himself up as he screwed open another mini-bottle. "She can tell me herself. She'll come back; she loves me. Why do you think she was at the center with me? And even if she gets doubts sometimes, she's got nothing without me. Her ass is mine just as much as the bank accounts are, and I guarantee you that prenup she signed is enough to keep her coming back to me even if love ain't. You just find her, and you'll see."

David slammed the door on whatever Raul could say next, and looked to his partner. Josh was breathing hard, leaning against the hall across from the penthouse's doorway.

"I don't know how you didn't kill him while you were in there. Fuck, man." Josh waved the crumpled picture in his hand and then stuffed it into his pocket. "I feel like I need to be decontaminated after sharing his air."

Despite everything happening, David felt himself releasing a quick laugh as they waited for the elevator. "You have no idea. But handing you a picture of his wife in the buff—that's a low I wasn't expecting. Saying I told you so doesn't quite cut it."

"Man…" Josh breathed out. The picture remained in his head, however briefly he'd looked at it. A full-length shot of the brunette he'd only seen fully clothed and taking care of Lauren, but in strappy black lingerie and sprawled backward on a bed, eyes closed. Having met the man who'd taken it, he doubted the woman even knew the shot existed. He'd thought to throw it back at him in the hotel room, but it was an old polaroid. Maybe it was the only one he owned. Just in case the woman was that lucky, Josh planned to shred it and toss it in the trash at their house, where nobody else could possibly chance upon it. "We find Lauren and his wife, we're gonna find a way to convince her to leave him. Find a way to set her up in WitSec to get her the fuck away from him if we have to."

In the elevator across from him, David nodded, but his eyes had already lost the anger their visit to the penthouse had brought up. His eyes were dark again, somewhere else.

"We'll look into their finances," Josh commented, half to himself. "Just in case. A guy like that, no telling what he's hiding. Could be something we can use to find her."

"Maybe so," David agreed doubtfully. "But she doesn't have her phones or any credit cards on her—all that stuff was locked up in the safes with the therapists, just like mine and Lauren's were. And from what Lauren told me, she was still with that joker because she didn't have anywhere else to go or the funds to make it happen. The center was a last-ditch effort for them to make a marriage work."

"Fat chance with that guy," Josh muttered as the elevator door opened before them. He thought back to the files, vaguely remembering that they'd been one of the later couples reported missing. He'd heard of them only after David and Lauren had gone inside. It had been the man's brother who'd reported them as missing, and he couldn't remember seeing anything about Adrienne's family in the file he'd gotten. That didn't mean they didn't exist, but it suggested they weren't nearby enough for the agency to have seen fit to question them.

Outside, Josh pulled up the file on his laptop while David checked in with Adrias and Barry. True to his memory, there was no mention of her family. She'd had something of a career as a graphic designer, but it had faded out a year ago for some reason that hadn't made it into the file. All of their finances were tied up in the center, just like those of the other couples who'd been inside, but Raul's penthouse suggested he must have had something lain away on the side, which didn't seem too out of character from what Josh had seen. Nothing in the file suggested criminal activity for either of them, though, even now that he went over it for a third time since Adrienne and Lauren's disappearance.

"Anything?" Josh asked when David slammed open the Mustang's door and then sank back into the passenger seat.

It took a minute for him to answer, and his voice was hoarse with anger when he did. "One of the paramedics remembered what happened. Two women on the side of the road; one of them was on the ground, apparently unconscious, and the other one waved them down. They thought she was injured. One blonde in her twenties; one redhead in her thirties or forties. Redhead was wearing a wig, but the guy noticed her real hair peeking out at the hairline once they were up close."

"Nell and the fake paramedic," Josh concluded simply.

David nodded, and Josh turned the key in the ignition. They had sketches of the blonde circulating, but until they got some sort of hit on her, there wasn't anything to do but head back to the house and wait for Barry to call.

Chapter 6

Lauren used the nail scissors to clip a few more ends from her hair, and then muddled the half-inch strands together with the honey powder mix, the strands of David's hair that Nell had kept, and some Sage and Bay Leaf. The mixing done, she poured the latest batch of materials across a small strip of muslin, dripped on some jasmine oil, and then added two shards of red jasper stone. When she'd folded over the strip of muslin a few times, making it into a strip of a pouch, she finally took up her needle and thread for the last time.

Nearby, Nell was putting the finishing touches on the other strips Lauren had already finished. Lauren worked on the last bracelet, but another bracelet and two anklets sat beside her materials already, all of them with jewelry clasps sewn to the ends so that Lauren could put them on and remove them easily for multiple wearings. In Nell's hands was the longest of the elongated pouches Lauren had sewn up—a necklace that would finish the ensemble.

"We could make them prettier if you like. Decorate the outside so it's not just plain old cream-colored muslin," Nell offered.

Lauren's eyes remained on the needle going in and out of the muslin pouch in her hand; she'd already pricked herself twice. "I'm not exactly wearing them for beauty, Nell." Lauren glanced up when the other witch didn't answer, and saw that the witch was frowning. "I don't get you," Lauren told her, putting the pouch down and stretching her hands. She'd never been much for sewing, and all of the detailed work they'd been doing that morning had left her with cramping, sore hands. The fact that she had to do it all while still getting used to the metallic shrug, and its constraint around her thumb and wrist to keep it in place, didn't help.

"There's nothing to get, Lauren. You're a witch, and our new coven can use you. This is what it takes. Plus, you need us, whether you want to admit it or not."

Choosing to ignore the last remark, Lauren narrowed her eyes on the other witch, trying to remember how Nell herself had treated her when she'd been at the warehouse, but she couldn't remember interacting with her at all. "Then shouldn't you be happy I'm on board? Shouldn't you be happy that Adrienne is already showing so much progress even though it's only been a few days of her working with Johanna? You're acting like you wanted us to refuse."

Tucking her red hair behind her ears, Nell got up from the table and went over to the butler's pantry nearby, where she ran water into a teapot and then put it on a hotplate. The woman drank more tea than a monk in India, Lauren thought, but she supposed there could be worse habits. When Nell turned around, she caught Lauren's eye and held it, but didn't come back to the table. "I want there to be another way, but because of your mother's spell, there's not. I don't want you to be anywhere near that man—as phantom or otherwise—so, yeah, I'm positive this is going to work, but I don't like it. I want you with us, Lauren, but I don't like even thinking of David Fredricks, let alone having him involved in your life going forward."

Lauren rolled her eyes and picked the pouch back up to finish sewing. Nell had always been unpredictable, but over the last few days, she'd seemed positively mercurial. One minute, she was grinning like a madwoman with a new toy. The next, she was sulky and annoyed. "He came after the coven because I asked him and Josh to help me when Melania threatened me. After I was told I wouldn't have a life of my own. If you hadn't sent that letter—"

"If? If! Lauren, stop making excuses for him." Nell came back to the table and sat down with a huff, and then she reached out and stilled Lauren's hands. When Lauren looked up, Nell's eyes were as dark and angry as she'd ever seen them. "This doesn't all come back to your mother, or to Melania. That man and his partner stole your magic. They did that because they wanted to do it. Because they don't believe there's any such thing as a good, decent witch, and they used your mother as an excuse to hurt you. And then, when that wasn't enough, he raped you—I saw it in his memories," Nell added. "I saw what he did to you, and I hate him for it even if you don't."

Lauren yanked her hands away from the other woman and stared at her. So, this was what had been floating in the air between them. "It's not... it wasn't that simple."

Nell scoffed, letting out a sharp, bitter laugh. "Right, it wasn't that simple then because you think you love him now?"

Shaking her head, Lauren tried to think of what she could say, and how she could say it, but no matter what she said, she knew she'd end up sounding like a horrible stereotype if she thought to defend him. And it wasn't as if he hadn't hurt her since then, which made this conversation all the more difficult. Did she love David? Yes, and however much that had to do with the spell, it wasn't something she could escape. And she felt sure, somehow, that he loved her, as well. He'd taken advantage of her too many times to consider now, but they'd been dealt lousy circumstances, and they were both struggling to navigate them along with the spell. Even after everything that had happened surrounding the case at the counseling center, she'd been confident they'd find a way to some kind of future together, some kind of happiness, and yet she couldn't even imagine what Nell would say if she knew the half of what he'd put Lauren through there. But in the beginning… in the beginning, when they'd first met at that bar, they'd just been attracted to each other. All of the things that had happened between them since were complicated and strange, and in some cases just plain wrong, but he'd never set out to hurt her like he had. Not in the beginning, certainly. And she couldn't put all of the blame on him when it came to that first time they'd been together. A lot of it, maybe—but not all of it. And that was what Nell was speaking of now.

"The point is," Lauren began, "I was only saying no because of Mom's spell. I was attracted to David from the moment we met, whether you want to hear that or not. I was attracted to him whenever I was with him." She looked back to the muslin, but kept talking when Nell didn't speak up. "I hated Mom for what she was doing—you know that. Hell, you and the coven didn't exactly love her, she brought so much attention on everyone. But I hated her for it. And that spell was the only thing holding me back from saying yes to David. You want to know the truth? If not for that spell, I would have tried to seduce him as soon as he took me back to that house, and maybe after that I would have run to the coven or to Mom to try to talk sense into her, or find some solution, and then maybe I even would have gone back to him if we could have found a solution. But none of that was an option because of that goddamned spell."

The teapot shrilled, and Nell let it go for a moment before turning back to it.

"You want to call it rape," Lauren continued, "I guess you can, but don't do it without keeping in mind why it was happening, and why I was saying no. What happened—the way it happened—had more to do with my mother than either me or David. I guess I never told him that, so you probably only saw guilt in his memory," Lauren added, her stomach lurching at the thought of it, and the mistakes they'd both made, "but every moment he touched me, I wanted to say yes. Consent is supposed to be simple—I guess it mostly always is. It either exists or it doesn't, right?—but in my case?" Lauren shook her head, and then put down the muslin pouch for a moment so that she could use the edge of her shirt to wipe sudden tears out of her eyes. "In my case, consent wasn't an option because I knew where it would lead. I knew where it was supposed to lead because of that spell. For fuck's sake, Nell, I wanted David. I wanted everything he did to me. I just didn't want to have no choice about my body's reactions to men and sex for the rest of my fucking life. I didn't want to have no choices about who I loved after one encounter. You don't think there was a good reason I was still a virgin at 25, when I met him? I'd made the decision to never have sex, to never get that close to a man. Any man. All because of my mom. You don't spend a decade planning on saying no, planning on never having sex and fearing the consequences if you do, and then suddenly forget all that and stop fighting it. Maybe especially if the whole reason you were so afraid is staring right at you."

"You're not making sense," Nell argued. "You said you wanted to say yes, and now you're saying you were always going to say no."

Lauren shook her head, finishing up the sewing before she set it down and took up the mug of tea Nell had just placed in front of her. "I did want to say yes. What I'm telling you—what I'm trying to tell you—is that I didn't know how. I didn't know how to say yes, and for whatever reason, in that moment, I didn't know how to tell him the truth. Or maybe I didn't want to because I knew that would end things—because I'm pretty sure… no, I'm a hundred percent sure… that he would have stopped if I'd told him I was a virgin, or about Mom's spell, or any of what I'm fucking telling you. But I couldn't. And because of the spell, I didn't even feel like saying 'yes' was an option."

Nell had gone silent, but when she spoke again, it was in a voice that was quieter than Lauren had ever heard her use. Almost apologetic. "I think Mary saw that," she said quietly. "We'd get drunk sometimes, and she'd talk about how hard that spell was on you. She thought it was the reason you never wanted anything to do with the coven once you reached the age where you might have joined."

Lauren sipped at the tea, which was a shade too weak, and reached for the sugar Nell had brought over. "She wasn't wrong."

"I never thought about it as your mom taking away your option of consent. I guess that makes sense. How you saw it. We all figured that was why you didn't go in for relationships, but even so, David was still wrong to push you like that. He's responsible for how things went."

Lauren waited until Nell looked at her before she answered. "No more than us, me and Mom. Mom cast the spell, Nell. I could have stopped him just by telling him about it."

"But then you'd have no magic," Johanna said from behind them, and both of the witches at the table turned to look at her. "So, take it for what it is. Both of you, stop worrying about the past. We've got a new witch to initiate."

It was a matter of a few moments to gather up the finished jewelry pouches and go downstairs to the casting circle, where they found Adrienne being fussed over by Evie and Sarah. The younger women were braiding strips of leather and flowers into her shoulder-length hair, and letting the materials trail down below her hair as if she were having strangely designed extensions put in. The dress she wore was flowy and red, heavy on material and gathered below her breasts as if it were some costume from another era. She looked up to Lauren nervously when she noticed her, but Lauren could see the flush in her cheeks betraying excitement.

"Is this happening?" Adrienne asked her.

Something in Lauren's mind snapped a little, compartmentalizing all that had happened before away from what was in front of her. This was a good thing in front of her.

Nell was helping with the preparations now, sprinkling a circle of powder in a large circle to surround the six of them and shut out the rest of the world for the duration of the ceremony, and Johanna was setting up a small slate in the center of the casting circle, with materials being laid out on a strip of ancient fabric in front of where Adrienne sat.

Lauren sat down, and reached out to take Adrienne's hand to begin helping. This was her first time being engaged in something like this, but she'd heard the stories and read the histories, and so it was all familiar. "It's happening," she promised her friend. "Are you happy?"

Adrienne gripped her hand, and then let it go as Lauren pulled away and began painting slight symbols onto her friend's skin with the pigments that Nell had laid out for them. "I am. I know I shouldn't be—God, Lauren, I know how we got here. And this is crazy. But I feel free. That's ridiculous, isn't it?"

Lauren couldn't find the words, so she simply kept painting along Adrienne's other arm, raising the sleeve to take these pigments up past her elbow. Her fingers were shaking and her throat was tight, but for Adrienne's sake, she could be happy for the moment. Above them, still fussing with Adrienne's hair, Sarah filled the silence.

"It's not ridiculous at all, Dri," she said, using the nickname she'd taken to adopting almost as soon as they'd met. "You're surrounded by powerful, independent women who care about you."

Lauren found herself nodding. "It's what a coven's supposed to offer. Support. That's what I'd always heard...."

"Her mother was a bad example," Johanna spoke up from the side, where she'd stood back to watch the proceedings with what Lauren could see was real satisfaction. "It will take time for you to learn, and for all of us to come together, but we'll do it. And we'll be better for it."

Adrienne glanced up and found Lauren's eyes, and must have read something more there. "Lauren, I know I'll be better for this," she said quietly. "I don't know how it happened, exactly, but I will be. I'm good."

Lauren swallowed the nerves in her throat and nodded. "I know you are."

Finishing with the final pigments, Lauren moved around to sit on the side of the circle opposite Adrienne. Her friend looked otherworldly, and her brown eyes were positively glowing with the magic that was already swimming in the air. Lauren herself could barely feel it, but knew that would change soon enough—when she got back to David, however that happened. For now, the image in front of her was such a far cry from the nervous woman she'd met at the center, who'd been so unhappy with that louse of a man she'd been with, it was enough to ground her. For the first time, she wondered if Nell was right. They'd talked so much over the last few days, and at first, the idea of being apart from David for any length of time had been a kind of pain in her whole body. She'd ached with the very idea of joining this coven and leaving behind the condensed sort of life she'd found with him. But it wasn't impossible that she'd been wrong all those years.

It wasn't impossible that her mother's actions, and Melania's leadership in the coven, had been such damning influences that she'd shut aside notions and plans that, realistically, she should have considered all along. Seeing Adrienne's excitement over the last few days, as the woman had seen into her own innate power and psychic ability, and spending so much time with these women… Lauren had started being able to see things slightly differently.

Yes, Johanna and Nell could be cruel and stubborn, and they had been to Lauren, but it was a cruel world, and they'd had their reasons. She couldn't defend what David had done to her in one breath and then refuse to do the same for them. And look how good they were being to Adrienne—even to her, considering the trust they had to build back between them. Evie seemed a bit thoughtless, but she was young, and so wrapped up in magic that she could barely think straight. Her mother had, apparently, tried to keep it from her all her life, and now that she'd been able to find a group that would allow her to embrace it and celebrate it… she was half in love with Nell and Johanna and anything they said, and Lauren doubted that would pass for some time. Lauren didn't expect to become friends with her, but she could tolerate her. Sarah was a different story. She was uncomfortable with how they'd brought Lauren and Adrienne in, and had made that clear. In her early thirties, she'd had enough time to grow into herself without the influence of a coven for the last five years, after her own had decided to move to

South America and she'd decided to remain in the States. She was thoughtful and smart, and Lauren liked her. She also liked the fact that the woman spoke her mind, even to Nell and Johanna. That was no small thing.

When everyone was seated, Johanna and Nell to each side of Adrienne, Johanna gestured for Adrienne to begin. Nodding, Adrienne closed her eyes after she'd picked up the large piece of lapis lazuli that had been set in front of her for that purpose. This would be her story stone, and once she was done tonight, a piece of it would be made into jewelry for her. When she took a breath to speak, the witches surrounding her closed their eyes.

"My parents named me Adrienne Alfano. I was born in Italy, but my family came here before I was two. I don't remember it. I grew up in California, but always begged my parents to move elsewhere. I was scared of the wildfires—it seemed like we had to evacuate every year, if not more than once per year—but I was the only one they bothered. My brother didn't care; he only wanted to be an actor, and was so focused on that, nothing else mattered. My mom was a hairstylist who made good money as a private stylist to B-list actresses, and my dad owned a landscaping company. They always expected me to move as soon as I turned 18, and I did. I left California and went to Michigan, where I'd gotten a scholarship to study graphic design. That's when I met Raul. He was five years older than me, and he had money. I don't know how we got so serious—he wasn't the kind of man I wanted to be with, but he was good to me at first, even if he wasn't very good to anyone around us. My parents came out, and they said I'd done well. He's good at impressing people when he wants to. Before I knew it, I was rushing my last classes and putting off graduate school so that we could get married. He wanted a big wedding, and I had to plan it with his mother. I kept telling myself things would get better, that he was stressed about a new job and that the wedding was expensive. I thought my parents wouldn't have approved of him if they'd seen anything to suggest he'd be bad for me.

"Things just kept going. Soon, we were married, and then we kept moving. I completed grad school online, but we never settled down anywhere. He was always looking for the next opportunity, and I didn't have time to find a decent job or make friends, so I just did what I could through an old classmate's agency; she'd been the closest thing I'd had to a friend for a while, and we'd never even met in person—only online. About a year ago, she sold the agency, and the new owner didn't have the patience for satellite employees, so I stopped…"

Adrienne's voice stumbled, and Lauren had to keep herself from opening her eyes and reaching out to her. That would disrupt everything, and she knew it was the job of the coven leaders to take charge of any interruptions or changes in the plan right now. They'd be comforting Adrienne now in the ways they could, Lauren knew.

And after a minute, sure enough, Adrienne began again.

"I stopped looking for professional design work because it was so hard to establish myself when we weren't setting down roots, and Raul discouraged me working anyway. He told me I was a failure, and I should just accept it—that if I'd been good enough at it, the work would have found me, but it wasn't coming my way, and therefore I wasn't good enough. And it was that simple. I started believing him. I worked at a coffee shop, and a shopping center, and then a daycare center. Anything to get out of the house and bring in a little bit of money; Raul made sure all of it went into the bank, and only allowed me to keep a small allowance, but I kept telling myself I'd start my own account. I didn't, though. Other things happened that made me want to just give up on everything. He had affairs, usually with his clients or their wives. And he didn't even try to hide it from me. He got abusive sometimes, but if I did what he wanted, we were mostly okay. For a long time, the worst of everything was his addiction. Gambling—casinos, races, whatever. He's too good at it for his own good. At one point, he sent us into bankruptcy and we had to move in with his brother's family for a while; I actually thought we'd settle there, but then he was back on his feet again and we were moving once more, before I'd even had time to find a job in design. That was our first bout with therapy, though—a counselor for his addiction, and it mostly did the trick until that wasn't such a problem anymore. He gave himself an allowance to gamble with each month, and it solved that problem.

"But there were still the affairs. The final straw was when I came home to find him in bed—our bed—with a teenager who was half my age. I doubt she was seventeen, even. He'd brought home the daughter of one of his clients this time. I went straight to a divorce attorney, the first one I could find, to try to figure out what I could do. My parents had told me I was crazy when I'd talked about leaving him in the past. They wouldn't help. The attorney said he couldn't help me without a big retainer, especially since I'd signed a prenup, but I went home and lied to Raul anyway. I didn't know what else to do. I told Raul that I'd found an attorney who'd help me for free, and that I was going to divorce him unless he changed. It was a bluff—all of our accounts were in Raul's name, and my parents wouldn't want me to interrupt their retirement lifestyle. Plus, they were still in California, and every time I thought of going back, I thought of those fires. That wasn't an option. Raul didn't call my bluff, though. He looked up options for marriage counseling, and that's how we ended up at the center where I met Lauren. And then, here, I met all of you."

Lauren recited the thanks for Adrienne's story along with the other witches, thinking it was no wonder that she and Adrienne had ended up connecting like they had, and that Adrienne had then been willing to fall into embracing this coven. What matter was it that they were living in a converted office building, sharing a room, when you thought about what she'd just come from?

In silence, they sat still in the room, but eventually Lauren felt the stirrings of movement and knew that Nell and Johanna were setting up for the rest of the ceremony. Slowly, she opened her eyes and looked around at the other women. Adrienne had been crying, as had Sarah and Nell—it made Lauren think better of Nell, to see that, and she kept revising her understanding of the woman. As might have been expected, Johanna was serious, and Evie looked to be barely holding in a grin—anything with magic excited her too much, Lauren thought.

With everything set up, Adrienne began showing them the spellwork she'd managed, in order of magnitude. She drew on the ritual words she'd learned and on the materials laid out for her in turn, first reading a memory that Sarah projected for her, and then lighting a small piece of parchment on fire with no tools but her words. Finally, Nell drew a knife along her own arm, and Adrienne mixed a healing potion and healed it so that the skin looked just as it had before. When all that was done, Adrienne's eyes were drooping in exhaustion and she was breathing hard, but a grin was on her lips.

"Adrienne, do you want to go by Adrienne Rivers, or by Adrienne Alfano, or by something else?" Johanna asked.

Adrienne had clearly expected the question, and she smiled tiredly in response. "The name 'Rivers' was the best thing about my marriage, and it's the name I want to put on a design business if I ever get around to having one. And it's how I got here. I'll continue going by Adrienne Rivers."

Johanna wrote the name into the front of a leather-bound journal, and then pricked her thumb with a pin, spread the blood around, and placed her thumbprint below it. One by one, the rest of the coven members did the same, Adrienne going last. Johanna handed the journal to Adrienne, smiling for the first time that night. "Welcome to our coven, Adrienne Rivers."

Chapter 7

David scrolled through the graphics that Barry had sent on, finally understanding why the tech wizard had decided to send them via email rather than just bringing them when he came by later that evening. The long and the short of his message was clear: They didn't know where Lauren was, and the data was all in. Either the witches had found a way to mask her tattoo, or they'd somehow gotten rid of it.

There were locations where the properties of her tattoo were showing up, but not in the size or amount or shape allocated to the metal on her skin. The closest matches were those lining up with other undercovers who'd already gotten the tech applied, but when it came right down to it, David only saw that as further reason for frustration. How could they so easily track the agents who'd been inked in recent weeks, versus the one person who should have been cemented in the system? Barry had assured them that the ink's signature wouldn't decay, and even offered the proof that the agent who'd been inked immediately after Lauren was still showing up as clear as day in the system. It wasn't the tracking or the ink, assuming the witches hadn't found a way to remove it—it was something the witches were doing to hide it.

Picking up his phone, he dialed Adrias, but only got the message service. "It's Fredricks, and I'm still waiting for that update. Call me back."

When he hung up, he looked at the clock for what was probably the twentieth time that afternoon. It was only four. Barry would be by in a few hours, and Josh would wander in then or before, but he had the house to himself until then.

In Lauren's room, he watered the cacti and ferns she kept, and then ran a dust cloth overtop of the hard surfaces in the space. He vacuumed the rug, then lit one of her incense sticks to freshen up the scent that usually filled the space. She'd be back soon, he told himself again, and it would be like she'd never left. Next, he unpacked the suitcase that they'd dropped on the bed the night before, hanging up and putting away all of the clothes that Lauren had brought with her to the center. His own suitcase still sat unopened downstairs, waiting to be unpacked. He doubted they'd have thought to gather any of their belongings if the center staff hadn't had them packed up and ready to move, but as it was, they'd left with everything they'd taken inside.

When everything was in place in Lauren's room, he turned off the light and moved to leave, but then came back in and sat on the bed. It felt like yesterday that he'd come in here and they'd made love again after everything that had happened at the warehouse. After everything then, and before everything else at the center. If he could have gone back to that day, and forgotten everything in between, he would have. Lauren's safety was worth more than the people they'd saved—to him, at least. He'd never forgive himself, or Josh or Adrias, if they finally found her and it was too late. What the coven had planned on doing to her before… he didn't know what had slowed them down then, but it wasn't thinkable now. The idea of them turning her into some sort of mindless slave? It was enough to make him want to throw up, or kill every witch on the planet. He couldn't live with himself or any of the decisions they'd made if that happened.

The front door opened and slammed shut, and David heard his partner dropping groceries on the island before he called out. "David, you here?"

He stood up and walked out to greet him, trying to put his earlier thoughts out of mind. They weren't giving up yet. "Barry with you?" he asked as he got to the kitchen.

"Coming by later," Josh answered, his eyes on the files David had left open on the laptop. "No news yet?"

David began pulling items from the grocery bags, sorting them on the counter. "None. I was trying to get in touch with Adrias to see if there've been any hits on that blonde's picture, or sightings of Everett or Wilkins, but he hasn't called me back. You talk to him?"

"This morning. No news then. Assumption seems to be that she's probably not in the system—we know witches usually homeschool their kids, and if this one was born off the grid and never entered the system, she might not be in any records."

David had come to the same conclusion, but since it didn't help them get any closer to Lauren, he kept setting it aside and hoping for something more to come of the search. Now, he sat at the island and watched his partner's expression as he examined the graphics Barry had sent over. There wasn't anything new there. "I've been thinking," he started, "that maybe I need to do what Lauren did."

Josh eyed him, and then turned to start putting away the groceries. "If you're talking about how she went in after you, you'll have to tell me how you even see that as an option. Lauren responded to what amounted to a ransom note. We went to a park where someone was waiting for her, as planned, and then she disappeared into the ether because of some retrieval spell that we couldn't track. I don't know how to break it to you, buddy, but I can't set up a spell to send you her way, and unless you're keeping something from me, you don't have the power to do that and we haven't gotten a word of communication from what's left of that coven. You a warlock now?"

David ignored the jibe. "But we could advertise we're waiting for them to contact us," David suggested. "That I'm here when they want me."

Josh looked up as if he was about to crack a joke, but his face flattened when he saw his partner's expression. "You want to do what?"

David got up and retrieved two beers from the fridge, and handed one to Josh. "I've been going over everything I heard them say in that warehouse. They were using me to amp up Lauren's magic. Now, maybe they've found some other way to wake it up, for whatever they wanted it for, or maybe they haven't, but her most direct connection to magic is through her mom's spell, and that spell runs through me, my connection to her. I got the impression that they needed me alive for that, and I can't see why that would have changed. Hell, maybe they hoped they could get both of us from the center, but when they had the chance to take Lauren and Adrienne, they cut their losses and ran with it."

Josh took a slug of his beer and then turned away. He kept putting away the groceries, remaining silent.

"What do you think?" David pressed him.

"I think you're nuts," Josh replied, not bothering to look at him. "And I think you're ignoring the obvious. If they haven't come after you again—"

"Don't—"

"Stop and think!" Josh cut him off in return. "You want to sacrifice yourself for nothing? If she's got no magic to speak of and they haven't said anything….

Dave, dude, it's been a week," he added, deflating. "They've had her for a week, and I know you don't want to hear it, but we don't even know if it's possible to…"

David didn't hear the rest. He'd already headed for the door to the downstairs suites, and he shut off Josh's comment with a slam of a door behind him. After everything Lauren had done for him, there was no way it was too late to save her. That wasn't an option. No matter what the coven had already done, and no matter what they planned to do, they weren't winning.

Downstairs, he opened up the small tablet he reserved for weekend email use and brought up the files from the coven members who he and Josh had set up with new identities after draining their magic. They'd settled one of them just a few hours away, and he pulled up her phone number first. If she didn't answer, he could show up on her goddamned doorstep.

When she did answer the phone, he reminded her who he was, and then he told her why he'd called.

***

Nell joined Johanna on the roof of the office building, first giving a brief look to the space above Lauren and Adrienne's room. The thatched plastic sheeting, metal shards spread thick below it, remained held down with heavy blocks of cement; it was still perfectly in place where they'd left it. With all of the weight on it, she couldn't imagine how much wind it would take to shift it or displace the metal below it, but it hadn't happened yet—and until it did, no satellite would be picking up Lauren's tattoo.

Johanna waved her wine glass at the other witch, gesturing for her to take a seat beside her on the patio furniture they'd set up almost immediately upon buying the building. It looked out over the cityscape of

Indianapolis, albeit from the outskirts of the city, and except for the fact that the light pollution bit into the power of the stars, it wasn't a bad view.

"You're never going to believe what popped up on the forum today," Nell told her, pulling her computer from the shoulder bag she'd been carrying.

Johanna poured her wine, pointedly ignoring the laptop. "Can't we go without using that damned thing for even a day, Nell? We've got enough on our hands with training Adrienne and keeping Evie in line. I don't think we need to rush to add anyone else."

"It's not that," Nell told her. Without explaining further, she pulled up the screenshot she'd saved earlier, and then shoved the laptop into Johanna's hands.

Johanna glared at her before even glancing at it, but finally relented and shifted her wine glass so that she could better balance the laptop in front of her.

"You see it?" Nell asked. "We're driving him crazier than I thought."

Johanna saw it. On the forum, Chloe Draymond's old screenname had popped up for the first time since she'd lost her magic, and for a very distinct purpose. The subject-line of the post read 'Att. Nell Everett and Johanna Wilkins', and the post itself was short.

> *Logging on to send through message of note from David Fredricks. His words:*
>
> *"If you want revenge, take it out on me. I was behind your coven's destruction, and I will destroy you if you don't let Lauren go. You let her go, I'll cooperate. You want a slave, take me instead of her. Or, tell me what you need to release her. I'm ready to deal or give myself up, so the ball's in your court. I'll be at the park where you picked up Lauren Sunday afternoon at 3, and every other day after that. Then again,*

you've got my address, so you know where to find me. Come alone, or don't, but show up; I'll be unarmed. – David Fredricks"

[This is the woman formerly known as Chloe Draymond. I am not associated with Agent Fredricks. He paid me in return for my posting this message. Please leave me out of future communications and understand that I have NO association with him or his agency. I hope you destroy him and Phillippa's bitch daughter.]

Johanna shook her head, a small smile growing on her lips. "I'm impressed Chloe found the spine to even share this message. I imagine she shit herself when that agent got in touch with her."

Nell took the laptop back and closed it up, then reclining into her patio chair and lifting her wine glass in sarcastic agreement. "What do you want to bet he blackmailed her into posting it?"

Johanna glanced back to the plastic as if to assure herself of its placement, but they'd measured it all multiple times and then double-checked with magic lines. It was where it needed to be. "I suppose that proves they're having no luck tracking the tattoo. The mesh is doing its job. Is she ready for tonight?"

"I think so." Nell sipped her wine, thinking of the conversation she'd had with the bitch earlier. Playing nice was becoming more difficult, but if they could heighten her magic and freeze it at high levels, or even bring her over to their side and keep her as an asset for a while, it would be worth it. "Between me working on her and Adrienne enjoying learning spellwork so much, she's starting to doubt herself. Bringing along that friend of hers was a stroke of luck. If I'm right, Lauren's already doubting that what she feels for him goes too far beyond the spell. Without him beside her at every turn, that doubt's going to grow, and since she won't be able to talk to him as a phantom, conversation isn't anything we have to worry about; I imagine she doesn't think too straight when she's in bed with him anyway. Plus, I don't know what happened to her with that man since we last saw them, but as hesitant as she is about talking about him or whatever went on, it wouldn't surprise me to learn that he himself gave her some reasons to wonder. Just think about what we know of what was going on there, Jo—it's almost a guarantee that he hurt her more. But if we can really turn her against him, and then show her the truth after she's helped us destroy him… talk about revenge. For us, for Phillippa, for Melania… all of us."

Johanna reached over and entwined her fingers with Nell's. "Funny, that we don't even have any need to bother with bringing him here, and he's just begging for it. We can let him stew in his paranoia and whatever else he's feeling for as long as it takes."

"As long as the plan works," Nell commented, and then tapped the laptop thoughtfully. "But it's nice to have a back-up. We'll have to thank him for that when we see him again."

Chapter 8

Lauren sat dripping on the side of the soaking tub, watching the water drain away. The bathroom was still steamy, and the scents of rosemary and honeysuckle permeated her every breath. Nell had told her to let her skin air-dry, so that was what she was doing. Her mind was full, so sitting still and waiting wasn't difficult.

The idea of what she was doing that night, and what she was hoping to happen, was somewhat beyond her. Her whole life, her own use of magic had revolved around plants, growth, and healing. Spells of control and psychic ability had been her mother's realm alone, and Lauren had barely paid attention to the lessons she'd been given over the years. She'd learned to recognize such magic and sense it—allowing herself to be trained in defense, essentially—but she'd never made any attempt to harness magic that didn't have to do with her own interests in flora and healing. The last few days had been a whirl-wind crash course in those spells which had been on the peripheral of her world in earlier years, and ignored ever since she'd left behind the coven in favor of college. And her brain had never been this tired out from science courses in the traditional world of learning; even the courses in statistics and software development, all of which had driven her crazy, hadn't been such a strain as all this. Not least of all because she wasn't sure she wanted to know it.

When the bath had drained, Lauren plucked the remaining honeysuckle blooms and shoots of rosemary from the porcelain, and threw it all in the trash. Nude, she walked into the bedroom she'd been sharing with Adrienne, grateful the other woman was staying with Sarah that night, and that they'd be setting her up with her own space tomorrow. It wasn't that they had any real secrets to keep from one another at this point, but Lauren didn't imagine she'd ever feel quite free enough to lounge naked in front of her or anyone else, and she didn't want to be worrying about the noises coming from her mouth if the night went off as planned.

In the slight chill of the bedroom, she lowered herself to the floor and began rubbing on the cream she and Nell had made that afternoon. It smelled of the same ingredients she'd included in her bath, but the work of stretching out her body and rubbing it in helped evaporate some of the moisture that had been holding to her skin. A glance at the clock told her it was still too early—David wouldn't be asleep yet, she guessed, and this wouldn't work if he wasn't—so she laid back on the floor rug and tried to relax.

The idea of seeing him, being able to touch him even if she couldn't speak to him, was enough to make her blood warm. Nell had assured her that David's experience of her wouldn't be like what she'd experienced with the phantom of Josh whose grip had been so cold on her arm, back when the witches had tried to tempt her from the ranch house all those weeks ago. Because of Lauren's connection to David—and because they'd had his essence to include in the spell, due to Nell's foresight—along with the fact that she was projecting herself versus someone else… well, all of that added up to mean that, if they'd done things right, she'd feel warm and real as long as it was only David she came in contact with. And as long as he didn't recognize in the moment that she was a phantom instead of a dream, and thus pull away from her or shut her out, they could spend time together and reawaken her magic without a problem. The magic would travel through her phantom to her, using it as a conduit, and it would be as if they'd been together in the flesh.

Nell had suggested she try not to wake him up. That she go into his room and soak in his presence, maybe lying her hand on his arm to soak in their connection more quickly and wake things up. Lauren had nodded, noncommittal, and acted as if that would be enough since it was clear Nell wasn't sure.

But of course, Lauren wasn't tricking herself into thinking she'd simply lay down beside him and let her skin charge from his presence, through the phantom, though that was certainly the intention of the spellwork. Her body had been desperate for him for days—for his touch, for his breath on her, for everything he did to her. The idea of just lying down beside him innocently, not even trying for more, was a joke. The spell was supposed to allow for as much physical contact as she accepted, and although Lauren knew there'd been safety features which Nell had built into things, to keep them from really communicating, Lauren wanted much more than to recharge her spells.

At the least, she wanted his touch, and his gaze on hers, and the sight of him reacting to her body and her magic. She wanted to feel him inside of her, pushing her and holding her, and she wanted the pain along with the pleasure of it all, as much as he could give her in whatever time they found together. Because despite the promises she'd heard, and the plans she'd heard, she had no faith in what was coming in the future. Everything in her was invested only in this spell, and in getting as much from it as she could. And while she knew she couldn't speak to David tonight, or communicate with him in any purposeful way without breaking the spell apart, she hoped she'd be real enough that he'd realize she was okay, and just keep looking for her. For tonight, she told herself that would be enough.

When the clock hit two a.m., Lauren decided it must be safe to try. Except when circumstances demanded it, she'd rarely known Josh and David to stay up past midnight. David liked to be in bed earlier, in fact, so that he could be up earlier to work out or head out the door for whatever case was calling. No matter how stressed he was with her here—and she knew he had to be, that he had to be searching for her—he was unlikely to be up at this hour.

Gently, she picked up the muslin jewelry pouches and put them on one-by-one. The anklets and bracelets fit snug against her skin, and the necklace had just enough give to make it comfortable and loose, hanging around where the neck of a t-shirt would have. With any luck, that would keep it from getting in the way or being so loose as to be torn away from her, though Nell thought they'd be okay even if it was torn off; more than anything, it was added insurance while Lauren got the hang of this spellwork.

The lights off, Lauren lay down on the tweed mat she'd placed on her mattress, and she focused on the physical sensations of her immediate surroundings. The slight stickiness of her lotioned skin against the mat. The roughness of the makeshift muslin jewelry along her wrists and ankles and neck. Her damp hair hanging loose by her face and against her shoulders. The feel of the air, warm enough on her skin now that she'd gotten used to it and dried a bit more. Anchored in her space, she next thought of the space she was seeking, and what it felt and smelled like. David's worn couch in his downstairs suite, and the roughness of its fabric, not unlike the mat beneath her. She thought of what the room would smell like right now, and imagined the left-over scent of David's cologne where it would linger on the couch. With that in her mind, she pictured an emptied beer can on the near side table, and the staleness of that smell. Keeping her eyes closed, she imagined the flat blackness of the space without windows, which David kept dark and silent, and she kept her awareness there, located in the sensations she was so familiar with from the time she'd spent down there, rare as it had been.

She breathed in and out in the space, imagining it, knowing time was passing, and speaking the words of the spell every so often. Nell had told her it might take multiple nights before it worked, but she was determined to give this her best shot now, tonight, and each time she felt herself slipping away from the physicality of the sensations she knew could place her there in his suite, she re-centered herself and pushed away sleep, reminding herself of his cologne, of the rough fabric beneath her that approximated his old couch, and the thick blackness of the air around her.

She was nearly ready to give up for the night, and allow sleep in, when she heard him snore.

She barely caught the sound, it was so slight, and then she only barely caught herself from jumping up and running to him—as if she could. Instead, she swallowed, and breathed out the second stage of the spell, word by word, meaning to anchor herself there for as long as the spell would last—hours if she was lucky, and minutes if not.

Slowly, she opened her eyes to the blackness. Her body felt too light, but of course it was pitch black and she saw nothing when she looked down at herself. Into the dark, she laughed, and the sound bled into the soft snoring she heard coming from David's bedroom.

By feel, she made her way around the couch and down the hall, hesitating only briefly when she came to his door. Worse comes to worse, he wakes up and shoots me, and I disappear. The thought made her smile, he was so close and she had so little to lose.

Inside, she wished she could turn on a light, but she knew she wasn't yet strong enough to interact with the space—it was why the phantasm of Josh had been forced to make her try to open the door, rather than been able to open it himself. She could be here, sort of, and she could interact with David in the space and against the surfaces his presence occupied, but that was it. At least until the phantasm was stronger. In fact, nchoring herself with him would be the only way she'd even stay atop the bed, Nell had told her, though she might get stronger with time.

At the bed, she reached out and found him by touch. He was on his back, in his clothes. Her breath caught when her hand landed fully on his chest, and she felt the rise and the fall of it as if through water. The magic reacted, pulsing in her long-healed palm, and she just caught herself from speaking his name. In the space of his bedroom, there was no sound from her heavy breathing, and that more than anything was what convinced her she was short on time.

As gently as she could, she rested one knee on the bed beside him, touching his ankle with her wrist, and then let her whole weight shift the bed. She could smell whiskey on him now, and realized he must have drunk himself to sleep; maybe that would help. Her magic was still so weak, even bolstered by the spellwork, she wasn't sure what would happen if he woke up before they'd had more contact.

Swallowing her nerves, she lay down beside him, getting as close as she could. He'd kept his clothes on, but hadn't bothered with the covers, and she wished she could see him. Since that wasn't possible, she closed her eyes and pictured what she was feeling. Her right hand slipped under his t-shirt, and she imagined it being the classic Van Halen shirt he liked. Her bracelet snagged slightly on his belt, and she paused, but he didn't wake up. She felt along his ribs, feeling the scar of the bullet wound she'd long since gotten used to, and the scar from the energy bolt that had torn into his side. He muttered her name, and she paused, but he remained asleep.

Keeping her eyes closed, trying to imagine exactly what he'd look like right at that moment, she reached up to his chin and felt along his jaw, appreciating the stubble that he'd been shaving away while they'd stayed at the center. He hadn't shaved for the last few days, she guessed. Magic was warming her arms now, coming up from her palms to her chest, and she felt herself making sounds of desire that didn't make it to the space of his room. Unable to resist pushing the spell further, she ran her finger along his lips and felt the dampness of his breath. Her magic tingled with the feel of it, and she began to warm with desire as much as magic.

She wondered if he'd taste the honeysuckle in the lotion when he woke up.

Swallowing the question, she slipped one of her legs over his, anchoring herself further, and rested against his side. Her body was open against him now, wet and waiting for him, and she could feel the magic bringing up desire in her blood, taking her breath away as it fought for more connection. It was pushing her to do more, faster, but her mind was stuck on the immediate feel of him breathing beside her, sleeping. Somehow, she hadn't expected to get this far, or for him to feel so real against her, and nothing she'd thought of in dreaming about this spell had prepared her for the question of exactly what to do now.

She let her leg rest fully on his, wondering at the fact that she could feel the fabric of his jeans on her skin, and then she shifted more fully against him, leaning against his chest so that her naked breast landed above his heart, and she could feel the beat of it beneath his t-shirt. With every second, the spell made the scene feel more real, and she realized that her imagination was helping it along, just as Nell had said it would. Her hand snaked along David's abdomen, holding him to her, and then she rested her head against his shoulder, her lips angled up toward his neck.

When his arm came down around her, out from beneath the pillow where he'd fallen asleep with it tucked beneath his head, she let out a shriek, and then laughed when there was no sound of it. This was so strange, but Nell had been right—David had just accepted her as part of some dream, and now they were together.

Her name came from his lips, only half intelligible, and his hand petted along her ass, fumbling for purchase before falling to the side and then coming back to her skin again, his palm bringing up magic through her skin with each press of contact. His movements were heavy, and she realized the spell of the phantasm she'd adopted was affecting him just as it had affected her. Still, she could enjoy this, and she only hoped he'd remember the dream and get some pleasure from it.

His hand fumbled over to her breast, groping her, and even as clumsy as the movement was, nothing like the way he normally touched her with such purpose and confidence, she gasped with the pleasure of it. Her skin was already heating with magic, reacting to him.

No longer hesitating, with his hands exploring her skin, she pulled his t-shirt up and pressed her cheek down to hear his heartbeat. Beneath her, he shifted, his hands moving away from her, and she sensed him struggling out of his t-shirt. And then her name was on his lips again, his hands fumbling against her skin, and she wanted desperately to kiss him, but she didn't think his dream would survive that—she wasn't sure her spell would survive his waking up tonight, desperately as she ached for it. Somehow, she also thought a kiss might make the separation more real, and suspected that she wouldn't be able to keep herself from trying to talk to him—really talk to him—if she kissed him and he woke up. She didn't want that. She didn't want to break the spell. She wanted whatever time she could have with him, right now and tonight. And if she said a word more than his name, with any intention of communicating some message, simple even as a hello, they'd be done.

His lips found her shoulder and nibbled at her skin, and she gasped with the heat that came up through the magic to greet his breath. It pulled her tighter against him, and she felt a new urgency in his body tensing against hers, as if his desire had suddenly woken up to hers.

Panting, she reached for the button of his jeans and pulled it loose, and the zipper came down more easily. His hands found her breasts then, and he twisted overtop of her so that she gasped. Words weren't coming from his lips, and so she imagined he must still be dreaming, thinking his body was with him in his dream and none of this was real. For a moment, she felt guilty for that, but then his lips landed on her nipple, biting down hard, and she shrieked silently into the air of his bedroom, gripping his arms for support. Instead of letting up, he sucked on her breast, pulling the nipple and areola into his mouth as his teeth bit down on the surrounding skin, devouring her, and all of her magic ballooned beneath his touch, heating up and warming her chest with the pressure of their connection.

Breathing through the pain, she tried pushing at his shoulders, but one of his hands came up to her mouth as if to cover it, two of his fingers finding her tongue, prodding her lips. Without thinking, she took the direction and sucked on his fingers even as she pushed at his shoulders, but when he finally lifted up and the sting of his bite was released, his lips landed at her neck and sucked skin between his teeth. She could hear him muttering her name when he released her, and wished she could answer, but the heat of his presence was winding through her body now, making it so that she could do little more than pant and lay beneath him with the power of it.

His hard dick was long against her thigh, even through his jeans, and she pressed her groin up into him, begging for it. They'd put some aphrodisiac into the lotion, thinking it would awaken the magic, and now she regretted it. Whether or not it was affecting him, it was affecting her. She couldn't think straight—couldn't breathe with the warmth and want running in her body— and when he bit into her neck, she sucked on his fingers and thrust up against him again, screaming into his hand when his other hand squeezed down on her breast. It was harder than he'd touched her before, she thought, but if he thought this was a dream, she suddenly realized there wasn't really any telling what he'd do. And, of course, there was the clumsiness of both their movements. She reached for his hip and her hand landed at his ribs, and the way his hands had fumbled at her side and her breasts and her mouth, she knew it was as if they were both delayed and moving in water, despite the heat and pressure of it all.

When he lifted up from her, she was afraid at first that the spell was breaking, and expected to wake up in her own room at the coven's building, but then she felt the bunching of his jeans against her ankle, and knew he was just pulling loose the last of his clothing.

He said something unintelligible when his hands landed on her hips, and then he was pulling her to the edge of the bed, spreading her legs. There was no finesse tonight, but she was desperately ready for him. When his body lunged against hers, filling her, she clenched her fists against his back and pulled him into her. He plunged into her again, pushing her legs wider with his body so that the magic ramped up beneath her skin, running along her core and rising to meet his movements. One of his hands yanked at her hair, forcing an arch into her back, and she screamed into the sensation of it. He thrust then, grunting with the force he put into it, and she realized he hadn't been fully hard when he'd first come inside her. Now, she felt the stretch and the ache of him filling her, and the magic rose through her blood to meet the pressure of it. There was a thickness to the air and to the feeling, and it made it harder for her to breathe with the power of it all, but the warmth was there, and so was David.

His hands gripped her ass, pulling her into him with each thrust, and she groaned with the pain and pleasure of it. Perhaps the violence of it wasn't what she'd hoped for, but the heat of the magic running through her blood made up for the ache. Suddenly, his lips were at her neck again, his dick pressing into her so that she couldn't move, and he bit down hard, both of his hands digging into the skin of her ass and hips. She bucked beneath him with release, magic bubbling in her blood with the orgasm as her whole body shuddered in reaction to what he was doing to her. Above her, she felt him stiffen suddenly when he came, but with more than the orgasm, and then he was rolling away from her, cursing in confusion as he woke up.

Panting in the bed, she froze. Her body was so heated, it was difficult to think, and her breaths seemed to be coming heavier with each moment, harder and harder as if the air were being sucked away from the scene. She heard him fumbling near the bed, cursing, and couldn't help herself whispering, "I miss you, David," even though she knew he wouldn't hear her. She put her fingers up to her neck, where there was still an ache from his lips.

She'd already felt the air shift, and she knew she'd left him behind even before the ache began to leave her skin.

Chapter 9

David did another circle of the park, forcing himself to examine each face he came across, but there was nothing suspicious to be seen. It was a normal Sunday. Parents with their kids; singles with dogs; groups of friends walking or exercising. No sign of Nell Everett or Johanna Wilkins or the blond who'd settled Lauren in the ambulance.

Outside the park's entrance, he took a seat on a bench and looked at his phone. It was nearing 5:30—hours past when he'd said he'd be there. With no messages from either his partner or anyone else, he sat back, feeling like he could go to sleep there if he half-tried. Despite it not yet being dinnertime, he was drained, and he still didn't understand what had happened overnight, or even if it was a good thing, a bad thing, or nothing at all. He couldn't get over the idea that Lauren had been with him in his room, absurd as that seemed. But he'd never had a dream as real as whatever it was he'd experienced; even calling it a hallucination felt too light in term. When he'd woken, he'd felt her—felt her in the way that he'd felt her in the center, with her magic pulsing around them and warming both their bodies with each move they made together. Felt her in the air. There'd been no sound in the darkness of the bedroom, and no body he could grip onto after he'd come back to his senses, but he didn't know how else to explain what had happened.

He knew that, if he brought it up with Josh or Barry or anyone else, they'd chalk it up to the whiskey, exhaustion, and wishful thinking. If not for the evidence, he'd probably have been with them on that—but there had been evidence, and he couldn't dismiss it like they would. His body had been wet with sweat and the stickiness that came from real sexual release, but there'd barely been a trace of cum on the sheets and his body, which didn't make sense if it had just been a dream. And the dampness on the bed hadn't only been from him; he'd smelled it, desperate for answers, and what he'd smelled had been liquid desire that could only have come from one place. Maybe the sweat had been his or maybe it hadn't— there'd been a sweetness in the air that he hadn't recognized, and it had even played on his lips—but the scent of sex in the air had been undeniable. In the bathroom, he'd searched his body for any physical sign of her, but there'd been nothing; he knew Josh and Barry would point to that as evidence of an erotic hallucination, but it meant less than nothing since Lauren almost never left marks on him. It was always the other way around, but for when her nails raked him, and that hadn't happened in the dream… or whatever it had been.

Instead, what had happened had been fast and violent, bled over from memory and taken into some territory that he didn't understand. He'd been dreaming of the drive from the restaurant, the night before they'd gone to the therapy center, but instead of taking their argument up to the hotel room, he'd driven them to a park and taken Lauren against the truck. They'd been arguing, and the angst of the fight had bled into the sex. He'd used her magic against her, taking advantage of what he'd only learned about her magic after that night and proving it was a dream in doing so. He'd been rough with her, biting and punishing in a way that had been purposeful, turning the fight into sex built of desperation and anger; outside of a dream, it wouldn't have been acceptable… especially when he'd been in his right mind, as he'd seemed to be.

And then, he hadn't been bending her backward into his pick-up's passenger seat. He hadn't been in the dark of a parking lot, biting into her and pushing her to climax around him, but buried to the hilt in her pussy within his own bedroom, over her on his bed as he pounded into her and came inside her, holding her to his body as she spasmed with her own release. The sudden violence of it all, and the fast change of scene accompanying their orgasms, had driven him away from her and into the dark of his bedroom. And then it had been over.

Just the thought of it all had his dick thickening with desire, but he didn't have any explanation for what had happened. He didn't know if some of Lauren's magic could have somehow been residual in him and only showed itself in making the dream more real than it should have been, or if he'd somehow brought her there to his room, or she'd somehow come to him herself. No matter how he considered the angles, it didn't make sense. If there'd been any reality to their encounter, any substance to the two of them in the immediate moment, why hadn't she spoken to him? Why hadn't he heard her? And if there hadn't been any substance… then what the hell had happened, and how had the scent of Lauren's desire ended up in his bed?

His phone pinged for the second time in as many minutes, and he finally fished it from his pocket.

Heading back to the house with dinner. Where are you?

He stared at Josh's message for a minute, and then typed back that he was on his way. He wasn't making any progress sitting at the park, and if his partner found out about the message he'd sent out via Chloe or what he was aiming for here, there'd be no shutting him up about it.

The drive to the house gave him enough time to determine that he wouldn't try to talk to Josh about whatever had happened the night before. Just yet, he couldn't think of any point to doing so. And since there was no witch who he could trust to tell him the truth in response to whatever questions he might ask—none barring Lauren, anyway—that meant he had to go off of what little information he had. If the night before had been a one-off, then that might be the end of it. Maybe he'd never know unless he got around to bringing it up with Lauren at some distant point. But if not… if not, he'd be prepared for it to happen again, and to take what he could from it.

Back at the house, he ate fast and made his excuses, feigning an exhaustion that was only half-real now that he'd come to some sort of a half-baked plan. Under the guise of bringing down another case of beer from his truck, he instead brought down supplies from the garage and began setting up, not allowing himself to drink anything but water as he did.

Between the door and the hallway, he sprinkled down solid lines of detergent powder. He hadn't wanted to use salt in case that would somehow impede Lauren, if she was somehow finding her way into his suite, but he needed something on the floor to show him that he wasn't going crazy. He sprinkled thin lines every foot or so, each one about two feet long, between the door to his suite and the hall to his bedroom, and then he used the rest of the detergent to sprinkle out lines that reached across the hall every four inches or so—no way would anyone be able to walk through the space without disturbing any of them. Not in the dark outside of his bedroom.

In the bedroom, though, he wanted some illumination. He didn't think he could sleep with the space fully lit, and he needed to sleep, but he turned on the lights in the bathroom and the closet, and left those doors wide open. He also turned on the nightstand's light, but threw a light blue sheet over it to muffle the brightness. From the closet, he took out the ropes and handcuffs he'd hoped to introduce Lauren to eventually, with some lighter intention in mind. Their purpose tonight had nothing to do with sex, though—if she'd somehow been there, and had then disappeared, it meant she hadn't had any choice about leaving when she had. Without any doubt whatsoever, he knew that. It seemed unlikely that silken ropes would help against whatever might have pulled her away, but maybe handcuffs with wards carved into them could keep any spell from shaking her back out of his grasp if she came again. Or at least slow it down. He tucked the tools into the nightstand's drawer, and considered whether or not there was anything else he could do.

The fact that he hadn't had anything to drink that night meant that he was as aware as possible; he'd not even taken Tylenol for the headache he'd had for most of the day, which he'd chalked up to stress and a lack of sleep. And he'd washed the comforter and sheets that morning when he hadn't been able to go back to sleep, even before the sun had risen, so if there were any fluids on the bed in the morning, he'd know they'd come from this night's activities and not before. He didn't know what else he could do.

In the shower, he leaned against the wall and thought back to everything he'd learned about Lauren's magic over the time he'd spent with her. It wasn't much. He knew its foundation was in the spell her mother had cast on her, and that it fed off of his connection with her since he'd been the one to activate it. What they'd experienced in New York at the center, though, had added new layers of complication. It fed off of their physical contact, it seemed, but the resulting magic also needed to be used, or it just festered inside her. The problem was, he didn't really know what that meant. The vines she'd created had burned her badly, but had the amount of magic she'd put into them just been too much too fast, or something she could have handled easily if given more space and time? And if she didn't use the magic that built up in her, how long did it last, or were their other negative side effects besides what he'd seen at the center? For that matter, had those side effects of lost focus and unpredictable emotion been entirely to do with the pent-up magic and their time together, or just as much an effect of what Shea and Toscano had been doing to her?

All of the stuff he didn't know was killing him, and they just hadn't had time to talk about it. Realistically, he wasn't sure even Lauren had all of the answers he needed now. And where did that leave them? Fighting a coven, and at the hands of a spell that neither of them entirely understood. Not to mention the fact that if anyone beyond him and Josh found out about Lauren's remaining magic, along with their relationship, they wouldn't even have the support of the agency in finding her. Hell, he might not even have a job, should that happen.

***

In the dream, David was lounging by the pool at the ranch house as the sun set. Across the yard, Josh and Claudia and others could be seen playing some yard game, but beside him, Lauren was sprawled out on a lawn chair that was the twin of his own. Her skin glistened in the last of the sunlight slanting into the area, and although David dimly recognized that the scene was new—that he'd been somewhere else, in some other scene and dream just moments before—it was comfortable. She was singing something under her breath, and her skin was feverish with the day's tanning as well as the magic running through her, which he could practically feel through the slice of air between them.

She looked over at him. "Do you think Josh and the others can see us?"

He glanced that way; he wouldn't have been able to make them out individually if he hadn't already known loosely what they were wearing, and they were focused on their games. "Not 'less they come back this way."

Sitting up, Lauren swiped at the sweat that had collected along her arms. "You want some lotion?" she asked, seemingly changing the subject.

"Sun's setting. I'm fine—" Whatever he might have said next died on his lips, succumbing to the realization that her offer had just been an excuse. Her eyes never leaving his, she lifted one leg carefully over his chair, and then lowered herself so that she was straddling it in front of him. He'd already lowered his own legs to the ground upon seeing what she was doing, and his toes brushed hers on the patio tile as she leaned forward over him.

Her hands were hot on his skin, massaging up above his knees and making their way under his boardshorts. When they were halfway up his thighs, she stopped, and she looked up and caught his gaze again, smiling. A moment later, she was lowering her face down to his crotch, breathing against the damp fabric, beneath which his dick was shifting with her attentions, readying itself for more.

Her breath was hot on the fabric, and David kept his hands on the chair, clenching its armrests as her fingers began massaging deeper into the muscles of his thighs, and she murmured and hummed against him. He didn't know what she was doing, but he could feel the heat of her from his knees up to his belly, and it was bringing up his blood. He sighed in reaction, and then he shifted his hips up when he felt her fingers on the waistband of his shorts, moving to tug them down.

Her lips came down on the head of his cock and sucked him into the heat of her mouth, and he groaned out loud with the pleasure of it. Her tongue exploring him as her hands did the same, moving between his shaft and his balls as he thickened and hardened in her hands and her mouth. He let one of his hands come to the back of her head and take hold of her hair, encouraging her to take him deeper, and she did. All of him wouldn't fit in her mouth, but she took him halfway and stopped, licking him and sucking, and he jerked in her mouth with the heat and the magic of it. There was a tingling heat to her mouth that was nothing short of ecstasy, and it was starting to hum through his blood so that his whole body reacted to her.

Unable to stop himself, his hand pulled her deeper onto his cock, and kept pulling her in even when she gagged and pushed back on his thighs, but he couldn't resist the heat of her. Knowing she must be wet for him, just waiting for him to fill her, made it all more desperate, sexier, and as she tried to get used to the rhythm he was setting for them, he let both his hands tangle in her hair and guide her. When he let her pull back from him, finally, he could feel her panting, drool wetting his cock and swelling the blood in his body to react to her magic. He felt tight, pressurized, and knew when he looked down that he'd see her wide blue eyes staring at him, and his cock pulsing between them and ready to stretch her open. Not ready to give up the sensations she'd been building in him, he tightened his grip on her hair and pulled her in again, and she moved into him without protest. Her lips and tongue moved up and down the vein at the underside of his cock, and then she took his balls into her mouth as she worked his shaft with her hands, jerking him more awake and ready. When he heard her take a deep breath, he knew what was coming and still groaned aloud with the pleasure of her taking the head of his cock back between her warm lips, and then sucking him into her mouth as she explored with her tongue. He tangled one hand tighter in her hair to guide her as his other hand found her shoulder, and then moved to caressing her neck and helping her to move back and forth, guiding her and pressing her for more even when he could sense she'd had more than enough. When she pulled back again, he let his cock jerk upward with her and held her to him, coaxing her mouth and lips to take him deeper as he pressed upward against her throat as she gagged on him.

His eyes closed, he felt the heat of her, and her nails in his thighs fighting against his pulling her in tighter on his shaft, and then, in a moment's time, he realized what was missing. He'd heard no sounds from her—no sighs of satisfaction or desire, no mews of pleasure or want, no grunting when he pushed her limits, and no whimpers of either pain or pleasure. He'd heard nothing.

His eyes jerked open, and the pool was gone.

In a moment's time, he'd released his hold on Lauren's hair and she'd jarred backward away from him to land kneeling between his legs, wide-eyed and panting in the dim light of his bedroom. Her face was damp with sweat and tears, her lips gasping for breath that he couldn't hear her taking. His sweatpants were discarded, half off the edge of the bed, and he'd already pulled himself up to recline half-propped against the bed's headboard. Breathing hard, he took in everything about the scene before him—Lauren, still out of breath and with tears and drool on her face, nude in his bed; his cock hard and ready between them; the odd fuzziness to the air around her and him; and the magic that he could feel running hot in her hand where it rested against his knee, holding onto him in a way that he couldn't quite describe.

His mind frozen, he tried for words and only came up with her name, but she didn't answer. She looked down, as if to evade his gaze, and a shudder ran through her. Heat or magic or desire or something else… David didn't know what it was, but he scooted forward and landed his hands on her upper arms before she could think to run.

Her gaze pulled back up to his, as if with effort, and he tried to ignore the heat of her magic pooling beneath his skin where they were touching. With both of them nude and the smell of sex in the air, his breath was coming hard as he tried to come to terms with whatever was happening. This wasn't a dream, but this wasn't simply her—the Lauren before him looked almost fuzzy, but felt real and live in his hands, which tingled with the magic of her, feeling energy more than heat.

She swallowed, and he suddenly noticed the odd necklace she wore, which appeared to be nothing more than a long twist of cheap fabric, but then she was leaning forward into him. Whatever discomfort he'd caused her in pulling her mouth deeper onto him was gone, and suddenly her lips were at his collarbone, her hands caressing his thighs and then moving to his dick, pumping it between them. He groaned her name, suddenly unable to think through the heaviness of the magic in the air, and she pushed him backward in the bed. Then she'd moved forward, over him, and her slick folds were coming down around his cock so that the heat between them and the gliding of their bodies was all that mattered.

David felt the lack of balance in her, the lack of confidence as she tried to get a feel for riding him from this angle, and landed his hands at her hips, helping her glide down further onto him. He still heard nothing, but he saw the 'O' of her lips signaling a gasp as he pressed deeper into her, her eyes going wider, and she bit her lip, propping herself above him with her hands on his chest before she could land all the way down on his shaft.

He felt her body adjusting around him, and the heat of her pussy swollen and wet around him, and focused only on watching her there above him, lost in the sensations. He couldn't hear her, but he could smell the sweetness on her and see the sweat beading along her skin with the pressure of him filling her and the effort of getting used to him. He reached up and ran his hand along one of her bobbing breasts, tweaking her hard nipple and then tugging at it. He didn't dare lift up and bring it into his mouth, not with her still perched like this and struggling to get used to him filling her from this angle, but he played his hand around her breast while his other kept her thigh anchored to his, waiting for her signal. His brain had kicked on enough to make him realize that maybe she could hear him, even if he couldn't hear her, and he whispered without being half-aware of what he was saying. Telling her he missed her. That he needed her. That he'd find her. And repeating her name. Questions could wait for later. Maybe she could mouth messages to him or write in the steam of a mirror even if she still couldn't talk to him for some reason. He knew he couldn't hear her—not her gasps or words or even her breath. But for now, he only needed her to know that they belonged together, and that whatever this was, he wanted her with him no matter what it took.

David didn't know how much she heard of what he said, if anything. He could feel the magic running hot beneath her skin, and could barely think, for how warm and pressing her channel was around his dick. When the line of her torso relaxed, however slightly, he let his hands go to her hips and guide her further down onto him until she was tight against him, warm and wet, with his dick bottoming out inside of her. He could see from her heaving chest that she was panting, gasping—maybe with the pain and the pleasure of it at the same time, but she stayed seated atop him with her mouth and her eyes wide open on him, her skin soaked with sweat. Tears, too, but he knew he'd let her guide herself down onto him, so he knew any pain was pain she'd welcomed in—or, maybe, the tears were for whatever else she was thinking or going through, or what was keeping her from being all here, but he tried not to think of that. He didn't know which was worse, the idea that the tears were related to him hurting her, however incidentally, or something else entirely.

When she shifted forward and he sensed the pulsing of her body coming in waves of pleasure more than discomfort, he gripped her thigh with one hand and moved his other hand to her ass, guiding her into a rhythm as she rode him, levering herself up and down on his cock as he pressed into her again and again. Groaning with the pleasure of it, he pressed deeper and felt her shuddering above him, a whole-body quiver of magic and orgasm running through her blood as her mouth opened in what should have been a scream of pleasure and release, but was only silence. His own roar of climax came seconds later, and he grasped her as tight to his body as their skin allowed, pulsing into her as she gasped for breath above him and his dick filled her with his cum, so that he knew it would leak out of her when they disengaged. Her pussy felt swollen around him as they both panted, eyes locked together, but he held his hands where they were, holding her body to him and treasuring the reality of it. There was a heated magic between them that swirled under the skin, and he could see the fever of it in her flushed face.

When she closed her eyes above him, he let her go and rolled her to the side as gently as he could, disengaging from her as he did. She was glistening with sweat and whatever moisturizer she'd used, and he ran his hands along her body, feeling the magic follow his movements along her muscles as she tensed and panted beneath his fingertips. Along with the necklace, she wore bracelets and anklets that looked to be made of the same twisted fabric, but which he instinctively understood must have something to do with her presence there. He didn't touch them. Instead, he swallowed down the fear of her disappearing and took a few long moments to sink his fingers into her moisture, feeling her natural wetness and warmth coated with his own cum, and then he ran them up along her body, to her breasts and her mouth, and he sank his fingers into the warmth of her mouth, knowing she was tasting him there again, even as he bent down and nuzzled at her neck, licking and sucking at her skin until he could feel her trembling with desire again. His dick was still hard, wanting more, but there was one more thing to do first.

Without warning her, he flipped back to the other side of the bed and dug his hand into the nightstand drawer, coming out with the pair of handcuffs he'd secreted there before. When he turned back to her, he saw her eyes hooded with desire go wide, and then her mouth opened in some form of protest, but he was already clicking down the handcuff around her wrist.

No, he realized in the next instant. He'd clamped it around the air that had been her wrist only moments ago.

She was already gone.

Chapter 10

Lauren jarred upright from the tweed mat, out of breath and heated. She could feel the whole of her body tingling with pleasure and magic, and the pain she'd felt in her core was gone, transformed into a simple and familiar warmth. Even the soreness she'd felt in her jaw had disappeared, though she could taste David in her mouth. Closing her eyes, centering herself, she reached beneath her pillow and gripped the hunk of gypsum she'd placed there to help center and then store her excess magic. If Nell was right, this would be the key to making sure she had access to magic when she needed it without her body ever being too overwhelmed. Until she attained more control and balance, this was the best safeguard to keep her feeling like herself.

There was an odd sort of give-and-take with the stone, where she felt as if it were reaching into her with some essence other than her own, pulling in more energy than she'd meant to give over, but the sensation was there and then gone again, just as had happened the morning before when she'd come back the first time. She ignored it, keeping the gypsum grasped in her fist.

Finishing the spell, she pushed the rock back under her pillow, ignoring the sense of unease in her gut. Sending heated energy into a mineral might be common sense, given her situation, but Nell kept talking about all this as if it were a long-term plan. As if she'd forever be visiting David like this at night, to keep her blood running warm with power. But that was crazy.

Still in her bed, she licked her lips, tasting him. She didn't know where he'd been in his mind when she'd first shown up. He'd been asleep in his sweatpants this time, silent—as if he were just there waiting for her. And there'd been some light, allowing her to see him; she'd been so thankful for that. It had felt natural to do what she'd done, pulling his pants away and then taking him in her mouth. Still in his dream, he'd become rough with her, pulling her down on him until she'd feared she'd choke or pass out, but he must have had more control than she'd realized, even in his dream. And then he'd woken up, and she'd been so frightened it would all be over, but the spell hadn't pulled her away. He'd known she wasn't a dream, too—from all he'd said, all he'd repeated, he'd known she'd been there. If only he hadn't tried to hold her there with that warded cuff, she knew she'd still be there with him, but that had snapped the phantom spell as cleanly as if she'd willed it to end in the moment.

Breathing deeply, she got out of bed and looked at the clock. Three in the morning, only—she'd gotten there faster, but stayed longer. Wound up from the adrenaline and the magic of the night, she went back into the bathroom to wash away the lotion that remained sticky on her skin. She wanted it gone—the smell of it, the feel of it, everything. It felt good, putting it on, but having it on her body afterward was surreal. She ought to feel sweat along her skin, or cum along her thighs, but instead she only had the slight taste of him on her tongue, where her taste buds and nerve endings remembered his presence more so than her actual body could.

It wasn't fair… or right.

In the calm of the shower, her mind went back to the look on his face when he'd awoken to find her there in his bed with her. It had been so good to see him—even better to see his eyes open and aware of her. But the shock she'd seen there had been laced with so many other emotions. Fear, maybe. Horror. Relief had been there, too, along with desire, but they'd been slow to overtake the others.

***

Later in the morning, Lauren sank down into the cushions of the sectional with a cup of coffee. Nell sat nearby going over an old journal, and Adrienne was just a hand's breadth away, having gestured her over. "Shouldn't you be sleeping?" she asked quietly.

Yes. Yes, I really should be. But instead of saying that, she shrugged. Nell hadn't had an answer for her when she'd asked about her own energy levels earlier that morning, and Lauren was too new to this type of spellwork to have any idea of what she ought to be expecting. But over the last seventy-two hours, she doubted she'd gotten more than four hours of sleep. She'd been too nervous to sleep well the night before they'd first tried to connect her to David through a phantasm, and then she'd been so high on adrenaline when it had worked that she hadn't slept a wink afterward. And last night, she'd slept for perhaps an hour or two after trying the spell again, and that was it. Yet, she wasn't tired at all—not remotely.

Adrienne took her non-answer for what it was and looked back to the closed journal in her lap. "It went okay again?" she asked next.

"Just like planned, except that he woke up this time, and I was able to stay around." Lauren smiled with the thought of it, blocking out the initial mix of emotions she'd seen on David's face in order to focus on the intimacy that had come after that. She sipped at the coffee in her hand, and only looked to her friend when she didn't answer. The look on her face took some of the smile from her face. "What? Everything went fine."

Adrienne looked over to Nell, and then brought her eyes back to Lauren's. "Well, if the first visit ended when he woke up, what did it this time?"

Across from them, Nell scoffed. "He tried to trap her, and failed."

Lauren grabbed Adrienne's hand to get her attention and shook her head, frowning at Nell. "It's not that simple. It was just a cuff. A warded cuff. It's not like he was trying to lock me up in a dungeon," she said pointedly, and although Adrienne couldn't know what Lauren was referencing or anything of the warehouse, Lauren knew Nell understood her meaning. What David may have attempted the night before couldn't be compared to what Melania and the coven had done.

Adrienne looked doubtful, but Nell met Lauren's gaze and gave a tight nod. "Alright, so it didn't seem any more serious to you than a sex toy, fine. But now he'll know he can't keep you there, and maybe you won't let your guard down and allow him to break the spell before you're ready."

Sighing, Lauren looked back to Adrienne, willing her to understand. "He must have sensed I was there the night before, and not wanted me to disappear again. That was all he could think of."

"I'm not bothered by him trying to put a handcuff on you," Adrienne said gently. A frown still turned her lips down, and her eyes ranged between Lauren and Nell, who already seemed to have lost interest in the conversation.

"So, what's bothering you, then?" Lauren asked, genuinely puzzled. The abruptness of her leaving had upset her own senses, but she couldn't see how Adrienne could be aware of that, let alone be bothered by it herself.

"I mean, that was it?" Adrienne began, stumbling. "I thought your relationship with him was… good. Solid. But it sounds like… it sounds like you guys slept together, even after he was awake, and he didn't even try to talk to you? Ask you where we are, or if we're okay, or—"

Nell slammed her journal shut, cutting Adrienne off. "Adrienne, that's enough."

Lauren looked up to see the red-headed witch's eyes were laser-focused on her friend, with an anger that she hadn't seen from them since she didn't know when.

"The spell doesn't allow for communication," Nell reminded her, more quietly. "And that's not the point of it."

Adrienne's lips pursed, and she went to speak, but then thought better of it. When she looked to Lauren, Lauren only gripped her hand as if to tell her to let it go, and shrugged again, still trying to sort out her own feelings. "He did say something when he first woke up, but I didn't understand him," she said, thinking only of the unintelligible words he'd muttered against her skin and praying that Nell wouldn't pry for more detail; she was paying more attention to Nell's reaction to her words than Adrienne's. She'd understood much of what David had said, but it was a godsend that she hadn't understood everything, and could thus tell this half-truth by focusing on what hadn't made sense. "We were focused on other stuff," she added, hoping it might change the subject.

Nell smirked, but Adrienne blushed and stood up. "Right, okay. I'm going to go find Jo and Sarah—they were supposed to be trying to figure out what went wrong with that spell I muffed earlier since I couldn't. Lauren, see you later?"

Nodding, Lauren watched her friend head off up the stairs. When she looked back to Nell, the other witch was still gazing at her, examining her, and Lauren once again remembered how the monsters at the center had sometimes reminded her of this witch. There were times when she felt so off-balance with the woman, as if she really might have judged her all wrong, and others when she felt like this. Like Nell was still a witch who Lauren would have been better off never meeting, let alone learning magic from. Even if that meant she'd have no magic.

"You can still feel the magic now?" Nell asked.

The hum was there in her blood, soft but constant. It hadn't been the day before, but her second visit with David had done it. She nodded. "It's not strong—I don't think I could do much with it—but it's there. And when I came back, I sent some of the immediate excess into the gypsum, like you said."

Nell's body relaxed back into the couch, as if she'd needed to hear Lauren say that again even though she'd told her the same that morning. "Good. That excess heat you feel immediately after being with him probably isn't magic you could absorb into your blood outside of his presence. It's more spell than you at that point. Sending it into the gypsum will let you access it when you need it." With that, Nell re-opened the journal in her hands, but Lauren cleared her throat to bring her attention back to her.

"What Adrienne brought up, about communication… I'd like to talk to him."

"Why?"

The scowl that had come to Nell's face transformed it, and Lauren had to force herself to keep facing the woman. But she had to. The expression alone was enough to assure her that she and Adrienne couldn't give up on walking away from this place, these women—not and remain good. "Well, why not?" Lauren tried. "Even if I knew where we were, I wouldn't tell him," she promised, wondering if her words sounded as false as they felt. "But I don't know, so what good is the safeguard, anyway? It's… it's odd to be with him and not be able to speak to him. It feels wrong."

Nell's eyes had gone back to her journal, but her body was still tensed when she answered, "He hurt you, and all you're doing is fucking him. Because I know you are—no need to try to hide that, Lauren. And if it's for the sake of your magic, fine. We'll support you using him for that. But don't think we're going to open up the lines of communication and let him coax you back to him."

Lauren leaned toward her, willing her to listen, but wasn't surprised when she didn't look up. Still, she tried again. "But if it would make me more comfortable, him more comfortable with me being there, wouldn't that be better for the magic? Couldn't we… get more power from each visit?" she pressed. "More magic for our use here?"

For a moment, Lauren thought the temptation of more magic per visit had drawn her attention—for whatever reason, she knew Nell was anxious to have her at full strength, and she doubted it was only for Lauren's own benefit, as Nell and Johanna claimed. But apparently that wasn't enough of a carrot, because the hardness she met Lauren's eyes with was complete. "You try to communicate with him, even the simplest thing, and that spell is built to cut out. You're not strong enough to change it, and even if you were, we wouldn't tell you how. It will sense your intention the moment you try to tell him anything. Anything at all, Lauren—you remember that. You try to tell him you're alive or fine, or that the fucking sky is blue, and you'll disappear faster than the words can travel. And it's for your own good, Lauren. He won't hear you, and I didn't think you'd be able to hear him, despite your connection—I'm glad I was correct. He's a liar. It's what he'll do. He'll brainwash you into coming back to him and then he'll find a way to steal your magic entirely, now that he knows how strong it can be. Don't doubt that."

Lauren swallowed down whatever protest she might have made. She wasn't entirely sure Nell was wrong about him being uncomfortable with her retaining magic, given the look she'd seen on his face last night, but even so, there were things here that she and Adrienne weren't being told. And they were still hostages, no matter how friendly the witches' behavior might appear. No matter how much Johanna and Nell insisted that the secrets and their being kept isolated was for their own good, and for the protection of their coven, Lauren had seen too much of the witches over the years to trust them easily, not with the way they spoke of Lauren's power and how pleased they were with Adrienne's coming along. And no matter how much Lauren learned of the magic she'd always ignored over the years, no matter how much more comfortable she became with this phantom spell or how thankful she was to feel the magic running consistently in her blood, too much of the spellwork felt wrong.

Nell met her eyes, and her look seemed to soften, though Lauren didn't feel pulled toward the false empathy she could see the other witch trying to radiate. "I know it's hard, Lauren, but it's for your own good. You'll be better off without him once all this is done."

Fighting her instincts, Lauren nodded, and then she stood up, thinking to go back to her room, but Nell waved her back down.

"I'm going to finish reviewing this, and then we'll examine those pieces of gypsum and your blood; I want to see how much magic you've managed to build up over two days. That might give us a timeline for when you can try some more challenging work."

Lauren stopped moving toward the door and came back to sink back down upon the sectional. The mesh of her metallic shrug caught on the fabric of it as she reclined, and she pulled herself free of the snag. The garment felt tighter than it had before, constricting just as much as any handcuff ever would, and she missed being able to glance down and see the tattoo that had given her so much comfort over the last few weeks.

We were afraid the witches could track my magic, and they did. Maybe David will find a way to track the phantom back to me if he can't find the tattoo.

That's not impossible. It can't be.

Chapter 11

David kept his head back on the passenger side's bucket seat, letting the Mustang's rumbling engine lull him into a doze. Although it was only five o'clock, it might as well have been midnight. He'd been awake for hours after Lauren had disappeared, and although he'd managed to sleep after that and only made it upstairs when it had gotten closer to noon, he felt like he could pass out at any moment. Coming out for dinner and drinks—with anyone, for any purpose—was the last thing he wanted to be doing.

Beside him, Josh was silent, and David guessed he must still be mulling over all of the information David had dumped on him earlier. There wasn't a whole lot to be said about it at this point. Lauren had left them no clues to her whereabouts, though they were both convinced she'd been at the center of the projection—or phantom or phantasm or ghost or whatever the fuck had been in his room—he'd interacted with over the last few nights. She'd said nothing, and not even left footprints behind in the powder that David had set out for that purpose. But he hadn't hallucinated it. Both of them had been able to smell the remnants of that flowery lotion in David's room, and Josh had even managed to put a name to it. He'd labeled it as honeysuckle immediately upon walking into the space, remembering it from growing up in Virginia; the scent had been as strong as the musk left in the air from what David and Lauren had done to each other, making it impossible to pretend that everything was some trick of David's mind.

And then there was the fatigue on top of it. David had been chalking it up to the midnight encounters and the stress of searching for Lauren and Adrienne, but now that Josh had pointed out how complete it was, how utterly wasted David felt, they'd been forced toward the conclusion that it was connected. David had slept that day, after all—maybe it had been in spurts, from around eleven at night to one in the morning or so, and then from around seven that morning till close to noon, but that should have been way more than enough sleep for him. He'd gone on far less, night after night after night. One night with three or four hours, and the next night with five or six at minimum, should have been more than enough. And it wasn't even close.

Eyes closed, he thought back over the afternoon and how little progress they'd made. They'd called both witches they'd put into WitSec, and each one had refused to talk. They'd denied knowing anything about spells related to phantom projections, and since the two of them had been dosed and in the agency's custody even before projections had been sent by the coven previously, back when the phantoms of their own visages had tried to lure Lauren out of the ranch house, it wasn't as if they could be called on a bluff. From what he and Josh had learned of the coven, more serious spells might only have been performed by higher-ups anyway, and Chloe and Lalita had been anything but. Josh had hit a roadblock in trying to research that type of spell way back when the coven had taken David, too, so there didn't seem to be much hope in them finding information on their own.

The Mustang rumbled to a halt, and Josh nudged his shoulder. "You awake? Aware?"

David grunted, releasing his seatbelt and stretching in the bucket seat. "Barely." He lowered the visor and shifted the mirror so that he could see himself. Then he buttoned another button on his shirt and adjusted his collar, covering up the hickey Lauren had left above his collar bone—the one other piece of evidence proving that he wasn't simply going insane.

"Sorry we have to do this, but they went to the trouble to track us down and drive out here."

"Yeah." David was already leveraging himself out of the low-slung car, stretching his shoulders and wondering again why Josh preferred this type of vehicle to a truck. "Where to?"

Josh gestured down the street as he fed some coins into the parking meter. "Red Water Pub. They're probably already there."

David glanced along the street, which was fairly empty. No surprise on a Monday afternoon.

The Red Water Pub was an Irish pub he'd been to in the past, mostly for craft beers and sports, but the food was good and the staff were fast—there were worse places he could think of to have an awkward conversation. Inside, his eyes hadn't yet adjusted to the light when two shapes pulled back from the bar and approached, just as Josh entered behind him. David stuck out his hand, but Phil surprised him by wrapping him in a quick hug instead and then stepping back with a clap to his shoulder. Christopher greeted him in the same way.

"We owe you too much for a handshake," Christopher told him bluntly. "Nice to see you again, Agent Devlin," he greeted Josh next.

David looked around the small group, but was saved from figuring out what to say when a waitress came up and ushered them over to a table in the back.

"We asked for as much privacy as they could give us," Phil explained as they sat down. "A spare hundred might have helped," he added when David glanced pointedly around them—toward the front half of the pub, most of the tables were taken, but all of the spaces around their own table were open, and he could already see a waiter waving someone off from coming back toward them, taking them to a bartop near the window instead.

David picked up the menu and glanced at it blankly before putting it back down. He'd thought he could do this, but sitting here in a restaurant like nothing was wrong… even knowing it wasn't the case, he felt like he was giving up on the investigation, on finding Lauren. When he looked at Josh, about a second away from making excuses, he saw in his partner's face that the impulse was understood, but needless. It was enough to make him swallow it down; as had been the case when they'd gone to see Raul upon his request, there was just nowhere else they needed to be at the moment.

"We never would have taken her for a government agent," Chris began, looking between them. "You guys maybe, but not her."

The waitress came for their drink orders then, and David managed to order an IPA despite the lump in his throat. When she'd left, he thought to lie, but couldn't quite find the will to bother. "She's not. You guys ought to know that."

Josh cursed beside him, and Phil's mouth pressed into a hard line, but Chris just looked back at him without surprise. "So, you two came in because it was your investigation and you guys thought you could keep her safe. And she agreed."

David glanced over to the bar, waiting for the beer, and Josh filled the silence, giving the two men a bridge-level view of how investigations had fallen apart in the past with agents being refused entry, but Lauren being in a relationship with David and also being with them in a sort of protective custody had made it seem like the only option at a certain point.

"My sister made a lot of calls, it sounds like, when I quit my job," Chris spoke up, his eyes on the beer that had just been delivered. "Reporting us gone to whoever would listen to her. Nothing seemed to make a difference. We weren't lying when we said we owe you a lot—more now, it sounds like. Everybody in that place does."

David took a gulp from his beer, wishing he'd ordered a coffee instead. "The women who were after Lauren before managed to track her down—they had a new accomplice we didn't recognize, and that's who we met at the ambulance. There was no reason to think she wasn't safe or that they could have tracked her to the center. But they did."

"She should have been safe," Josh added, "and what happened wasn't anybody's fault. We'll find them. It's just gonna take some time."

"Yeah, that's why we're here," Phil said quietly. David looked up at him, but he kept going. "When we heard an agent and a civilian had gone missing, from the first ambulance to leave the place, Chris was desperate to track you guys down. I told him we oughtta let it be, but… you should hear it from him."

David looked at the ex-teacher, waiting, but he remained silent. His husband nudged him.

"Chris, we drove here. They'll either think we're crazy or they won't. You gonna tell them or you want me to?" Phil demanded, an edge of frustration leaking into his voice.

David finished his beer in a few gulps and watched as Chris did the same. Beside him, Josh gestured to the waitress for another round for just the two of them. "Chris, I don't know how you'd know anything that could help us, but if you do…"

"How long have you been with her?" he asked, seeming to stumble over the words.

"What?"

"How well do you know her, is what he's asking," Phil put in, sighing. Discomfort was written over his face.

David looked sideways to Josh, but saw that his partner was just as confused as he was. "Look, guys, I don't mean any offense, but you said you wanted to meet up to say thank you and check in about the girls, and it felt like we owed you the time, but…"

"Fucking tell me, alright? If you're serious about finding them, talk," Chris bit out, leaning forward across the table. "How well do you know her? How much do you know about her?"

Josh's hand landed on David's bicep, keeping him from rising, but it was a close thing. "You said you owed us," David said flatly. "Excuse me if I don't want to go into the details of—"

"She's a witch," Phil interrupted him. The other three men turned to stare at him, and he shrugged. "You two want to fight about how well you know her and who's got a right to her secrets, it's your bag, but I'm invested in you guys finding her, and I don't particularly give a shit if two shady government types think me and my husband are crazy. So, fuck it, I'm telling you. She's a witch."

David felt himself deflating, leaning back into his chair. When the waitress came with the next round for himself and Chris, he took a gulp and nearly let it drop to the floor rather than getting it to the table. "She told you," he muttered. "She wasn't supposed to use her magic or tell anyone."

"You knew?" Chris asked belatedly.

Phil sighed. "I told you, you idiot. You saw them together. And her not being an agent sealed it. You think he would have brought a civilian in there, otherwise, she had no way to protect herself?"

David looked between the men and then glanced to Josh. "I thought we kept the secret. If I'd known—"

"She didn't know I knew," Chris cut him off, calling their attention back to him. The flush to his face had faded, and the easy calm David was used to seeing in the other man was back, if tinged with worry. "So, don't blame it on her if it was meant to be kept quiet. She didn't tell me, and she didn't know I knew. Ask me, I doubt Adrienne knew, and they got close fast."

"When did you find out?" Josh put in, even before David could think how to respond.

Chris looked back to David, squinting his eyes in thought. "You remember the night Shea told you she might keep Lauren without you, if you tried to leave? When you guys started getting a feel for the real ring of the place?"

"That was only Saturday night of that weekend," Josh commented, thinking backward. "End of the first full day."

Phil nodded, picking up the conversation. "While I was talking about that escort to you and Van, Chris was still with the girls. He figured it out then."

"My sister, who reported us missing?" Chris said quietly. "You..." he broke off, looking over to Phil, who looked between the two agents with a frown on his face.

Josh picked up on the concern before David. "Whatever you guys tell us, about your sister or anyone else, it'll stay between us. We just want to track down Lauren and Adrienne. Anything that'll help. But if you guys figured out she was a witch, it can't hurt us to know how. Maybe others did, too."

Chris nodded. "My sister practices some. Not much—she doesn't belong to a coven." He must have seen David flinch, because he nodded. "Knowing what I did, I kind of figured Lauren's old coven might be behind the kidnapping, given all the agents around that place and how easy it seemed to go off. I'm sure there are some good ones out there…."

"But they're bad more often than not," Josh finished for him.

"Yeah. Seems like a witch on her own is an amazing woman—least, my sister is, and Lauren is—but you put a bunch of 'em together, I don't know."

David took a gulp from his beer and found his voice. "No, we get it. We've seen it. And you're right to guess that Lauren doesn't belong to one now. There are good covens out there, but most of the covens that form and stay formed are the ones where witches are looking to pool power and get more control than they need. And you're half-right. We think it was Lauren's mom's old coven that's behind the kidnapping, but even though we know some of the women involved, we haven't managed to track them down yet."

Chris took that in, and then spent another few seconds gathering his thoughts before he kept going. "So, that night, Lauren was pretty shook up. And I didn't mean to, but I let slip that Phil had learned something dark—what he got from that escort. I'd been putting off telling anyone; didn't know how to, really. And Dora and me were hoping Adrienne would get out of there, but Lauren saw through my bullshit, and then all of the girls were determined I was gonna tell them whatever I knew." His eyes shifted to Phil, and he half-smiled. "I'm shit with secrets, man, you know that."

Chris looked back to David and met his eyes. "I had a hard time telling them. At one point, Lauren reached over and took my hand—innocently," he emphasized, and

David waved him off. "I felt calming energy like when my sister used to help me through anxiety attacks. I'd never been entirely sure that that energy was real instead of imagined. El's always pretty cagey about what's magic and what's not when it comes to healing—that's what she does," he added. "And I didn't recognize it at first, I was so upset, but when I was talking to Phil later on, I realized what I'd felt. It was just like what my sister used to do for me. Thinking of it, I realized Lauren must have been sending some calming energy, some of her strength, into me and Dora and Adrienne while we were all sitting there together. I could be wrong about her doing the same for them that she did for me, but looking back, it feels like the girls should have been a little more panicked after what I told them, especially after Lauren flat-out demanded that Adrienne not leave until we all decided to do it together. And we were okay, that night. Like it was just another night."

"Another night in hell, yeah," Phil muttered.

"So, that's how you knew," Josh pressed. "She didn't tell you or do anything spectacular?"

A small grin came to Chris's mouth. "Spectacular like all those fucking vines that appeared out of nowhere, you mean?"

"Yeah, like that," David said flatly.

His smile disappearing, Chris shook his head. "Not that I saw."

Phil suddenly reached for his drink and downed it, though he hadn't touched it up till then, and then he raised his voice and called the waitress over. Something in his tone brought her over even before anyone else at the table could speak up, and he ordered four shots of whiskey and another round of beers for them before gripping his husband's shoulder. "Sorry, Chris."

Glancing sideways, Chris raised his eyebrow. "What?"

"You came here to tell us she's a witch," Josh explained, even as David caught up. "But we already knew that. If that's all you came to tell us, we're probably no closer to finding them."

Phil frowned, and then nodded at the waitress when she came with their drinks. "We hoped it would help, knowing to look for a group of women she'd been involved with in the past."

"How long were you there with Adrienne and Raul Rivers?" Josh asked after a moment. "Can you tell us anything more about her?"

Phil shrugged, looking to his husband. "Chris knew her better than me, but I can tell you she's a good person."

"A good person?" David echoed. "We saw that with Lauren, I guess, but if you're bringing it up now... what do you mean?"

Chris got up abruptly, excusing himself, and the table went quiet for a moment. Phil looked after him, and then turned back to face David and Josh. "He was really hoping we could help, and he takes his sister's secrets seriously—it was hard for him to tell you she practices. The fact that maybe we told it for nothing...."

"I get it," David told him, "really. We've got secrets to keep with Lauren, too. But what were you saying?"

"There was this one night," Phil answered, "when Chris was all worked up about some group therapy session. Jace had been trying to get everyone worked up, I think, and tried to get the group brainstorming—man, this sounds even more fucked up now that we're away from that place—anyway, he was trying to get them brainstorming about revenge. What they'd do to people who'd hurt them, spouses and anyone else. Adrienne went off on him. Only time Chris had seen her lose her shit, he said. Didn't matter that she pretty much hates Raul and just doesn't like to admit it; she tore Jace a new one for suggesting that they should even consider imagining hurting people who'd hurt them. And it wasn't a karma thing for her; she was just flat-out horrified that Jace would suggest it. Chris got a kick out of it, though he was pretty upset by some of the ideas flying around that night, too."

David stared into his beer. Realistically, the idea that something like that might help them somewhere down the road seemed far-flung.

"The point is," Phil continued, "she's good. Good like your Lauren. Maybe that'll matter," he added, shrugging.

"It can't hurt," Josh said.

Chris came back to the table then, his phone pressed to his ear. "You guys had any contact from Lauren at all?" he asked. "Any letters, signs, whatever? She said she'd been spending a lot of time in a new garden she'd built at your place—any weird stuff happening there, maybe?"

David frowned, working to catch up with the conversation, and then glanced sideways to Josh. He was still trying to figure out what to say in reply, and how much to tell him, when Chris took David's hesitation as answer enough and went back to his phone call.

"Sis? Yeah, they have, can you come tonight?" He looked back to the men at the table. "Where do I tell her to come to?"

Chapter 12

Josh finished pouring a coffee for David as a knock sounded at the door, and he called over his shoulder for the Rollysons to come on in. For himself, he took a beer from the fridge, and then he raised a hand to the visitors when they came up to the island.

"Coffee for me," Phil said. "I gotta be back in the office in the morning."

"Beer," Chris said. "I'm off till Fall."

"Right," Josh said, getting the drinks. "You gonna be able to get back to your old school?"

The man shrugged, pushing his hand through his hair as he took the beer. "Looks like it."

Phil took a seat at the island and rolled his eyes. "He's being modest. They need good teachers, and he's one of the best. You'd think I'm the workaholic because of my job title, but he's the one who'll be working sixteen-hour days and weekends once the school year starts up."

"You think you guys'll find 'em?" Chris changed the subject, catching Josh's eye.

Josh saw that he looked to his partner first, but it seemed clear David was struggling to stay awake even with the caffeine in front of him, so he answered for him.

"Yeah, we will. Somehow. We'll fill you in when your sister gets here, but we're confident that, at least as of last night, Lauren's okay, and if she's okay, I don't know why Adrienne wouldn't be. And if they're okay, that means we still have time to track them down." He didn't add that he could think of any number of reasons that Adrienne wouldn't be okay, if pushed, but the fact that Lauren hadn't looked grief-stricken when she'd come to David was the best sign they had of her safety. And if they hadn't found Adrienne's body yet—which they hadn't— that also seemed like a good sign. The witches would either have been interested in taking her alive with Lauren or not, and they easily could have left her disabled or dead in the ambulance, but they hadn't.

Chris took a swig of his beer, nodding. "El should be here soon. Listen, though, about Adrienne… she's the other reason we wanted to come talk to you guys. You met her husband, right?"

Josh couldn't think of a polite answer, but his expression must have been enough of one.

"Yeah, so you know what he's like. Thing is, part of the reason Adrienne was still there when you guys came around was that she's got nowhere else to go. He still wants her around, and her family thinks he's the Second-fucking-Coming—sorry," he added, seeing his husband cringe, "but she's never managed to put any money together that doesn't have Raul's name on it. We wanted to let you guys know that, when you find her, we'd like you to tell her she can come stay with us. We've got a basement we're working on shifting into a guest space, and she'll be welcome if she needs a place to stay while she gets her feet under her—away from Raul, I mean."

"I'll make sure we tell her," Josh promised, thinking back to what they'd seen of the woman's husband. "David and I joked about getting her a new identity if we had to, given what we've seen of the jerk."

Phil grinned. "I knew I liked you, mate."

They'd never gotten around to ordering food at the pub, so Josh turned to putting together some sandwiches as the conversation went on. David eventually moved over to the couch and reclined there, but the time went fast as they waited for El, who was coming from a few hours up the highway, a little bit beyond where Phil and Chris lived.

When she arrived, Josh saw the relation between them immediately. Though El's hair was curled and bleached blond, she had the same facial features of her brother and was nearly as tall. She also wore platform sandals and a sundress—Josh couldn't imagine a women who'd look less like a witch, but she had an infectious smile, and hugged him and David both upon greeting them.

"Anything I can do," she told them, accepting a cup of coffee when Phil gestured. "So, what sign have you seen of her?" she asked next, taking a seat on the sectional beside David.

He looked lost for words, still half-asleep, so Josh took the lead once again as the other men perched at the nearby island. "She's been showing up at night as a sort of apparition, phantom, something," he said, and tried to ignore the shock he saw fall over Phil's face. "I haven't seen her because we don't have security cameras set up downstairs, where our rooms are, but David's seen her the last two nights. They've…" he stumbled, thinking of what David had implied more than what he'd said, and finished awkwardly, "interacted. Physically."

Chris spoke up from behind them, "Can we not have details? If that's okay?"

"No details," David echoed quietly. "Point is, I could feel her, not just see her."

El looked thoughtful, but unsurprised, so Josh went on as she sipped her coffee. "David laid out some detergent powder on the floor, trying to catch her footsteps and make sure he wasn't hallucinating, but there were no footsteps at all, even where she must have been stepping. But we keep some handcuffs with warding on them—warding against spells," he clarified, seeing Phil's confused look, "and when David tried to put one on her wrist, to keep her from leaving since we figured she must be getting pulled away somehow, she just disappeared."

"And you're sure you're not imagining her?" Phil asked from behind them. "Dreams can be pretty real when you're stressed, and no offense, David, but you look fucking wiped."

"I'm not imagining it," David said, sitting up straighter and taking a swipe at his eyes. "Josh smelled her perfume—some kind of honey."

"Honeysuckle," Josh clarified. "Probably some lotion, it sticks to the fabric down there so much. And she left a, uh, mark on David, too."

El's eyes got slightly wider for the first time. "She tried to hurt you?"

"A hickey is what he's talking about," David said with a shake of his head. "She didn't have any weapons and didn't try to hurt me. Just… she seemed to want to be close."

David went quiet, and Josh took a breath to try to center himself. He only knew what they were hiding second-hand, but if they wanted this to go anywhere…. "It's a long story," he began, focusing on El, "but Lauren lost direct connection to the magic in her blood. Long before she came to the center. Because of an old spell, though, well, it wakes up when she's around David. We have reason to believe that maybe the witches are pushing her to come back here—or allowing her to come back here at night—because it's the only way she can have access to her magic, by having some contact with David."

El had gone slightly rigid beside them, looking between them, and Josh saw what was coming before she said it. "I've seen rumors online—of a government agency that's found a way to take a witch's powers. Are you… is that you?"

Chris rose behind them, cursing under his breath, and Josh interrupted whatever he was about to say. "We won't hurt you, El. We won't do anything to affect your magic. We're just trying to find Lauren and Adrienne."

The blond witch's face had gone hard, and she put her coffee cup on the table and rose to pace across the room. She stopped at the window and turned to face them, but she'd closed herself off some, he could already tell.

Fighting the urge to stand up, knowing it would only escalate things, Josh blocked out the murmured curses coming from his partner and focused on talking to El. "Look, you're right, okay? That's our agency. But using that mix on Lauren was a mistake. Her mom was killing people—she killed forty-some men that we know of over the years—and it seemed necessary; at that time, we had every reason to believe Lauren was connected to her coven and complicit in the murders even if she wasn't directly involved. But the stuff our agency came up with, it's only going to be used on witches who are breaking the law from here on out. We've been working to make sure more mistakes don't get made, I promise, so it'll only be used when it has to be. And I'm not talking traffic tickets, El, I'm talking murder. Real criminal activity that endangers lives. You don't have to be afraid of us."

El stood still stiffly at the window, and Chris and Phil were standing by the couch now, looking around the group. "Sorry, El," Chris spoke up. "I didn't know. But I saw what Lauren did at the center—she's got magic now. And these guys... they're the only way we got out, sis. Them and Lauren."

Josh didn't bother pointing out that the magic Lauren had was only related to David, and that the potion they'd put into her had worked. He had as many regrets about that whole mis-step as David did at this point. "I'm just saying, we won't hurt you or affect your magic in any way. And we won't give any of your secrets away—we promised Chris that, and we meant it. But if you can help us, anything you can do… we're out of leads right now," he finished. He glanced to his partner, who'd slumped down again to place his head in his hands, elbows propped on his knees. He'd already given up on El helping them.

After what felt like minutes, El shook her head at Chris and signaled they should sit down. She pulled the ottoman slightly away from the sectional, giving herself more space between herself and the men even as Chris and Phil came around to take a seat, and then she sat down again. Smoothing her dress down, she focused her eyes on David, and then she leaned forward and placed one hand on his knee, leaving it there until he shifted and looked up at her.

"I don't know if I should help you, but I believe you don't mean me harm. Will you let me read your emotions? I need to know—I need to know for sure that you love this girl before I help you find her. I don't even know if I can help, but if this is all some trick to get her back even though she doesn't want to be here, I can't be a part of it."

"What do you need?" David asked, and Josh felt the tension in the room decrease another notch.

She looked over at Josh. "Chris said that Lauren was keeping a garden here, and I didn't bring any supplies with me. You mind if I take a look at what she's got and see if I can save us some time?"

Josh led her around to Lauren's gardens, where she picked some Mugwort, Lemongrass, and Peppermint, having to explain to Josh what the Mugwort was along the way. In the kitchen, she set water to boiling and asked Josh for Bay Leaf and Cinnamon, which he got for her.

When she seemed to want privacy, he left her to the kitchen after showing her where the mugs were.

Back on the sectional, he listened in as David finished telling a PG version of what Lauren had been through with her mom. He didn't fault his partner for it. Every indication suggested that these men were the closest things Lauren had to friends at this point, outside of Adrienne, himself, and David, and they obviously had open minds. If it helped David to get everything off of his chest, classified information or not, he wasn't going to argue.

When El came back, she had two mugs. One, she handed to David, and she kept the other for herself. "Drink it," she told him simply, and he did. Sitting beside him, Josh got the scent of David's tea, which was lighter in color than El's. It smelled something like Sage, though he knew they hadn't picked any. He glanced to Chris, but the utter lack of concern on his face took his blood pressure back down. If he trusted Chris and Phil, which he did, then he had to trust El.

When both had drunk their tea, David looked a bit more hesitant, but he sat up straight when El directed him to, and held her hands as requested. "I just need to know how you feel about her. That's all. Just think about her—no specific memories or scenes. Just her. Make sense?"

David nodded and closed his eyes, and Josh watched as El closed her eyes, as well. For what felt like too long, they sat like that in silence, and he finally had to turn his eyes to the window and focus elsewhere.

A deep breath beside him signaled that whatever had been happening was over. He looked back to his partner, who was swiping a hand across his eyes. "You okay?" he asked.

Nodding, David stood up. "I'm getting a whiskey."

El asked, "Make it two?" and Josh looked over to her. She looked more open now—relieved, he thought. David called back to ask if she wanted hers with soda, and she said yes before meeting Josh's eye. "Okay. I don't know if I can help, but I'll try."

Phil got up for more coffee, and came back in just as David was handing El a drink. "I pass approval?" he asked her.

"You love her," she agreed. "That's good enough for me." She took a sip of her drink, then glanced around to the group again. "Okay, so… she's coming into the house at night as something. Probably a traditional phantasm since that's a relatively simple spell in a situation like this, and I'm not seeing any evidence to the contrary. I'm guessing you've got wards, but if she was living here already, as Chris said, then those wouldn't be affected by her energy in any form. I take it she didn't tell you anything about where she and Adrienne are being held, or I wouldn't be here?"

David sat back and shrugged. "She doesn't say anything. I can't hear anything from her. Sometimes, I've seen her mouth moving, or felt like I should hear her because of… what we were doing… but there's no sound. I can't even hear her breathing—I've tried."

El frowned across from them, resting her whiskey on her knee. "That's odd. Phantasms can usually communicate sound just fine if they're done skillfully, from what I've heard. I haven't made one, understand— but I've studied plenty of books that covered them." She thought for a moment, and then asked, "Was it that you couldn't hear anything at all? Like you were in vacuum?"

"No." David took a sip of his drink and forced himself to sit up straight, willing himself to wake up. "I could hear just fine. I heard myself, and my steps on the floor, and the bed creaking. I could hear the air conditioner, too," he added upon a moment's reflection. "I just couldn't hear her. Not anything she did, not anything she said. Not even her breathing," he repeated.

"Well… that's not anything to do with the phantasm spell, from anything I've ever heard. It must be something added in. Maybe she wasn't the one who made the spell, and someone added in some silencing element she didn't have any control over," El guessed.

"That would track," Josh agreed. "Her focus, from what she says, has always been on plants and healing. She wanted nothing to do with her mom's coven growing up, and when we had those phantoms we mentioned show up here the one time, it didn't feel like she knew much more about them than we did."

"They didn't talk, either, though," David put in. "You sure that's not normal?"

"The reason phantasms are often thought to be silent is because they can only speak with the voice of the person behind the spellwork. If Lauren looks and feels as real as you say, and her skin was warm instead of cold," El provided, waiting for David's nod before she continued, "then that means Lauren has to be at least mostly responsible for the spell. Maybe it's not all her behind it, but she's part of it. There'd be no reason for her to keep silent unless that were a secret."

"So, with the phantoms that came here who looked like us—"

Phil rose, heading to the kitchen. "Sorry for the liberty," he explained when Josh paused, "but I need a drink for this. Chris might have grown up with this, with his mom and El, but I sure didn't."

Josh nodded—he could relate. He looked back to El. "Those phantoms that came here looked like us, but they wouldn't have sounded like us? That's why they wouldn't speak to Lauren?"

"Exactly." El took another sip from her drink and then kept going once Phil had returned. "If they'd said anything, it would have broken the illusion because Lauren would have heard the voice of whatever witch was behind the spell. And because neither of you was involved in making that spell, it was less real—the skin that touched Lauren was freezing cold, you said. And they looked almost glitchy. David's getting a realer, human-feeling version of Lauren only because she's directly involved in the working of the spell. She's at the foundation of it, and it's her intention to be here herself. But if she doesn't have the experience to fully understand what she's doing on her own, then she's depending on another witch to help her. Whether they're telling her or not, that witch must be adding in another element to the spell, to keep you from being able to hear anything she says."

"Well, if she can't tell us anything, I don't know where that leaves us," David commented.

El's expression was thoughtful, and she took a moment to answer. "Is she wearing anything?" David hesitated, glancing over to Chris and Phil, and she continued, "I mean, just in general. I don't care if she's showing up in jeans or lingerie, guys, trust me. But if she's wearing anything, that might help."

David released a breath, and then admitted, "Not much. She's got some sort of odd jewelry on—a necklace, and around her wrists and ankles, too."

"Like jewelry you'd buy in a store?" El asked.

"No, nothing like that… it looks like plain old fabric. Just twisted or sewn up into strips. I don't think it's tied—I think I saw actual jewelry clasps on the ones on her wrists, at least—but it might as well be, it's so simple."

"That's probably some part of the spellwork, though," El told them. "Anything else?"

David was already shaking his head when Josh thought of the fake wedding rings the two of them had worn into the center. His partner still wore his. "What about the rings?" he asked.

David looked back at him blankly, and Josh pointed to the wedding band that remained on David's finger. He hadn't bothered to take it back to the office yet. "She still had the wedding band and engagement ring on when we put her in the ambulance; I noticed them when I was carrying her downstairs."

"I don't… I don't know." David closed his eyes and tried to think back to the night before. He'd been so focused on her, and on the odd bands of fabric, he hadn't thought to look for the rings. Hell, he hadn't had any reason to. "Maybe?" he replied. "I think so?"

El smiled. "Well, if she is, that means she can wear something else if she wants to—jewelry's no different from clothing. Maybe she could write something on her clothing that would allow you to find her, or wear something to point you in the right direction? Can she hear what you say to her?"

David shook his head. "I'm not sure. Until this morning, I wasn't even sure I wasn't hallucinating."

"Just in case, you shouldn't depend on being able to tell her that," El suggested. "If you're open to it, I think we ought to assume she will come back, and I think you ought to write her a message on the wall. 'Write your location on a shirt and wear it here,' or whatever."

"I thought you couldn't read in dreams?" Josh interrupted her.

"I think that's an urban myth," Chris commented.

"And this isn't a dream anyway, right?" David pointed out. "Plus, we've got nothing to lose."

"Okay," Josh said, "so, that's something we can do, anyway. Another thing…" he began, and then glanced at his partner, who just raised an eyebrow at him.

"Don't hesitate on my account, man. Spit it out."

Josh nodded, and looked back to El. "This guy is barely functioning. He's exhausted. You don't know him, but he can function on no sleep at all, and he's been sleeping. I think... I think something about what's happening is draining his energy. Is there anything we can do about it?"

"Besides caffeine," David added.

"All spells take energy from somewhere," El pointed out. "Something in the spell being used here must have the energy drain redirected, so that it's coming from you instead of Lauren. My guess is, if you're feeling so drained as you look, she's not feeling any effects at all. You've got the ingredients here that I'd need to redirect that drain, and I can do that..."

"But then it would all be coming from Lauren," David concluded.

"I'm afraid so." El shifted, adjusting her skirt as if she were suddenly uncomfortable. "I wish I could tell you another way, but if she's the one actually working the spell, the energy has to come from either you or her. And this sounds like a strong, long-lasting spell, so we're not talking about a small amount of energy being used for it. I can help you shift it, but that's all. The only other thing I can suggest is that you tell her not to spend so much time here, or else ask her not to come so often, assuming this keeps going on."

David was shaking his head, and Josh didn't blame him. Given who Lauren was with, they didn't want to drain her of whatever energy she had, and they couldn't ask her not to visit David unless the energy drain got to be debilitating.

"Lauren's got plenty of healing plants growing," El said after a few seconds had passed. "I could prepare some brews for you so that you have something other than caffeine to bolster your energy and get it back faster. That would only do so much, but it's better than overloading your system with chemicals, and it would help some."

David nodded his head, and then he stood up. "Thanks, that would be good." He met Josh's gaze, and nodded.

"You guys get her whatever she needs. I'm gonna go paint a message on my bedroom wall."

Chapter 13

When Lauren got to the door of David's room, she saw him already starting to sit up in bed, blinking himself wearily awake. He looked exhausted, with circles under his eyes, but his gaze came straight to the door to focus on her. For a moment, her breath caught, and then she saw him pointing up above his head. With a glance upward, she noticed what she hadn't seen before—in big black letters, he'd painted a message for her.

Tattoo not working. Wear something we can track.

"Can you understand me? Hear me?" he asked, already getting up from the bed and coming toward her.

She stood frozen at the doorframe, fighting the impulse to answer him. The whole reason she'd made an effort to come when he was asleep was to catch him off-guard, and because it was supposed to be easier for the spell to home in on him if he was asleep. He asked again, repeating the question, and suddenly she couldn't help it; she gave in to the impulse to nod her head, even as he stepped within arm's reach—and then she was gone.

Back in her room, on the lower bunk she'd been sleeping in each night, reclined on the tweed mat they'd picked to mirror the rough fabric of David's old couch.

The head-nod alone, little of it as he'd probably seen, had been enough of an attempt to communicate that it had shaken her out of the spell, and she hadn't even gotten close to him. But that message… if the tattoo wasn't working, what on earth would he be able to use to track her? She'd hoped he'd be able to use her magic and that tattoo, but if not that, what?

The lock on her door clicked, and even before Lauren had been able to grab a blanket to cover herself, Nell had stepped inside. She wore loose sweatpants and a t-shirt that served as her pajamas, but she looked wide awake.

"I was passing by and I felt the energy drop off," Nell told her, though Lauren could hear the lie in her voice.

Lauren pulled a blanket over top of herself, more upset at the intrusion than the lie. Once the spell had begun working, she'd figured they had some way to keep track of the energy and how long she spent with him. It made sense that they wouldn't leave her quite so much to her own devices. "He was awake when I got there. I couldn't keep from shaking my head at him when he… when he asked if I could hear him," Lauren finished, realizing her mistake already.

Nell's eyes moved over her, flat and analytical, and Lauren fought to keep her breath even.

"It was a simple question," she tried, her mind racing with what she could say without lying. "I could read his lips since he kept repeating it." Which was true. She'd been able to read his lips and hear him.

"And you shook your head, and were back here."

Nell moved closer, staring at her. Lauren forced herself to nod, hoping she could sell the half-truth. "I don't even know if he saw me shake my head," she added, "it was so fast."

Lauren couldn't think of a way to stop the other woman from approaching, and soon Nell had sat down on the bunk beside her, humming something to herself. She couldn't help flinching away when Nell's hand came down on her arm, gently, and she breathed through the threat. Whatever Nell was doing, Lauren couldn't do anything about it at the moment but wait it out.

"And he was awake?" Nell asked. "That's odd, but I'm glad the spell still worked."

Lauren breathed out when the other witch took her hand away, and offered a half-lie. "He was waiting for me," she said, though she knew he'd somehow been awoken by her approach, even if he hadn't been able to hear her. "But he looked exhausted, Nell," she added. "I'm worried… it made me worried that maybe I shouldn't go each night. I know you said it would be okay, but—"

Nell stood up, already heading back to the door. "He's fine. It's fine. You need to build up your magic, and that's best done with consistency. The spell isn't using up any more energy than is normal. Your boyfriend's probably just drinking too much or fucking around." Nell had turned back to her in time to see Lauren flinch, and a smile tilted her lips. "With any luck, he'll realize that you can't communicate with him and stop asking you to, and that will make this easier. Try two more times tonight, and then you can give up if he keeps trying and you can't resist attempting an answer. He'll figure out he's chasing you away quickly enough," Nell added. "Alright?"

Lauren swallowed, and forced herself to nod, and finally Nell left.

There'd been a threat in Nell's words that Lauren didn't entirely understand, and she was over her head in terms of the spellwork. She'd just have to trust that she'd recognize a problem if she and the spell truly did start taking too much energy from him, and hope Nell wouldn't find a way to force the issue if Lauren chose to stop.

Nell had locked the door from the outside, but Lauren walked over and slid home the deadbolt she'd requested be placed on the inside. Johanna had balked at it, but given in when Lauren had pointed out that the witches were strong enough to move it with magic if they really wanted to. It still made her feel better, even if it could give her only an extra few minutes or so of privacy, at best, if Nell or Johanna truly wanted entrance. The chore done, Lauren walked over to her dresser and went through the drawers. All of the clothing she'd been given here was expensive, soft and comfortable, but none of it was particularly distinct. Certainly, none of it was hand-crafted or location-specific in a way that she imagined could help David and Josh find her. The closet offered nothing more noteworthy when she paged through it.

Grunting in disgust at the futility of the search, she went back to her bed and reclined on the mat again. The lights had remained on tonight since David had taken to leaving the lights in his suite on after her first night's entrance, so she simply closed her eyes and tried to imagine the dimmer lighting of his bedroom, and the hall just beyond it. The knowledge that he must still be awake and waiting for her distracted her, so she got up and stretched, and re-applied the lotion before she lay down again, focusing on her own breathing before she went back to imagining the space of his suite.

It wasn't sound that alerted her to the change in space this time, but the smell of incense in the air, and she opened her eyes to the dim light of David's living room. She could smell Sandalwood, though she didn't see its source. Sitting up, she looked around, but everything was still. She hadn't noticed the scent when she'd appeared earlier in the night, and realized now that it must be something he and Josh had set up—that they'd somehow found a way to sense her showing up, allowing David to be up and waiting for her. As if to confirm her suspicions, he appeared at the door of his bedroom even as she turned toward the hall, and she swallowed down the emotions that were trying to bubble from her mouth. She couldn't let herself try to talk to him. She just couldn't.

Tonight, he wore black sweatpants that hung low on his hips, and there was stubble on his jaw. His hands were fisted at his sides, but his stance was relaxed, as if he only didn't know what to do with his hands or how to treat the moment. But there was a smile on his lips, and none of the horror of the night before.

Walking up to him, she saw him looking her over as if trying to find some injury, but he was so aware of her that it took her breath away. It was as if she was there with him, totally, and without the spell. When she got to him, he picked up her hand in his and held it between their faces, calling her attention to it. His fingers rested on the wedding band and engagement ring that she still hadn't taken off, odd as it had been to wear them at first.

Her eyes went back to his, and even though he looked exhausted, a calmness exuded from him—one she hadn't seen on previous nights. Thinking of the message, she wondered if that was it; if he thought he'd found a way she could signal him, but there was no way she could tell him otherwise.

Keeping herself silent, she let him lead her into the bedroom and push her to sit on the bed. She watched as he pulled her hand sideways and away from her lap, treasuring the heat coming from his touch. He placed it on his pillow, pressing down to communicate that she should leave it there, and then he pulled a camera from his pocket. Bringing it close to her hand, he focused and took a picture. Then he twisted the rings on her finger, and took another, and repeated the process twice more until he'd gotten pictures of the rings from four different angles. Her hand was relaxed now, and she understood what he wanted in the moment, though she didn't see the point. Seeming to hesitate, he looked back at her, and then he put the camera away and sat down beside her on the edge of the bed.

Her hand had already warmed with his touch, and now she leaned her body into him and breathed in his scent. She tried to forget everything but the sensations between them as his arm wrapped around her and pulled her in to his side, his other hand clutching hers against their thighs, covering the rings.

"I think you can understand me, but can't talk to me, and that's okay," he started, and she had to fight the urge to nod against him. "If you can sell these rings, or convince someone to do it for you, do it. The diamond's worth something, which might make it tempting, and the money doesn't matter to us, so whoever sells them can keep it. The point is to get them out there, into the public sphere. If you can get them into a pawn shop, we might be able to track you through them." He went silent, as if taking a breath, and she pressed herself closer to him, hoping he'd understand the pressure as her understanding him. His hand tightened on her shoulder, and she hoped that meant he did.

He nudged her chin up, shifting her gaze to the closet. He'd opened up the door wide, and on the inside of the door where ties normally hung, she saw that he'd hung up some shirts. One was a t-shirt that had a slogan for Ralph's Pizzeria, where the guys liked to get pizza, and another was a hockey jersey for some NHL team. Still another t-shirt read 'Blueridge Larks' and had a number beneath it, so that she guessed it must signify some sports team from David's past. "Place names," he said quietly. "Anything we can track."

Once again, she fought the urge to nod, but what was the point anyway? If she'd been able to communicate to him that she understood, that was all well and good, but none of this helped her. She hadn't seen any of the women in the coven wearing anything but casual, normal clothes—nothing that gave a signal to place or time or name. And it wasn't as if she could ask for something like that. Hell, even if she could have talked to him, what would she have said? They were in a nondescript building, probably one made for offices, and being controlled by Johanna and Nell? He and Josh had probably guessed as much already.

Wishing she could just have a normal conversation with him, about anything at all, she instead turned her head sideways and met him in a kiss, pushing her hand against his chest and taking in the feel of the magic's heat rising between them, relishing the skin-to-skin contact. His tongue dipped between her lips, pushing against hers, and one of his hands tangled in the back of her hair, levering her up against him.

When he pulled away, she was breathless, and licking her lips with the taste of the herbs he'd had on his lips— he and Josh must have been experimenting, she thought, trying to find a way to talk to her or help David keep up his energy, and the idea of it made her want to cry, but David was already moving beside her, pulling her up toward his headboard. "Just spend the time with me tonight," he whispered to her once she'd landed beside him, his arm wrapped around her, and she didn't fight him as he shifted them down toward the pillows and spooned behind her, wrapping his arms around her so that he could pull her into his body. "Relax, baby. I just want to be with you, so just relax." His breath was on her neck, warm and tingling, and she closed her eyes to simply enjoy it. The magic was running through her body, reacting to him, and having his heart beating hard against his chest pressed to her back was enough for now.

His hand ran up and down her side, wandering from her knee up to her chest and back, and the magic followed his touch. Bubbling and heating in her blood, it teased her skin into arousal and left her trembling against him, but he kept his hands to her side, and to her head and her stomach, and talked to her all the while as she tried to soak herself in the sound of his voice, curled against him and clutching his hand.

She lost herself to him whispering to her, telling her he loved her, and fought the despair pulling against the magic in her blood. This wouldn't be forever, she told herself, pressing herself tighter into his arms and sinking into the warmth bubbling up between them. This was all they had now, but he'd find her. This wouldn't be forever.

When drowsiness began pulling at her, she welcomed it. Going to sleep in David's arms, in the heaviness of the spell's air and the heat of her magic reacting to him, hadn't felt like an option until now, but his gruff voice against her neck and his hands on her skin were everything she'd been wanting and missing. There was desire at her core, wishing they'd done more, but that could wait. She just wanted to lie there with him and forget the world for a while, enjoying the heat of what they had without the pressure of anything else, or anyone else. Lying naked against him, it was easy to forget all of the rest of the world, and sleep came fast.

Waking up to her room without him was slow, and she felt his absence more than her own magic. Not bothering to open her eyes yet, she reached for the gypsum, but then she realized there was no need. The magic was in her blood, but it was relaxed—there was no excess heat running through her body or pushing her to find a use for it, and no lack of stability to what she could feel. More than she had in days, she simply felt like herself, like she'd felt when she'd been around David in those last few days at the ranch house before they'd left on that blasted case. Stretching, she shifted sideways and looked at the alarm. Nine in the morning, nearly. She wondered how long she'd remained in David's bed, and how long he'd lain awake beside her. Whether the spell had worn off, or whether one of them had done something to cut it out.

Either way, it didn't matter.

When she got out of the shower, Nell was waiting for her, sitting on her bed and holding the gypsum that Lauren had had no need for that morning. Averting her eyes, Lauren went to the closet and pulled out the metallic shrug.

"You didn't have any extra energy this morning even though you spent most of the night with him," Nell said, unmoving. Normally, she'd have been approaching Lauren already, helping her get into the tight tangle of fabric.

"That's a good thing, isn't it?" Lauren asked, forcing a levity into her voice. "I'm hungry—help me with this?"

Finally, Nell set the gypsum down and stood up. She held the shrug behind Lauren so that she could drop both of her arms into the sleeves at once—it was too tight to do anything else—and then pulled it up snug around her shoulders. The locks were out of her pockets a second later, and she latched the first one at Lauren's neck even as Lauren fit her thumbs through the holes at the bottoms of the sleeves. The garment felt tighter on her throat every day, she thought, though it hadn't shrunk and she hadn't gained weight. She was simply more aware of it, and everything it represented. She held out her hands to Nell silently, and Nell latched the final miniature padlocks into place. Instead of stepping back and leading her to the door, though, her hands came down on Lauren's wrists and held them between them. Nell dug her nails into the fabric so that they tented into Lauren's skin tight enough to make her whimper, and then she stared into the other witch's eyes.

"What changed, Lauren? This is about building up your magic. If you spend a whole night with him, only to come back in the same stasis you were in before, we're wasting time," Nell hissed, pressing her nails deeper into Lauren's skin.

Lauren pulled back from her, but the other witch didn't loosen her grip. "We… he… we only laid down together. My magic got enough. I got enough magic," she stumbled. "Nell, you're hurting me," she pleaded, pulling away again.

Nell finally released her, and Lauren fell back into the dresser they'd been standing near, doing what she could to massage her wrists through the rough fabric encasing them. "Our point, Lauren, is to make you a strong witch worthy of your mother's power and worthy of being in this coven. That's only going to happen if you take this seriously."

"I thought you didn't even want me having sex with him," Lauren reminded her quietly. She glanced to the door, praying that Adrienne wouldn't walk in on them— the other girl had relaxed into the atmosphere of the place, and at least for now, that seemed best. If Adrienne didn't act like a threat, Nell wouldn't treat her like one.

"I didn't," Nell acknowledged. Turning away, she walked back over to the bed and picked up the gypsum, and she hefted it in her hand as if determining its weight. Then, she turned back to Lauren. "This was supposed to be as full as the stones you filled the last few nights. That's the goal. So that after a while, we can use these stones to sustain and balance your magic in your blood without David being involved anywhere near so often, if at all. With any luck, we'll be able to balance out the magic so that it becomes self-sustaining, held at a level that will be useful to you and to the coven. That needs to happen. If that means sex, fuck his brains out, Lauren, but

I expect you to keep filling a stone each morning so that we have the power stored up for when it's needed."

Chilled by the coldness in Nell's words, she looked for some slip of kindness in the other woman's eyes, but there was nothing. This was the cruel woman who Lauren had caught glimpses of as a girl, when she'd plotted with her mother and they'd applauded each other's games at the expense of others. This was the woman Lauren had instinctively feared for as much of her life as she could remember, and she had more power in her blood than Lauren could ever hope to have without more training and without David by her side.

Lauren felt for the magic in her blood, pulling at it, and wondered how much she could do with it, assuming she determined what to do that might help. She had no books to consult, and Adrienne had, so far, learned nothing of a spell that could be used as offense or to combat their imprisonment here, no matter what the witches called it. She had nothing to use against them. She swallowed, watching the threat on Nell's face as the woman examined her.

"You can't have it both ways, Nell. I know you want me in the coven for my strength, but if you hurt me, you won't have me at all. And I won't hurt David just to feed into the coven's power. I won't overdo it or… or… or make myself nothing but a conduit for my mother's power."

Nell's eyes narrowed, and Lauren realized she'd come closer to the truth than the other witch had wanted. In another moment, Nell was in front of her, eye to eye and snarling.

"You're assuming we'll hurt you. You're assuming you have some choice in all this. Use the spell and collect power, and do what we've talked about, Lauren. You don't want to cross us." Nell took a step back, and then walked to the door and turned back to her. "David's too important for us to threaten him right now, given what he means to your power; I grant you that much. And you're right that we can't hurt you and still bring you into the coven. But why in the goddess's name did you think we brough Adrienne along if not to ensure your good behavior? What do you think we'll do to her, Lauren, should you stop cooperating?"

Chapter 14

Lauren pressed another stone of gypsum into the potion that Nell had brought to the kitchen, holding it in her hand beneath the surface of the fluid and waiting until she felt it humming against her skin, waiting for an infusion of energy to be offered. When it felt ready, she pulled it out, dried it, and placed it in the shoebox of stones at her side before taking up another one. Perhaps to make a point, Nell had told her she wanted a whole month's worth of stones prepared.

The thought was both overwhelming and something of a reassurance. It meant that Nell planned on Lauren visiting David each night for at least another month—that was a lot of time in which she and Adrienne could search out a way to signal him, and a lot of time for David and Josh to spend searching. At the same time, he'd looked exhausted last night, after only two nights of the spell feeding her energy into a state of overload. She'd known it was taking its energy from him, and now she suspected that it might have been pulling more energy than needed in order to feed into her magic. She hadn't realized that before, but if lying beside him for a night hadn't been enough to overheat her, or at least get her to the saturation point she'd found at the center when they'd spent so much time together, then her blood was already balanced—it was the spell that was pushing for more magic, more energy, and Lauren knew David would start suffering for it.

And yet, she had no answers.

With the last gypsum stone prepared, she rubbed the ends of her sleeves and her hands dry as best she could after dumping the remains of the potion into the sink. A glance at the door of the kitchen told her it was still locked, so she moved over to the pantry and began taking some inventory of what they had. She'd promised to help Adrienne and Sarah with dinner, and didn't particularly have any desire to knock for Evie's attention at the door only to be escorted down to hang out with Johanna or Nell until the hour got later. They had plenty of pasta, and everything needed for a simple goulash, so Lauren decided to go in that direction. If Adrienne and Sarah had other plans, then she could set it aside later and they'd eat it tomorrow instead, when it would be just as good after sitting for a day. Falling into the process of cooking, she lost herself in her work and moved through it quickly. She was just finishing pre-cooking the beef and adding in the pasta when Sarah came in with Adrienne following right behind her, the two of them stopping in their tracks upon seeing Lauren's progress.

"We just asked you to help! You prepared all that gypsum and then made dinner on top of it?" Sarah asked, coming over and taking an exaggerated sniff of what was in the pot. "It smells amazing."

Lauren shrugged, weeding away the last of the seeds from the peppers she'd cut before adding them into the casserole dish. "I didn't mean to take over, but I finished up with what I was doing and was already here. If you two have other plans, we can save this for tomorrow. I needed something to do," she added, when Adrienne took a closer look at the dish's contents and then raised an eyebrow at the array of spices set out on the counter.

"Where's the recipe?" Adrienne asked.

Lauren smiled, remembering that Adrienne had told her she had a whole collection of cookbooks and couldn't live without them. "In my head?" she replied, slipping the casserole dish down into the oven. She turned back to the other girls and glanced at the clock. "If you want to just go with this, it should be plenty."

Sarah laughed and wrapped one arm around Lauren, guiding her over to the table. "Well done. And Nell went out to get some apple pie for dessert, too—this'll be lovely. How about some wine while we wait for it to cook?"

Lauren was about to agree, and then she glanced to Adrienne, realizing the opportunity she'd been given. "How about a beer instead?" she asked quickly, knowing there was no beer in the fridge behind them. She started to rise, but Sarah waved her and Adrienne to take a seat.

Turning back to Adrienne, Lauren began telling her about the recipe in detail, waiting for the coming interruption.

"We're out here, but I know we've got some beer downstairs," Sarah announced. She headed for the door, and hesitated only briefly, but Adrienne took the hint.

"You don't mind, Sarah?" she asked. "I'm so tired now, I don't think I slept at all last night, after all, but I hate for you to have to…"

Sarah waved off the comment, smiling. "Just don't get into trouble, okay? Evie'll hear you if you need anything, so just bang on the door if you do. I'll just be a minute—you sit."

A moment later, Sarah was out the door and they heard the lock on the outside slide shut. Adrienne pulled Lauren into a hug, kissing her cheek before pulling back and staring at her. "You okay? We haven't talked alone since before you started going to David."

"I know—listen, are you leaving the building at all? With Sarah or anyone? Can you?"

Adrienne pursed her lips and shook her head, glancing at the door. "Sarah took me out yesterday, to help her harvest some herbs from a garden they've got outside, but I didn't see anything to tell us where we are, and I didn't see anyone else but her. We're just in some city's outskirts, but it could be anywhere. I couldn't even catch a glimpse of any street signs. You were hoping I'd called them?"

Lauren swallowed the hope that they'd been giving Adrienne freer rein and shook her head, looking down to her rings. "I can't talk to David, but I can understand him. He can talk to me. They're having trouble tracking the tattoo, but he told me they could maybe track these rings if we could get them into a pawn shop," Lauren explained.

"You want to sell your wedding ring?"

"It's not mine, Adrienne—we're not married."

"Oh, right… I forgot." Adrienne sighed, looking down to her own ring. "I wish I weren't and you were, Lauren; that would make a lot more sense. I don't even know why I wear it at this point," she commented, and without further ado, she slipped it from her finger.

Lauren looked at it for a moment, and then back at her own, but she left them on her finger. No point in giving them up if she didn't need to—real or not, they were still a connection to David. "He also suggested trying to wear something to give them an idea of where we are, but I don't know what that would be."

Adrienne raised an eyebrow.

"A hockey jersey, restaurant t-shirt… whatever," Lauren said. "We don't have anything like that… right?"

"Not that I know of," Adrienne agreed.

"But, hey," Lauren said quickly. "You're doing okay? With all this, I mean? You're okay?"

Snaking her arm around Lauren's shoulder again, Adrienne gave her another quick hug. "I'm fine. This is all pretty fascinating, honestly. If it weren't for how we got here…" Adrienne trailed off, scowling. "But we'll get out. I'm just a little tired of being babysat all the time."

As if on cue, the lock outside the door snicked and Sarah maneuvered her way inside with two six-packs of beer. Adrienne hurried up to help her, grabbing one and heading to the fridge while Sarah detoured to hand Lauren one of the lagers. Lauren made a show of hurrying to take the cap off and taking a grateful sip. "This is really refreshing, Sarah, thanks," she told the other witch as she and Adrienne came back to sit down with their own bottles.

Sarah's eyes went right to Adrienne's wedding ring, which had been left to sit on the table. "Don't get me wrong, Dri, because from everything I've heard, I'm glad to see you've taken it off—but are you sure?" she asked, picking up the ring and eyeing what was, admittedly, a giant diamond.

"I'm sure," Adrienne told her.

Distaste was so clear in her friend's voice, Lauren couldn't help laughing. "Sarah, if you'd met Raul, you'd understand."

Adrienne took a swig from her beer and agreed, "I want nothing to do with him—not the ring or anything else of his money." She paused, and her eyes came back to Lauren's for a moment, squinting with thought. "Hey, you know… you guys have done so much for us, weird as the start was," Adrienne commented. "I mean, look at these gorgeous clothes?" She plucked at the expensive sweater she wore by example, and then held out one of her feet to model the heels that had become her favorites. "What about you and the others sell it?"

Sarah's mouth dropped open in surprise, but Lauren jumped on the idea before she could say anything. "That's a great idea! And mine, too! This is a real diamond, I'm pretty sure, and the gold's real, but David and I weren't even married—they were just part of the charade we were putting up for that center. I've kept them on mostly because I didn't think to take them off till now," she added. In another moment, she'd twisted the two rings from her fingers and plopped them in front of Sarah.

The witch looked between them. "You two really don't want these?"

Adrienne and Lauren both shook their heads, and Adrienne went so far as to reach out and close Sarah's fist over her own ring, which had still been in her palm. "I never want to see it again," Adrienne promised. "You'd be doing me a favor by selling it and applying whatever you get to the upkeep of this place."

It took a moment, but then Sarah nodded, seeming pleased with the idea. "I'll see what Johanna thinks. I don't think the coven needs the money, but it couldn't hurt, and I know she'll be glad to see you giving up the attachments."

Sarah tucked the rings into her pocket, and Adrienne shot Lauren a fast smile.

They had a better chance now than they'd had thirty minutes before, and that was something.

***

David tried to be optimistic about the idea he'd given Lauren, but it was hard.

That diamond ring was something, sure, assuming Lauren could get it on the market, but David knew there were too many loopholes to even consider depending on it. For one thing, even if they got the images out to all registered pawnshops and jewelry stores that would pay for used rings like that, hearing anything would depend on those stores not just paying attention to the communication, but caring enough to contact them and trusting that they'd not be penalized for the good Samaratanship. Even with the promise of an additional reward beyond the rings, and assurance that the jewelry hadn't been stolen and was simply related to a missing persons' case, that seemed like a big ask. And that was assuming that the witches would not just want the rings, but aim to sell them sooner than later. So, as much as it had been nice to have something to offer Lauren as an idea, and as much as he wanted to believe they had a lead, he knew better.

Realistically, they had shit.

He looked again at the map and data in front of him, zooming in on various points where the metal had been picked up. "Am I reading this right?" he asked Barry. "We've got over six thousand points of possible contact to check out?"

Barry reached across the island and pulled the laptop around so he could read it. He typed in some numbers, and then shifted it around so that David could view the screen again. "Without parameters, yeah, but realistically, we're talking about two-thousand-seven-hundred-ninety."

"Because that's so much better."

Josh sat back down on a stool, staring at the screen from over David's elbow as his own eyes glazed over and he sipped his coffee. "How did you narrow it down that far?" Josh asked.

"I'm going by amount now instead of shapes. Let's assume that the only way they can hide the metal from our tracking systems is by obscuring the shape of it somehow—interrupting the data transmission to make it look different, although I don't know how they'd do it—or else masking it with larger amounts. That means we can eliminate all traces of the element that are showing up as being smaller than what Lauren carries with her. Trace amounts, in other words, that are related to single pieces of decoration on jewelry, figurines, whatever, or that were accidentally transferred away from larger stockpiles through accidental contact."

"You're telling me the amount of metal on Lauren is more than you'd have in a bracelet made of the stuff?" David asked, suddenly awake.

But Barry was already shaking his head. "You've gotta remember the type of metal we're dealing with. It's too weak to make jewelry out of—there'd be no point. Could the metal in Lauren's tattoo make a bracelet if we somehow extracted it and melted it down for that purpose? No, of course not. That would absolutely be toxic. But it's not strong enough for that type of use, is the point; it would be like making jewelry out of cardstock that was insanely expensive. So, the primary use of this metal is decorative—to add another element to some other metal that's being melted down for jewelry or a picture frame or whatever, and give it more depth, or to add some decorative element to a single piece of jewelry. You can spread it around to cover as much of a surface as you want, but you have to have a base, and a little bit goes a long way. We used more in the tattoos than we absolutely needed specifically because of the purpose of the tattoos and how easy this stuff is to pick up against other elements, but relatively speaking, there's not a ton of it out there."

"So, you're telling me there's no way they're just hiding the metal from us entirely, and one of these—what, two-thousand-some dots is definitely Lauren?" David asked.

He watched as the tech traded looks with his partner, and then shrugged. "I mean, if not, we don't have anything to go on, so we have to think that's the case, right? But yeah, I think that's what's likely."

David waited for something more definite, but from the looks on the other men's faces, he realized nothing was going to be forthcoming. They were narrowing down to these dots based on an assumption of what the witches could and couldn't do, just like he'd asked Lauren to sell that ring based on the assumption that they'd be able to track it. They were still grasping at strings.

He pushed himself up from the table and went to retrieve some more of the tea El had made him. He'd already gone through a quarter of it in just the last day, but she'd promised to come that weekend and bring a stockpile—assuming they needed it. Another fucking assumption, but he had a hunch this one was correct.

"I'm heading downstairs to try to catch some shut-eye before Lauren comes tonight. You guys let me know if you find anything worth following up on."

David left the room without anyone protesting, finally allowing himself to give in to some of the exhaustion he'd been feeling all day. Even though he and Lauren hadn't done anything more than rest together overnight, it had drained him, and while he could feel El's concoctions making some difference in the hours after he drank them, he suspected they were only shoring up a dam of exhaustion that would, eventually, break down and overtake him. That's how it felt anyway—like he was just pushing back the inevitable need to collapse. And what would happen if he did? Lauren could come to him in his dreams, and he didn't want the spell to start overtaking her, so where did that leave him? If he ended up basically comatose due to the energy drain, and the spell kept on sapping what little energy he had….

He pushed the thought to the side and let himself fall back into the bed, closing his eyes against the light filtering through from corners of the room and his covered bedside lamp. None of that was worth thinking about. He needed to sleep.

When he woke, Lauren was there.

Kneeling between his legs, she had one of her hands clutching his left thigh and the other holding his shaft as it hardened, her lips in an O around his head as her eyes watched him. She must have pulled away his sweats while he'd slept since he wore only a t-shirt now, and he lay still where he was and watched her working his dick, their eyes locked together.

As the tension in his body grew, he finally gave in and reached for her. She pushed herself down onto him one more time, taking him deeper while his hands rested on her arms and he let out a curse of pleasure, but then she rose up and he was pulling her up his body. She was naked but for the strange, home-made jewelry he'd talked over with El, and before he could forget, he grabbed for her hand and looked for the rings. They were gone. He looked back up to catch her eyes and see if he could discern what that meant, but she only wore an uncertain smile. If anything, it seemed to reflect the uncertainty he'd felt earlier in the day.

With her sitting on his thighs, her hands exploring his abdomen now, he let himself enjoy the heat of her skin and the feeling of his dick against her slit. He moved it over her wetness, feeling the warmth of her body reacting to him as he made them both squirm, and finally she rose up again and, this time, sank herself down onto him, enveloping him in that tight warmth he found himself craving even when he was too tired to think. Before she found her balance, he'd caught her hips and twisted them sideways, landing on top of her and pinning her to the bed. He could see he'd taken the breath out of her, but he caught her mouth in his and pressed in hard for a kiss as he let himself take her, pinning her to the bed. He felt her body's heat rising to him as he breathed her in, and her pussy pulsing as she got used to him again, taking all of him. Slowly, he moved his mouth sideways so that he could suck on her neck as his hands found her breasts and he began pressing in and out in a slow rhythm, playing the magic up and out of her body as if it were sweat or words.

Too soon, he felt himself straining for control as she gasped beneath him, and he pulled up onto his elbows to lock eyes with her. Her pupils were wide, her mouth gaping and shaping words he couldn't hear, but he could tell she was close. Thinking only of that, he took a deeper breath and held himself bottomed-out inside of her, pinning the two of them together as the magic boiled and heated between them. When the heat was almost unbearable, he pulled nearly all the way out and then dropped back into her. He couldn't hear her, but he could feel her screaming a release beneath him, and that was when he let go and came in a jolting eruption of energy and need and desire. Her body spasmed around his as he locked his lips against hers and gripped her body beneath him, enjoying the heat of her as it rose to his touch.

His breath calmed before hers, and he rolled sideways off of her, hoping she'd stay long enough to fall asleep with him. The previous night had been good—lying curled together with her in his bed until they'd both been asleep. He didn't know when she'd disappeared from his bed, but it must have been in the early hours of morning.

But instead of spooning up against him like the night before, her back to his chest, she turned into him and curled her leg over him once she'd caught her breath, and her hand came to rest on his dick, still hard and ready even if the rest of him was exhausted. He groaned, though he didn't know if she heard it or understood the emotion behind it, and reached down to wrap his hand around hers, stilling her exploration for the moment.

"Give me a few minutes," he muttered, still catching his breath.

For a moment, he thought she'd lay back down, but instead she bent to take his cock in her mouth again, and the warm pressure of her lips around him told him just how ready they both were for another round. Resting his head back, he let himself begin a rhythm with her, and let his hand fall down into her hair to guide her as they moved together, rocking in the bed. He let her do most of the work, toying with her breasts and the flesh of her arm as she moved against him and took him as deep as she could. When he tensed and came into her throat, his hand still tangled in her hair, he could feel her fighting to remain fixed to him and taking everything, with the magic heating both of their bodies and still, he felt, demanding ever more. When she came off of him gasping, he was already half-asleep.

She landed against him length-wise this time, but without the curious tension he'd felt urging her on before. He wrapped his arm around her, and didn't bother speaking. Her heart was speeding in her chest, and it seemed as if every inch of her glowed with the warmth of the spell they kept on awakening. But he didn't have the energy to do more than look again at her naked finger, where the rings had been twenty-four hours before.

Her lips came down on his chest, warm and wet and soft, and he held her tighter before he fell back into dreams.

Chapter 15

"Still not feeling great?"

Lauren took the can of ginger ale from her friend and just managed to resist the urge to grunt rather than speak. "Better than yesterday, but no, not really."

Adrienne patted her shoulder and took a seat nearby on the sectional which Lauren had occupied all day. The other woman opened up her own book as she got comfortable, and Lauren guessed that her friend would make more headway today than she herself had. And her fogginess at this point was more truth than act, though she hadn't expected it to work out that way.

Some forty-eight hours ago, when she'd returned from David's room after having seen what a toll the spell was taking on him, she'd wracked her brain for some way to give him a break without Nell wanting to take it out on Adrienne. When she'd found herself wishing for the ability to feign sickness—yet another convenience that her mother's spell had long disallowed—she'd realized the clearest option was to make herself sick.

And so she had.

She'd started by drinking more coffee during the day than she normally would have, and quietly confiding her plan to Adrienne—though, in doing so, she'd understated how exhausted David was, not wanting her to realize the full truth of all that was happening. Then, she'd had two over-full glasses of wine with dinner, and when Adrienne had all but demanded they all celebrate her mastery of some semi-difficult spellwork that Sara had been helping her with, they'd had their excuse to get into a bottle of tequila. It had been easy for Lauren to let herself get out of hand and relax into the revelry, and nobody had seemed surprised that she'd woken with a massive hangover the day before, not even having attempted to visit David. Nell had been as hungover as her, in fact, and both of them had spent most of the day in bed, ill and completely out of sorts. Adrienne and Sarah had been mostly unaffected, though Evie had moaned more than once that she felt as if she were dying.

Last night had been a more difficult prospect. After lazing about for the whole day, Nell and Lauren had both remained ill, but Johanna—who'd not been around for the revelry, for some undisclosed reason—had pressed Lauren to at least try for an overnight visit with David. She'd begged off, citing queasiness and the fact that she didn't think her stomach could handle the scents of the herbs required, let alone the spellwork, and Johanna had reluctantly let her off the hook. But Lauren knew tonight would come alongside that much more pressure for her to visit David, and she desperately wanted to give him at least a third night in a row of rest. Much as she wanted to see him, much as her body was urging her to see him, she knew he needed it.

Her thoughts were still on him minutes later, when Adrienne's whole body jerked where she sat with her book, her eyes flashing up to focus on some distant point of her imagining. Lauren's hand stilled, halfway to her mouth with the can of ginger ale, and she was just about to ask what Adrienne was thinking of when the other woman's gaze came back to her. And she grinned.

"What?" Lauren asked. "What is it?"

"Your shrug," Adrienne replied, putting her book to the side and sitting up to lean forward toward Lauren, cross-legged and with the appearance of an excited child. "I've never seen anything like it," she added.

Lauren looked down at her sleeves, trying to see it through Adrienne's eyes. It was pretty enough, she supposed, but also incredibly restrictive, and her skin felt abraded by it far more than she could describe or chalk up to—

"The metal," Lauren whispered. She locked eyes with her friend, the realization driving away every remaining bit of fogginess she'd felt as a hold-over from the liquor and subsequent hangover.

"If he sees it, he'll know how they're hiding us," Adrienne whispered, her voice barely audible.

"And it's got a shape," Lauren said, barely containing her excitement. She glanced sideways, reminding herself they weren't alone, but Evie and Sarah were fully focused on whatever spell they had going in the circle across the room, with not a thought to the two women reading and chatting on the sectional.

Lauren looked back to Adrienne, who'd taken the hint from Lauren's glance at the other witches and wiped away any trace of her earlier grin. "Even if he can't figure out who made it, where it came from," Lauren concluded, "the metal is wound into the whole of the fabric in strands—that's how it works. He can use the shape of it like they've probably been trying to use the shape of the tattoo."

Adrienne opened her mouth to speak some reply, but the door to the stairwell creaked open just then, signaling someone's entrance, and the woman instead twisted her hand against the cushions of the sectional and offered a quick thumbs-up.

Johanna stopped beside the couch, eyeing Lauren, and she seemed to eye even the half-full can of ginger ale with some suspicion. Lauren, for her part, willed herself to lose every ounce of the energy that had just filled her with Adrienne's idea, wishing they'd been given just a little more time before getting interrupted. Finally, though, Johanna seemed to come to whatever conclusion she'd been approaching, and she turned to cross the small space and take a seat on the opposite side of the sectional from where Lauren rested.

"I want the two of you to listen to me—no arguments," Johanna began. "None of what I'm about to say is up for debate, though we'll get to a point when I'll ask for a decision. Understood?"

Lauren could feel Adrienne staring at her, but didn't bother glancing her way. She knew, as she felt sure Adrienne did, that the speech of their so-called coven leader just now had been for her benefit alone.

"Understood," Lauren breathed out, pulling herself into a straighter seated position and putting her book aside.

"Nell and I understand you're worried about the effects the spell is having on your agent friend, and that any attempts we've made to sway your loyalty, up to this point, have had little to no success."

Lauren heard Adrienne's intake of breath, but she willed her own face to remain flat, expressionless; she didn't know if she succeeded. Still, she remembered Johanna's instructions and remained silent. The women in charge of the coven were smart as well as driven, and there'd never been much chance of Lauren tricking them into thinking she was on their side rather than David's.

"And, for now, we accept that," Johanna continued with a frown, adjusting her black sleeves in a way that made her look ever bit the annoyed Sunday-school teacher, inappropriate as the comparison might be. "I also understand you are still hung over—slightly, just like Nell is—and I imagine you're hoping to stretch that bit of irresponsibility into another night spent away from him. So be it. That leads me to what I'm about to say. Nell and I have been wanting you to take faster steps toward realigning yourself with the power you're capable of, which you so unwisely—if understandably—walked away from at a younger and more innocent age." Johanna paused, letting the full implications of the word sink in until Lauren felt a fire-hot blush in her cheeks and her chest. "But your mother is gone, and she was the reason you turned your back on your heritage and organized magic. On the sisterhood of a coven. Our coven. But that is the path you are on with us, despite any other plans you may have had in the past, and I believe you're moving toward accepting it. Your actions, though, belie that fact, showing your reluctance to take that next step in our coven's development. In fact, in my opinion, our coven's greatest obstacle at the moment is you."

Johanna had gone quiet, but Lauren had begun to see where this was going. They at least wanted to play at making a peace with her. "I'm not... trying to hinder the coven," Lauren said gently. And it was true, really. She wanted them to be found by David, so that she and Adrienne could get away, but she would have been just as happy if they all could have decided to live and let live. To go back to the way things had been at some far distant moment in the past which she could hardly remember, when the coven had left her to her own devices and she'd left them to theirs.

"But you're also not so anxious to join us, and that's what we need to remedy in order to have our coven at full strength," Johanna continued. "That agent, and your affection for him, are holding you back rather than simply feeding your magic, and there's no denying it."

"You're proposing some sort of compromise," Lauren surmised, when it became clear Johanna was waiting for her next reaction.

"I always said you were too smart to have come from your mother," Johanna told her, a slight sneer to her lips. "But yes, you're correct. You've focused almost entirely on healing magicks—growth and herbs and medicines and what have you. That's commendable, of course, and necessary to some extent—every coven needs a healer. For us, that may well be you. However, it's time that you stopped shying away from moving beyond that."

"I've been studying—" Lauren began.

"You've been procrastinating, more like," Johanna argued. She glanced to Adrienne again, as if including her in the meat of the conversation for the first time. "So, let's get to it, alright? You both understand well enough that magic can feed from emotion and connection. I want to see you take that to the next level. I want to see you feed from memory—negative memory, in particular. To be able to let your magic gain from such memories and use them for additional power. And then I want to see you, Lauren, push another, and their emotion."

Lauren felt herself paling, her body tensing. "What sort of emotion? I won't... Johanna, I won't try to control someone's mind. Maybe that was my mother, at times, but it's not me."

Johanna smiled, almost as if she were humoring her, but Lauren felt Adrienne going rigid nearby, and she tried to console herself with that fact. However excited Adrienne might be about experimenting with magic, this was still a line for her, as well. The coven hadn't corrupted her completely. Not yet, at least. And Lauren wouldn't let that happen—not to either of them, she promised herself.

"That's not what I'm speaking of," Johanna replied, as if she didn't even sense the new tension in the space. "I'm only talking about pushing emotion to a more significant depth than it may have reached prior to your involvement. Elevating feelings where they might barely have existed otherwise. Annoyance to anger, as it were, or mild amusement to outright mirth and joy. Surely, you can bring yourself to such an attempt as that?"

Lauren hesitated, looking for the catch. Put like that, what Johanna had just suggested didn't sound too... wrong? It wasn't right, certainly, but it wasn't close to what Lauren might have expected the woman to demand of her. She glanced to Adrienne, who looked torn between confusion and concern—like her. Turning her eyes back to Johanna, Lauren swallowed and then made herself answer. "And if I agreed to try, to go along with that and expand my... magic use, what would that mean? What would your side of the compromise be if I stop, as you say, procrastinating, and get to this next level you're suggesting?"

"We'll let you off the hook tonight. Tomorrow, as well, if you succeed. Nell assures me that you have enough magic stored away to allow for these spells and more, and that you have plenty to spare. That being the case, I can see some merit in giving you—and your agent—" she added, though spite dripped from her lips as she did, "...some modicum of a reprieve. I assume that would be a bargain to your liking?"

"And I'm not agreeing for Adrienne?" Lauren asked. "Just for myself?"

Johanna shrugged, looking to the other woman. "Adrienne, you're making great strides, but you're not ready for this quite yet. You'll be an observer only in what I'm proposing, until you're ready." Her eyes came back to Lauren, flattening with some emotion that Lauren couldn't quite determine. "Well?"

It seemed too good to be true, actually. Two more nights for David to rest was more than she'd thought possible to achieve. "I'll do it," she agreed quietly, working to keep her face expressionless and avoid giving away the feeling that she'd gotten the better of the coven in this deal.

"And I do want to hear from you that you won't object or interfere," Johanna commented, looking to Adrienne.

The other woman glanced to Lauren, but must have seen some version of reassurance there. Whatever she'd needed, at least. "You have my word," she agreed.

***

Lauren attempted to still her own breathing, blocking out the rhythmic chanting of the coven around her. This was the first time they'd all been gathered in a casting circle again since Adrienne's initiation, but the circumstances were so different. All her life, Lauren had promised herself not to work even remotely dark magic, and working magic from negative memories and feelings was as close as she'd come. Spells were driven by intention. Wanting to heal someone, to grow something, or even to escape some malevolent person or space... all of that was positive. This, though, would mean imbuing a spell she cast with ill thoughts, if not ill will, and she'd never crossed into that territory. Not on purpose, not accidentally.

"Focus on some moment that did you wrong. Something which you wanted to go another way," Johanna intoned. "Live in that moment. That space. Just live there and don't yet ask it for more."

Easier said than done. Lauren knew what the witch was doing, not starting with people. She'd escalate later, but this was more neutral territory. Less threatening.

Still, she appreciated the easing into what Johanna had planned, if that was truly where she was headed.

Taking the cue, Lauren reminded herself of the purpose here—giving David more of a break, and ultimately getting them out of the coven's proximity—and focused backward in time. A moment was all she needed. Some ill moment... a moment that had done her wrong, as Johanna had just put it....

The fire in the woods, she realized. Back at her family's first home.

She'd been in her backyard, minding her own business and playing on the swing set her father had built her. And then she'd seen something odd in the woods behind their house. Some flickering shade that didn't belong. Investigating, she'd soon discovered a group of neighborhood kids building a fire for no apparent reason. And it had been entirely too close to the trees surrounding it, just asking for some dire consequences. She'd hidden for what must have been ten minutes—fighting the urge to flee and leave them to their mayhem, as well as the urge to tell them they were being reckless and offer to help put it out. None of the kids had ever made any sort of overture of friendship where she was concerned—her mom was weird, and she was shy, which made her off-limits when it came to the gangs of kids that roamed the neighborhood in packs. She'd gotten over the jealousy of it years before, but it generally led to her avoiding them if she could now, and here she felt like she couldn't do that. She'd just gotten her courage up, and moved to approach them and appeal to their better judgement, when firefighters in full gear appeared from the other direction and accosted the group. Before she'd gotten the breath to speak, the group of children had seen her reacting, read the larger situation for what it was, and turned on her.

"She did it! We were just about to try to put it out!" one girl had screamed in defense.

Embarrassment and horror had frozen her, and although she'd gotten the sense that the firefighters didn't believe the traitorous group of neighborhood children who were so utterly united against her, she'd stood there with them silently as the firefighters had put out the flames and given them all a lecture on safety and what might have been. They'd also taken down the children's names and phone numbers, and Lauren had guessed that most of the other children lied about that yet again. Afterward, she'd stalked from the woods alongside all of the other kids, in a sort of shocked stalemate, but the horrified betrayal she'd felt had stuck with her for days afterward, and surged up again each time she'd seen any of those kids again.

Now, she forced herself to linger in that time—in those feelings and moments—concentrating all of her energy on that time of her life.

Johanna's voice intruded only slowly, as if from a distance, and it took more minutes still before Lauren managed to force her own eyes open. She felt like she was in a fog, looking on from another space and time, but Johanna was grinning at her from across the circle, and when Lauren looked down at her hands where they rested on her knees, she saw them glowing with a red energy that, once upon a time in her long distant past, had been a familiar sight in her own mother's hands. The horror she felt on recognizing it brightened the glow, sparking the element of discomfort now running hot in her blood, and she heard Adrienne gasp beside her.

"Now, we put words to that energy you've drawn up," Johanna told her, "and then you'll learn to call it up at will."

Chapter 16

Finishing his second circuit of the park, David wasn't surprised to see his partner waiting for him on a bench near the parking lot. It had only been a matter of time before Josh figured out where he was disappearing to, and likely why.

Without bothering with a greeting, Josh stood and handed him a water bottle as he approached, and David took it with a quick nod of thanks. "Figured you'd catch me here eventually."

"Barry found the message you got out on the message boards last time he was looking for chatter. Anyone tell you lately that you're an idiot?"

David shrugged. That wasn't news, and he didn't have the energy to argue.

"Raul hired a private investigator. Guy called me this afternoon and said he wanted in on the investigation. You believe that shit?"

David turned and started walking toward the cars, and answered when he sensed Josh following behind him. "Sounds like he's just as much of a douche as the guy paying him."

"Heh. Working on it, yeah. Since I had him on the line, though, I told him to look into Adrienne's ring—see if there's any way to track if it gets sold, any pictures they might have taken for insurance, whatever."

David glanced back to his partner as he reached his truck. "I hadn't thought about her ring going out with Lauren's, but I guess there's no reason for her to keep hers since she clearly wants to part ways with Raul. How are you thinking they could track it, though?"

Josh leaned back on his mustang, which was parked only a spot away from David's truck. "Some newer diamonds have laser coding. And Raul seems the type who might have major insurance on a purchase like that, so there could be pictures on top of any trace code."

"And it's probably more expensive than what Lauren wore," David acknowledged, thinking about how Raul did seem like the type who'd want to show off his wealth in that fashion. "Well, see you at the house?"

"Soon. I'm gonna run by the office first."

David nodded and then got into his driver's seat, where he waited for Josh to pull away first. He himself wasn't in any hurry. In the privacy of his truck, he took a second for himself, trying to assess where his energy levels were. Every night spent without a visit from Lauren was, undeniably, providing him with three times the rest he'd been getting otherwise. He still wasn't back up to speed, but he'd been able to make a few circuits of the park without totally wearing himself out. A few days ago, that would have been impossible. He would've come to the park, found a bench, and watched for Nell and Johanna from one stationary spot, having to be satisfied with simply remaining awake. That's how bad off he'd been.

He only hoped that Lauren wasn't suffering in return for this reprieve that he was getting.

Last time they'd been together, she'd seen how much the nights were taking out of him. He knew she had, much as he'd tried to hide it, and that killed him.

But if he was right, that hadn't really been news to her. So, what did that mean? Had she finally seen something on that last night that had told her she had to give him a break? Or was it that this break had always been in the plans, or was just a matter of some opportunity she'd suddenly been given? He wished he knew it had been her choice, at least, and that she was okay, but there was no way to tell until she got in touch. Maybe not even then if she still couldn't communicate with him at that point.

Resigned to the fact that the witches wouldn't be showing up that afternoon, and that he'd have to live with his unanswered questions for at least a while longer, he resolved to do what he could to put it all out of mind as he got his truck into gear. As he would have expected, the drive back to the house was uneventful, and he was quickly settled back at the kitchen island, pulling up progress reports related to the metal tracking.

They were going on the assumption that Lauren remained in the continental United States. So far, research had eliminated most of the southeast—where there hadn't been many flares to check out to begin with—as well as much of the Atlantic coast. A good majority of the tracking flares were off to the west, scattered through California, Oregon, and Washington, but they were starting to focus search teams and research on the Midwest, moving steadily west from the center, based on the assumption that the witches would have been smart enough to have a set-up waiting, and would've wanted to move Lauren and get her resettled as soon as possible. He thought that made sense, and hoped it would have to Johanna and Nell.

Truth be told, it was going about as well as could be expected. Faster, even. Because even with a missing 'assett'—and god, how David hated Lauren being referred to in such simplistic terms—and two witches who were firmly planted on the Most Wanted list, they were still limited by resources. It took manpower and time to get warrants for searches, and a lot more of the same to perform actual searches. There was no point in going through locations so fast that they could miss Lauren entirely, but with some of the target locations having actual goddamned mines attached to them, that meant a slow process. All they could do was prioritize and keep things methodical. Careful.

And hope they wouldn't run out of time.

When Josh walked in with a bag of take-out and a stack of files under his arm, David hadn't gotten much further in looking through the latest reports. There was no real point to reading all of the reports listing 'No New Leads or Findings—and logically, he knew that—but with nothing else to do, he kept hoping he'd see something which might have been missed by other operatives and techs, if only because of his personal experience with the coven.

"You good?" Josh asked, dropping his burden on the counter.

"As I can be. Anything new?"

But there was no point in giving voice to it, really. The answer showed on Josh's face.

By the time they went through the motions of eating a meal and catching each other up on the various sources which had, so far, offered up a lack of new leads, David felt years older. Sharing the responsibility of a case had always helped him sleep in the past, and Josh was a damned good partner, but the sheer lack of progress was killing him. After eating, having a beer while staring at the computer screen for a while longer, and trying fruitlessly to come up with some new plan of attack,

David was wiped enough that he admitted he might as well go to bed.

But he didn't sleep well. It had nothing and everything to do with Lauren, of course—she never showed up, but his body and his mind expected her. Over and over again, he woke up to feel the side of the bed, and look around the room and eye the hallway, only to have to close his eyes in resignation. The fact that he still woke to his alarm without any trouble the next morning, aware and ready to get moving, was proof enough that his energy levels had mostly returned.

In the shower, he leaned back into the tiled wall and thought about the showers he'd shared with Lauren at that therapy center from hell. For years, he'd written off shower sex as more trouble and risk of stupid injury than it was worth, but the thought of Lauren on her knees before him, his hands fisting her hair as she learned to pleasure him with her mouth... now, it made him want a bigger shower. Where they could start like that, and then he'd lay her down on a tile floor and take her as water pounded down on the both of them.

Fisting his hand around himself as he braced his head against one arm, set against the wall, he pretended his hand was Lauren's, and that the heightening steam was only a symptom of her magic rising around them. He pretended she was moaning before him, struggling to take all of him because she wanted only to please him, just like they'd been together not two weeks before, and with that, he erupted against the wall, yelling out with the force of it. He kept his eyes closed afterward, unwilling to let go of the illusion just yet.

By the time he opened his eyes and stood straight, centered back into the reality he had to deal with in the absence of Lauren, the water was running cold and his fingers were pruned with moisture.

He'd promised to call his partner If there was anything to report from the night, but instead he ran into his partner in the kitchen. The mere fact that David was there to pour some oatmeal into a bowl this early, as Josh was making coffee, was testament enough to clarify that the night had been unremarkable.

"I'm gonna stick with the plan and go into the office to help Barry coordinate search teams," Josh commented. "Anything else you want me to work on if you're still planning to catch up with El?"

David started to nod, and then thought again. "I'm still going to see El, yeah, but listen... I was thinking about what the guys said about Adrienne getting worked up about revenge. Revenge in general. That's the coven's thing, don't you think? What got all this shit started, with them not being able to just live and let live, right?"

Josh pushed a mug of coffee toward David and sat down on a stool. "I guess. So?"

"So, something El said struck me, about covens and power. Let's assume Lauren's alive and basically fine. She can't leave, yeah, but she's fine. If that's the case, there must be an endgame. What is it? It's not revenge anymore, but that's what we've seen make them tick, so she has to fit into their plan somewhere."

"Okay. Endgame... it wouldn't be taking Lauren's power for themselves or they would've done it already, assuming they could."

"They were breaking her down when they had us," David said slowly. "And Nell hated my guts, but I don't think she hated Lauren's. Melania was the one behind that whole scheme of taking her will."

"And Melania's dead," Josh finished for him.

"Exactly. Which leaves Nell and Johanna in charge— at least as far as we know, and it's hard to imagine they would have convinced witches who are senior to them to join in on hijacking a woman they don't even know, let alone when it involves an attack on federal agents. They wouldn't be able to hide that from them with Lauren around. So, let's assume Nell and Johanna are in charge. And they weren't out to kill us—I think we know that for sure, because they had that opportunity as soon as we put Lauren in that ambulance. They didn't take the opportunity then, and they've had their chances to grab me, too, but that's not happening, either."

Josh shifted on his stool and raised an eyebrow. "Are you getting somewhere with this?"

David swallowed, thinking about the worst-case scenarios that he'd been considering the night before, when his brain had been awake and running, unwilling to sleep. "Optimal revenge is what I'm getting at. As their endgame, I mean. Adrienne's good, right, and that's the thing she wouldn't take as motivation. That's what I keep thinking. That was where she drew the line, even when she was in a situation that scared her at the center—she still wouldn't cross that line. So, simplifying it? Nell and Johanna are bad, and they've been motivated by revenge from the start—at least partially. Far as we're concerned, Devlin, what was the worst-case scenario even before we really got to know Lauren?"

Josh's eyes widened, and he put down his coffee cup hard enough that it spilled. He didn't move to clean it up. "That she'd go bad, like her mom."

David nodded, grimacing. "And I can't think of a better act of revenge on us, can you? Now that we've gotten this close to Lauren? Turning her bad?"

"Revenge on Lauren, too," Josh said. "That was always her worst fear, turning into her mom or letting her mom's actions define her." He paused, staring at the spilled coffee, and David let him have the time to come to the conclusion he himself had reached only that morning. "So, that's it. That's the endgame. They're trying to turn her bad."

"But they won't," David said. "So, that's how much time we've got. However much time they spend trying to do it, and failing, before they give up."

Josh finally moved to grab a paper towel, and began mopping up the spilled coffee as he spoke almost to himself, putting into the air the same question David had had revolving in his mind. "Okay, so now we know the endgame. We just have to figure out how they'll try to get there, and how long they'll spend on the attempt."

***

El had gone overboard, and David was grateful for it. If Lauren's visits started back up, he'd have plenty of formula to combat the night spells' energy drain, and if what they all hoped for instead came to pass, and they found Lauren sooner than later before the formula could even be needed... well, then it would keep in storage or he could even have it distributed among other agents—compliments of a witch on their side of the aisle whose identity he and Josh would just keep to themselves.

He stowed the fourth—and last—cooler in the bed of his pickup and then headed back up to the bohemian witch's porch. Her family was away for the day, though Paul and Christopher were visiting in the kitchen and currently helping her clean up all of the bowls and cutting boards she'd used in the final preparations for their lunch, as well as the last rounds of mixing she'd done for his own supplies. When he got back into the kitchen, she was settling down at the island—clearly waiting for him—and the men were pulling a round of beers from the fridge and distributing them around their small group.

"You've done a lot—I won't say you've done too much, I so appreciate it," David admitted, "but it's a lot. More than you know." He took a sip of the beer Christopher had pushed toward him and then settled into his seat. Across from him, El simply offered a smile. She was more relaxed than he'd seen her previously, and the comfortable kitchen reflected her friendliness. Fresh flowers and herbs were everywhere to be seen, hanging from pots that came down from the ceiling on sparkling clean chains and strips of braided cloth, growing from the windowsill planters, and even coming up from trellises in one corner. He knew Lauren would love the whole space, and only hoped she'd get a chance to visit it one day—not to mention meet this woman who'd already worked so hard to help them.

"I still think we ought to work on using meditation to help you bridge the spell's power over you, but you said you have something else you want to talk about first?" El prodded him.

He nodded, and then glanced to the other men in the room. "Something you said about Adrienne—and her reaction to thoughts of revenge—got me and Josh thinking. It might be partially a guess, but I think we know the coven's endgame in kidnapping Lauren." He took another sip of his beer, almost expecting to be interrupted, but the others only waited on him to continue. "I think they want to turn her to their side—recruit her, so to speak."

"She'd never turn against you," Paul said immediately, shaking his head at even the idea of it.

"I agree," Chris put in, and then he looked to his sister. "If you'd seen them together... it's like you and Jamison. Me and Paul. There's no question of her turning against him. She just wouldn't do it."

"I hope you're right—and I think you are," David said, trying not to get caught in the feeling of relief he was experiencing, knowing that everyone who'd been around them, so far, agreed on this point. "But I don't think the witches have accepted that. Hell, if Josh and I are right, I hope they haven't, because it buys us time."

David focused back on El, and then went on. "So, that's the question. If a coven were going to convince a witch to join them—a witch who was definitely, absolutely disinclined to join them—how would they do it?"

El's brow was crinkled in thought, and she remained silent as Paul broke in. "You said something in our conversation made you think of this, but Adrienne's not a witch. Does she play into this theory you've got? Or, if not, what did you mean?"

"Not much—rather, I should say I'm not even sure of the connection, beyond that it was our conversation that helped us get to this conclusion," David admitted. "You guys mentioned that Adrienne reacted negatively to a conversation about seeking revenge, to understate things, and I was thinking last night about how Lauren would feel about that. About revenge. Both of these women, Adrienne and Lauren, are good people. One of Lauren's greatest fears was always... well, to lay it all out there, her mom was a killer. Literally. That's how we met, remember," David added more quietly. "Josh and I were after her mom, on a case. And at first, we thought—before we knew Lauren, I want to emphasize here—we thought that maybe she could go that route. Become bad. But the more we got to know her, the more we knew that could never happen. Am I making sense?" he asked suddenly, seeing from Paul's face that he might not be.

"You're rambling a little, maybe, but it's fine," Christopher told him, reaching out and clapping a hand on his forearm, squeezing slightly. "You're saying Lauren couldn't be bad, that they're good, so...."

"So," David said, trying to pull his thoughts together, "that would be the coven's ultimate revenge is what I'm saying. Against me for going after them and Lauren's mom, tearing up their coven. Against Lauren for rejecting them. If they could pull her to their side—and I don't think they could, like you guys said—but if they could, that would be the ultimate payback. The ultimate revenge. Yeah, I don't know what they'd do after they got her to their way of thinking, or after they figured she just couldn't be corrupted and it wasn't possible, or how Adrienne would fit into that... but that's the best guess we've got for what they're doing. And it makes sense," David added, "because if they'd wanted her dead, they could have made that happen in the ambulance, but they didn't."

He took a breath, swallowing the last of his beer and closing his eyes for a second. "And you guys don't know this, but I offered myself up in trade, too. Put a message out on their network and tried to get them to go for it, and we've got every reason to believe they saw it. So, they could have gotten to me, too, and didn't."

"Damn, man," Paul said under his breath, though none of the other three individuals gathered around the island looked surprised.

David only shrugged. "Thought maybe it would work. It didn't." He looked up and around the small group. "So, I think that's their revenge, trying to get her on their side. But how, El? That's what I can't figure out. If we can get an idea of how they might try it, that might give us a step up in finding them. So, yeah... that's the question. How would they even try to do it?"

El looked back at him thoughtfully, playing her fingers along the mouth of her beer bottle. "If she's as good as you say, and predisposed to be against them, to distrust them... they'd have to trick her. Or at least lower her defenses and lull her into adopting some of their practices, I imagine." She met David's eye. "You say she hasn't been to visit in a few nights?"

"Three," he answered without having to think about it.

El seemed to hesitate, taking a glance at her brother before speaking, and when she did answer, she did so gently. "Perhaps it's a deal, then—in part, at least. She cooperates with something they're doing—and I imagine it can't be too horrible a something, given what you've told me about her—in return for giving you a break. She must know the spell's been tiring you out. If they've been compelling her to visit you every night somehow until recently, giving you that break might be enough of an impetus to have her cooperate with them. Even if she'd otherwise be inclined to refuse."

The idea made sense, and he guessed Nell would appreciate the idea of trading their peace of mind away. But it would be a temporary trade. "So, you're saying they'd need Lauren's help for... something?" he asked. "What couldn't they do on their own if they're more powerful than her to begin with, though?"

"It is possible, no matter their personal levels of power," El told him. "There's a reason witches choose to belong to covens to begin with. It's not only safety in numbers, but power in numbers. Five witches can each work five smaller spells, but have greater difficulty with a more serious one. Or, even if one witch alone wouldn't have difficulty enacting a larger spell, it might be weaker, less effective, or not so long-lasting as they'd like, and any of that could be remedied by teaming up with another witch and joining powers."

"And in any case, five witches could do a difficult spell with no problem," Christopher concluded. "Not near the effort it would take from one witch alone."

"Exactly. It's not rocket science," El allowed, smiling at her brother with the joke. "But," she added, frowning, "that wouldn't get her to their side in the long run. It wouldn't change her loyalties. That goal would... well, it would take corruption of a sort," she finished with a shrug.

Her eyes had gone uncertain, and Paul was fidgeting while David waited, feeling tension in the room growing.

El seemed to sink into herself until Christopher finally got up and pulled some more beers from the fridge, passing them around before he broke the silence.

"Spit it out, El. What are you thinking?"

She looked around, and then twisted the cap from her second beer and took a sip. "You guys know the whole example of a frog in water, right? I hate it, but it's useful. You drop a frog in boiling hot water, he leaps out straight away, barely worse for the wear."

"But you put him in regular water at room temperature," Paul went on, "and then raise the temperature slowly up to boiling, then the water boils him alive and it's too late for him to escape by the time he realizes the danger, assuming he ever senses it at all."

El nodded. "Magic can be like that, I'm afraid. Witches fall into black magic, guys. They don't wake up one day and say, 'Damn it, I want to be evil now.' At least, not mostly. They don't start by brainwashing someone to commit murder, in other words."

"They start by brainwashing someone into throwing a punch," David suggested, still not really seeing the point. Lauren wouldn't commit a crime, period. Not just to give him a decent night's rest, certainly, and he wasn't sure she'd do it at all.

"No," El disagreed without pause. "Not even that, David. They'd start by persuading someone to even think about throwing a punch. Not brainwashing them into doing it, but tempting them into thinking about doing it, into seeing themselves as someone who would. They'd simply persuade them to consider it. 'Don't commit murder—don't even throw a punch; just think about what it would be like to throw that punch. That's okay, right?' they'd ask. 'We all occasionally, once in a blue moon, consider some violent act, right? So, you can do that? Think about it?' That's where they'd start—with something that's mostly acceptable, like imagining an act. If you get someone to accept the first step, then they can consider the second. Then the third, and then the fourth. Persuading someone to maybe consider throwing a punch is step one. Brainwashing someone else into committing murder... call that step fifty."

David swallowed some of his beer. "That's what you meant by corruption—taking such baby steps, she doesn't even realize it's happening. Okay. I can see how that makes sense."

He paused, thinking about it. Thinking about how he'd spent time pushing Lauren, himself. Pushing her boundaries. This was no different, and it made him feel sick. But that wasn't what mattered right now.

He met El's eyes, willing her to be able to answer his next question. "How, El? How would you do it?" She looked away from his gaze in a way that made it clear just how uncomfortable the question made her, but he let it hang in the air anyway.

After a few more seconds passed, Christopher reached out and put his hand on his sister's shoulder. "If you can't answer, I understand, sis, but Lauren... she's good people. If David's asking, it's because it might matter, so if you can help..." he trailed off, looking to his husband for some answer, but Paul only shrugged.

"We won't be mad if you can't do it," Paul said quietly. "It's okay."

David bit back argument, but he could see the struggle on El's face. Pushing her wouldn't get them anywhere, so he only repeated the question, and then offered a 'please' that, even to his ears, sounded more like begging than anything else that had ever passed through his lips before. Somehow, it did the trick.

She got up from the island and got herself some water, and then came back to sit down and met David's eyes. "This is because you've asked... you understand I'd never do this to someone?"

Relieved, he nodded. "I can see you're uncomfortable. I trust you're like Lauren, El, I do. Whatever you tell me, it won't leave this room unless I need to share it with Josh, and even then, it would be him only. I swear to God this won't come back to bite you. Please, trust me on that."

It took another few seconds, but finally she sighed, and nodded. "Understand... I don't know Lauren or these witches. Talking about the strategy in anything like this is uncertain. But, if it were me? I'd start with something small, but build to something that was personal to her— and make sure that was in the back of her mind the whole time, as much as I could make it so without being obvious. I'd look for where she already had passion. Something they could use." El looked at him, considering, and then shook her head as if changing her mind internally. "It's not you they're using in that way or you'd have sensed some change in the way Lauren's looking at you. So, let's take romantic passion out of the basket. And it's not familial, either, if her mom was her only relative..." she inclined her head at David as if for confirmation, and he gave it. "Okay, so... something else. You've told me she's interested in healing. There's nothing I can see them using in relation to that, not if they want to corrupt her in some fashion. That's too pure a passion at its base. What else?"

David waited for El to go on, and when she didn't, he finally asked, "What else, what?"

"What's she passionate about?" El prodded him. "A cause? A dream?"

He looked around the group helplessly, but as he might have guessed, the men were as lost as he was. And he knew Lauren best, after all. "She, uh, likes plants," he tried. "And she cares about the environment's potential for healing, finding natural cures and all that, but she's not a part of a formal group related to it. At least, not that I know of," he added.

El frowned. "What about a cause she's against? Something she's passionate about fighting?"

This isn't getting us anywhere, David couldn't help thinking, and El must have read it on his face, because she leaned back in her chair again as if to give up that line of questioning.

"Okay... what about a person?" El asked. "Someone who's hurt her? I don't imagine it could be the witches, though it sounds like they'd fit the bill—at least, I don't know how they'd use that emotion against her in this way if they want her on their side. But.... Maybe an ex-boyfriend, or a roommate who she ended on bad terms with, or some professor who treated her unfairly?"

David was about to say that he didn't know enough about her earlier life to know of any such person, and to say there'd only been him in her life since he'd known her, but he caught the negation on his tongue just in time. Thinking of the bruises she'd worn when she'd first come back to the house, after calling Josh for help, he wondered what she did think of that man who'd hurt her, assuming he crossed her mind at all regularly. How much anger was she harboring for him, still? Any? He'd assumed she'd mostly left it behind, but.... "There was a guy," he said quietly. "Not an ex, but some date who attacked her one night. I don't know his name."

"Well," El said gently, "if you can find it, that's where I'd start." She glanced over to Christopher, and then to Paul, before looking back to David. "I make a point of not holding grudges or regrets, but that can be hard. I've had decades of practice, and it's still hard when it comes to some things. Something like that—a physical attack—would be hard to forget, no matter how badly she wanted to. If the witches know about it, they could potentially use that negative emotion." El paused, hesitating again, and then looked around their small group. "If she had the chance, do you think she could bring herself to hurt that man who hurt her?"

David frowned, pushing back in his seat and finishing his beer. Christopher shifted uncomfortably, and it was Paul who finally spoke up. "Lauren's strong, confident. If a guy hurt her badly enough—or hurt someone she cared about—I could see her losing control just enough to retaliate. There's some steel in her. We saw it at the center."

El nodded, and then reached out and gripped David's hand. "Start there, and get to that man before she does to keep an eye on him if you can. If the witches can sway her to hurt him, that's the water beginning to boil. But if you're already there watching him, worse comes to worse, you'll be in a position to stop her. And get them back."

David swallowed, and it seemed that all of them agreed—silently—to let the train of conversation die there.

Christopher and Paul turned the conversation away to some new herbs that El had growing, and David didn't fight the move. Within the time-span given to another beer by the rest of the group, he made his excuses, thanked El once more for her work on the strength-giving concoctions she'd mixed for him, and headed out the door.

He was at his truck door when El came hurrying out of the house, waving him to a stop before he could leave.

"David, one last thing!" she called, and he stopped with his hand on the door.

"Just think of something?" he asked. "A magic bullet, maybe?" And though he'd meant it to come out as a joke, he was too tired—too overwhelmed by the thought of trying to not only dig up the guy who'd hurt Lauren, but potentially protect him from her—to make the joke sound like one. It rang hollow in the air, and El put a fast hand on his wrist and squeezed something like understanding into the gesture.

"Not quite, but I didn't want to bring this up in front of my brother and Paul. David... if you don't mind me asking. You and Lauren are pretty passionate—in the bedroom, I mean?"

David felt his eyes narrowing, staring at her. "I'd say that's none of your business if I were talking to anyone else."

El blushed, and took her hand from where it had rested on David's wrist, but she stepped closer rather than backing away. "If there's a way—and you needn't tell me, but I feel like I have to say this—David, if there's a way for you to, uh, heighten that, you might temporarily overwhelm the spell. Make it possible for Lauren to say something to you, communicate something if she had the wherewithal to do it."

David stared at her, his brain spinning. "You mean like... what, X—ecstasy? A drug?"

She shrugged, the blush growing brighter. "I don't know. You're not physically together; if you were, then yes, sure, X, but that's not an option—and I'd never tell a federal agent to use an illicit drug," she stammered, her eyes going wide as she suddenly realized what she'd said, but he waved off the concern and she took a deep breath before continuing. "No, I mean, that's not an option, but if you can think of something else. Something..." she looked away, bit her lip, and then shook her head as if pulling herself out of whatever discomfort she kept creeping toward, "—a way to, I don't know, heighten things. You could try some incense that would heighten passion, but we don't know if she can smell, and I rather doubt she can. So, maybe something she... particularly likes? Taken to another level? Or combined with something else... she really likes?"

El blushed deeper and glanced toward the house, as if doubting whether she should have come outside.

Before she could flee, David grabbed her forearm gently, holding her there. "Okay, if not a drug... you're talking about pleasure? That's all?"

El shrugged helplessly. "It's an idea, David. Spells—even like the one that Lauren's using—are only made to take so much. If you can communicate to her that she might have a few moments extra to communicate something to you when her body is really overtaken by magic flowing into the spell, into whatever they've got holding the power for her—because there must be something they're using for that, since she hasn't visited you in a few nights and is presumably still using magic—well, that stream of magic is only meant to do so much. Only meant to hold so much at once. If it's so busy taking magic in, it might be too overwhelmed to police whether or not she's actually trying to speak or communicate with you vocally, at least temporarily."

David let the idea settle into his head, and nodded in something of a daze as El told him again that it was only an idea, but was something she'd had to mention, and then he watched her hurry back to the porch and disappear again. He was leaving with one idea for where to head Lauren and the witches off, and one idea for how he might allow her to say something to him, however fast or unthought. Even aside from the supplies in the back of his truck, that was a lot more than they'd had going for them that morning.

Chapter 17

Lauren woke slowly, her mind fogged with all of the memories they'd been working through. It was a lot to take in, given that their circle the other night had been so successful—as Johanna and the others had put it, anyway. They'd worked through most of the night and slept the next day, and then they'd had another, shorter session the previous night, after Nell and Johanna had decided it made sense to wait on a 'real-world' test of using the emotion.

That had meant two more nights for David to rest, and Lauren knew she ought to be glad about that. She knew he'd needed the time. But now... now, Lauren just wasn't sure she'd made the right decision, giving in to Johanna. It was true that they hadn't done anything wrong. They'd gone through what felt like all of Lauren's worst memories in one way or another, though—including the night that that man had raped her after she'd gone out to the bar. Even if she hadn't really been able to tell the other women about the experience, so much as stumble through a few details and remember it. Jerry, his name had been— that had actually come back to her afterward, in a haze of horror that had hit her only after she'd been slowly walking back to her room. But in the course of all that, and in the aftermath, it was as if she felt the memories living in her now. Almost like when she'd been at the center with David, avoiding the use of her magic and feeling it pulse within her blood as it built up. This wasn't the same thing, but it was similar enough that it frightened her.

And the idea of pushing emotion onto others, which had at first felt relatively harmless, the way Johanna had described it, now seemed something more... more devious. More... bad.

There was no other way to describe it, she supposed. The very idea of it felt bad.

Still lying in bed, she thought about the day ahead. She'd survive it—she knew that. And it would get her and Adrienne out of this damnable building, too, into the fresh air, but that didn't seem like enough of a payoff at the moment. The one thing keeping her going, really, was the idea of the oncoming night, when she'd get ready to visit David as usual, but then put on the metallic shrug and hope that was just the key he and Josh would need to track her down. That idea of Adrienne's felt like a lifeline, and she only hoped it wasn't a fool's hope, to think such a slight thing could save them.

By the time Nell had come in to lock the shrug onto her, Lauren had re-steeled her resolve, and the other woman's biting banter didn't bother her. It was what it was. Nell may have been putting up a friendly front at first, or attempting to, but the other woman's old, truer nature had been coming through lately. She needn't hide it anymore, so far as Lauren was concerned. The threats hung in the air now, blatant and demanding, and any pretense there'd been of Lauren one day being a free and equal member of their coven was only distantly remembered. She'd never entirely believed it was an option, not really, but some part of her had hoped for it, particularly when Nell had suddenly seemed more sympathetic to her—more human. That sentiment was barely a memory now.

In the kitchen, she recognized the nerves on Adrienne's face, but didn't have the energy to reassure her. Everything she had in her was going toward keeping herself standing up straight and thinking forward. And Adrienne didn't need to know the crux of it... that if Adrienne herself hadn't been weighing in the balance—which Johanna reminded her in every neat, overly practiced glance she offered—Lauren likely would have given up already. She'd have lain down in her bed and refused a single spell more. Not for the coven, not to see David. She was that tired, and that fearful of what was coming. Truly, she wasn't even sure she'd have tried carrying the shrug into a dream tonight, had she been able to give up on cooperating with the coven and not feared repercussions.

Once they'd eaten, the witches tied Lauren and Adrienne's wrists without fanfare, using simple ribbons and promising that it was more for ceremony than anything, meant as a simple reminder that they were still initiates of a sort. Sarah alone looked apologetic over the gesture, but she didn't argue with the others.

There was no question of who was in charge here.

At the door Lauren knew to lead to the underground garage, they put heavy cotton hoods over her and Adrienne's faces, blocking any chance of their seeing where the car might be headed. Lauren thought she might cry then, when the black cotton blocked out her sight, but she just managed to hold it in. No sound or word came from Adrienne, either, and Lauren found herself smiling briefly, thinking of the strength they were showing.

Time passed, but Lauren couldn't tell how much. Johanna and Nell cycled through what felt like an endless train of conversations, but never made an effort to include

Lauren or Adrienne. Apparently, they sensed the other women were in no mood to talk. And somehow, that only made Lauren more nervous. If this really wasn't a big deal in terms of magic, as Johanna had kept insisting, wouldn't they be attempting to put them at ease? Joking or trying to work up some of the camaraderie they'd so often tried for over the previous days? It seemed like it, and as a result, the trip didn't sit well with her. When they finally parked, they remained sitting in the car for what felt like ages more, supposedly waiting for Evie and Sarah to catch up. They'd traveled along in another vehicle, and had gotten separated somewhere along the road. The sound of another car pulling up on Lauren's side, and then the beep of a horn, signaled their arrival, and then the doors were being opened.

Nell pulled the hood from Lauren's head, next reaching across her to tug away Adrienne's. They were in a good-sized parking lot, a road leading off from each end. In front of the cars was a picnic area, and Lauren saw a variety of recreational grounds placed around it—tennis and basketball courts, a couple of playgrounds, and trails leading further off into the distance. Families and groups were scattered everywhere—even among the opposite side of the road, which was solidly lined with trees, but had various signs and trail heads leading off into the foliage. For just a moment, Lauren thought about making a run for it or screaming for help, causing a scene, but she could only imagine what Johanna and Nell would do in response. With a fast-offered spell, they'd be able to cut her scream off in an instant's time, and as far as making a run for it... well, she and Adrienne were outnumbered, and it wasn't as if Lauren had any idea where they were or in which direction to run.

She shared a quick glance with Adrienne, but it was clear enough that the other woman had reached similar conclusions.

But there wasn't more time to consider it all, anyway.

Sarah was there wrapping an arm around Adrienne's shoulder, guiding her toward a big picnic table set up beneath a wide-branched oak tree. Evie called to Lauren from the back of the car they'd driven, and Lauren joined her obediently. In the trunk, she saw a few coolers and a grocery bag, and she took the bag from Nell when it was handed her way. The other witch walked beside her, jabbering on about nothing and carrying one of the coolers as they headed toward Sarah and Adrienne, who were brushing pine needles and leaves from the table and attached benches.

It felt domestic—insanely domestic—as they set up their picnic. The witches had brought sandwiches, fruit and vegetable trays, water bottles, and even wine and the ingredients for a strawberry shortcake dessert. They were planning on being there a while.

When Lauren took a seat beside Adrienne, she'd just about gotten up the nerve to say they ought to get on with whatever they were there for when Johanna pressed a water bottle into her hands and told her to drink it. It was marked with her name, and Lauren saw a cloudiness to the water, but Adrienne was already drinking the one she'd been handed, and suddenly, Lauren simply couldn't see any other choice. She drank the water.

What she expected, she didn't know. The world didn't spin, or even seem to change.

Before she knew it, she was eating a turkey sandwich and nibbling on carrots and broccoli dipped in ranch dressing. The witches around her—excepting Adrienne—chatted as if they were on the most normal outing in the world. Lauren found herself watching a young family near the playground some fifteen or so yards away from their picnic. The man and woman—the parents, Lauren assumed—were fussing over a baby in a carriage. Two boys who looked to be maybe five and eight years old were chasing each other around the whole area, up and down and around the swings, jungle gym, and slide. No other children were nearby, and they were taking full advantage of that by making the space their own.

Gradually, Lauren became aware that the play was getting rougher. The younger boy, who'd been doing most of the chasing, was shoving when he caught up to his brother—and doing it hard. When he pushed him so hard that he fell outside of the play area, catching his ankle on the edge of the enclosure's wooden barrier and tumbling down with a startled cry, it seemed almost inevitable.

He turned over, rolling sideways, and Lauren saw blood trickling down from a large raw spot at his knee, where it looked like he'd scraped aside most of the skin. The younger brother, largely unaffected, stood to the side and watched as his brother sobbed and his parents came sprinting to the boy's side.

The mother knelt by the fallen boy and worked on comforting him. Meanwhile, the father gripped his other son's elbow and dragged him back toward where the baby carriage still sat. The boy's face remained stoic, but the father was apocalyptic, screaming about rough play and how often they'd told the boys to be careful with one another and how it would be a month before they came back to the playground and a month before the boy would again be allowed his video games. Other park goers were moving farther away from the scene, as if to pretend they couldn't overhear the family drama. Through it all, the youngest boy's face remained weirdly impassive, even up to the point when his mother came back over and began visibly working to calm her husband down. She gestured at the older boy—who was calm again, now that the immediacy of the pain had passed, and to the baby carriage, so that Lauren assumed the baby must have begun crying, though she couldn't hear it over the adults' yelling.

Eventually, the commotion calmed entirely. The man's face remained red, but the woman was able to herd him and her children into a mini-van that sat near the witches' own vehicles, and then they were gone, and the silence in the park seemed almost supernatural after the excitement had passed.

When Lauren realized she was still staring at the vacant spot the family's mini-van had left in its wake, she gradually turned her attention back to the witches surrounding her. Adrienne was looking down at a glass of wine she'd clenched her hands around, but from the angle at which she sat, Lauren could see tear tracks on one of her cheeks. Sarah looked uncomfortable and was staring off into the distance, but the other witches were all in varying states of glee, wearing coy smiles or, in Nell's case, an outright grin.

Lauren's eyes were heavy, though. She couldn't quite piece together what it all meant. After a moment, she reached out to Adrienne and gripped her forearm, drawing her attention. The other woman looked up at her, and her lips moved, but no words came out. More tears leaked from her eyes and she looked back down at the table.

Lauren slowly turned her eyes back to the other witches gathered around the picnic table. "What did you do? ... ... What did I do?" she added after a moment.

"We didn't want her to distract you while you were focusing," Johanna said, so sweetly that her tone all but guaranteed that Lauren couldn't trust a word that came from her lips. "You're learning to move emotions around, dear—escalating them in one party while drawing them from another. And that went so well, Lauren! On your first try, even," she cooed.

Adrienne shook her head, and Lauren simply closed her eyes, blinking away her own terror and frustration. How had she let herself fall into this? And what part had she just played in that boy pushing his brother, or the father yelling at him so violently? All of it to the extent that they'd muted Adrienne, expecting her objections.

"Rest until we've got another good candidate to try," Nell suggested.

And it said everything about how tired Lauren was, how heavy and dimmed her eyes were, that she could do nothing but nod and rest her head down on her folded arms upon the picnic table.

***

Riding back to the coven's home base with a hood over her head, there was barely a thought in Lauren's mind. She was drained. Numb. There'd been a point in the afternoon when her heart had ached and her mind had been swimming in a swamp of confusion and horror and pain, but at this point, she had nothing left to feel. After more so-called exercises, they'd apparently decided she'd be allowed the drive 'home' to decompress and left her alone, the witches' voices drifting in the air of the SUV, and with Adrienne remaining silent through it all. They'd given her some sort of muting potion to keep her from disrupting the afternoon's plans, and she'd yet to see it leave her system. The rest of their time at the park was a block of concrete in Lauren's gut still, so she could understand the feeling.

In fact, she thought their time at the park might remain a cinderblock weighing her down for the rest of her life— that's how she felt now, even when they'd left it behind and she was back to living beneath a hood of cotton. She felt sick, disgusted with herself, and a sob broke from her suddenly when she thought of the look David might have

188

had on his face, had he seen her at work today. Her sob went ignored, and that only seemed to reinforce the depths she'd sunken to.

It lived in her, hard and unrelenting. The memory of what she'd done—she, her mother's daughter, after all.

After some time had passed of her resting at that table, her head in her arms, a hand had landed solidly on Lauren's shoulder, and she'd understood it was time to come back to life. There'd been two men playing basketball, joking around like teenagers. At the witches' subtle prompting, Lauren had messed with their emotions—influencing and feeding and pushing and pulling, more aware of what she was doing now than she had been with the family, until one of the men had begun laughing near hysterically at his own cruel jokes, and the other had been stalking back to his car in frustration. She thought their friendship might have been ruined—or, at least, tainted forever. Next, there'd been a couple who, until Lauren had turned her attention to them, had been speaking together quietly at another picnic table. One had been quiet and regretful, the other sorrowful. She wasn't sure what would have happened if the coven had never looked their way, but as it was, they'd come to the park as a couple, and they'd left in a manner that suggested, clearly enough, that the relationship was over. The responsibility of that—the horror of that—weighed on Lauren like an anvil of the heaviest metal that had been dropped upon her soul and left to rust.

Now, when Johanna began speaking to her from the front seat, it took minutes for Lauren to process the sound, and minutes more for her to understand her.

"Choose anger or sorrow," the witch said from behind the wheel, and Lauren somehow knew that she'd already said it repeatedly—over and over again, Lauren guessed.

"I don't understand," Lauren finally whispered, when it became clear the woman wouldn't stop until she'd responded.

"Anger or sorrow!" the woman snapped back at her. "You've learned both well enough. You're going to make someone feel one or the other. Choose. Now."

Swallowing a protest, Lauren stared into the flat blankness of the cloth covering her head. There was no point in arguing. Now that they'd muted Adrienne against her wishes, without her consent, all pretenses were gone. They'd punish Lauren's friend if she refused to cooperate, and everyone in the car knew that without it being spoken aloud.

"Anger," Lauren announced. "If you're going to make me push one of those... anger."

Really, there'd been no choice. Maybe anger was its own kind of murky pain, but sorrow was an emotion of such depth, Lauren didn't want the guilt of causing it— not if she could help it. Maybe if the witch had told her to choose between rage and sorrow, there'd have been a harder choice for her to make, but whether by luck or design, that wasn't the case tonight.

When the black hood was pulled from her head, Lauren found herself standing arm in arm with Nell in a crowded parking lot for a chain restaurant. She knew it for its namesake, its cheesecake, though it had been years since she'd been inside one. Beside them, Adrienne was being bundled from the vehicle and pulled into lockstep with Johanna in the same fashion. "You try to cause a scene or call for help, Lauren, and you'll regret it," Nell whispered in her ear, gripping her arm tighter for a moment as if for emphasis. When Lauren didn't answer right away, Nell squeezed harder, and Lauren finally nodded.

It was just the four of them for a booth, though Lauren noticed Sarah and Evie enter soon after them and take a seat at the bar, in clear sight. The restaurant was fairly crowded—it was late in peak dinnertime for the restaurant, from the looks of things, and lots of the tables' occupants seemed to have come just for dessert. Johanna ordered for the four of them—wine and a couple of appetizers—promising the waiter that they'd also be ordering dessert and offering a big tip if he'd only make sure to give them their privacy. With the twenty-dollar bill she pressed into his hand even upon making the initial order, Lauren imagined he'd do his best to make the woman happy.

When he disappeared into the maze of aisles surrounding them, Johanna leaned over the table and met Lauren's eyes, holding her gaze in what might have been intimate connection between two other women. "Anger," Johanna said quietly. "We're going to choose someone, and you're going to create it."

"Here?" Lauren choked out, glancing around. Tables were packed all around them, with restaurant-goers, waiters, and bartenders constantly shifting the traffic patterns in some version of organized chaos. Blocking it out for a moment, she searched the walls for any indication of where they were, but she got nothing. This was a chain restaurant which, she was fairly sure, could be found in just about any major city in America—and a lot of the minor cities, too, in the middle of the country and places where she'd visited, at least. Its décor was unremarkable, and meant nothing, and she hadn't had a chance to look for some specific sign on the menus before the waiter had whisked them away.

"Here," Johanna said. "Look at the tables across the aisle from us, and let's choose from that group. You, Lauren, I think. You choose."

Lauren did as instructed, and immediately eliminated two of the three tables within easy, clear sight of them. One of those eliminated held a family, and the other a couple—she'd done enough interfering with families and couples for one day. The other booth was catty-corner to theirs, and held six women crushed together for what Lauren guessed must be a girls' night out. The women were dressed in what might, for one person alone, have been seen as work attire—but, taken that all six of them together were dressed just a touch too sexily for work, seemed more certain to be focused on a night out which they'd dressed specially for. They were probably in their late thirties, Lauren guessed, and there was nothing remarkable about any of them.

"The women," Lauren said quietly. "One of them. Does it matter which one?"

Across from her, Johanna smiled. Lauren chanced a glance to Adrienne beside her, whose eyes were down on the table and whose lips were in a tight line—she still couldn't talk, it seemed. Nell looked anxious, her gaze darting around, and Lauren suspected the woman was waiting for her or Adrienne to try something. That seemed hopelessly pointless, though. Guaranteed, the witches had some plan for if it happened, and Adrienne would be sure to pay the price for whatever she attempted.

Johanna nodded to the waiter as he delivered their wine from out of nowhere, and then he disappeared. She sipped at hers, pressing a glass into Lauren's hand, and took a surreptitious look behind her at the women's table. "How about... go for the one in the blue. She looks utterly bored and calm. Let's put some emotion into her." Johanna glanced sideways at Nell, and added, "Text Sarah and Evie the choice so they can keep an eye out. If you sit a bit more sideways, do you have enough of a view?"

Nell shifted sideways in her seat and sat with her back to the booth's end, one leg and knee pulled up in front of her on the seat as she reclined, the wine glass balanced on her knee. The booth backs were low enough that Lauren could see she had an easy sight of the other table, and Nell nodded to confirm it as she took out her phone to, presumably, text the witches at the bar.

"You want me to just... create anger?" Lauren asked. "Not a transference like at the park?"

"You can do it," Johanna encouraged her. In another moment, she'd dipped her hand into her purse and pulled out one of the small stones which Lauren and Nell had been using for magic storage. "For a bit of extra power if you need it, given the drains of earlier in the day," Johanna allowed, pressing it into Lauren's free hand. Automatically, Lauren wrapped her fingers around it. "Now, focus. Think of anger, of what it feels like... consider it. Live in it. And then... push."

Lauren gripped the stone tighter as she sipped again from her wine glass, and she shut out the feel of Adrienne shuddering beside her as the other woman took a few frantic gulps from her own glass. The memory that came to her wasn't of when she'd most recently felt anger—not at all. The restaurant's setting had brought to mind her last time out for dinner, and how David had played with her emotions and vulnerability, setting her up to be the ideal woman the center would take. He hadn't warned her, not nearly enough, and when she'd realized the full nature of his plans, the anger and humiliation had been practically insurmountable. Perhaps, in the moment, humiliation and sadness had outweighed the anger only because of her love for him, but the anger had been there, strong and constant, and this restaurant—being pressured again to behave in a way that she didn't want to, when surrounded by smiling, carefree people who'd have been horrified not just by what was happening to her, but who she even was—brought all of that back to her.

She lived in the moment, as Johanna had instructed, and then, as she'd been told... she pushed.

Drinking down her wine as the proverbial liquid courage, she at first noticed nothing. The woman dressed in a blue, silken dress blinked as if in surprise after Lauren first sent the emotion her way, and then she seemed to settle. The waiter brought their appetizers, and Lauren found herself munching on a bit of pita dipped in spinach and artichoke dip almost without thinking about it. She was curious, after all. At the park, she hadn't meant to do what she'd done—not really. It had been automatic, and she'd been drugged. This was more purposeful, and as much as she didn't want to have to do it... there was a part of her that was desperate to know whether or not she'd succeeded. In the car, driving from the park, she'd felt like her mother's daughter—more than ever. The possibility that she was capable of creating negative emotion out of nothing at all... well, that would be proof, wouldn't it?

The women kept talking, first about some TV series they were all addicted to and then, more specifically, about men who were in their lives, though Lauren couldn't quite parse out who was dating casually, who was seriously involved, and who was married—it was all a slew of names, and it wasn't what she was worried about. Slowly, the woman in blue became quieter. She spoke less, and her movements became more sporadic, more jerky. She sipped her cocktail more quickly, and jabbed at her dessert more purposefully. From across the table, Lauren heard Nell grunt in some sort of agreement, but Lauren didn't spare her a glance.

Suddenly, as if out of nowhere, it happened. The woman in blue erupted, loudly enough that Lauren jumped and there was a brief quiet from surrounding tables as others tried, and failed, to ignore her. "You slept with him, didn't you?!?" the woman hissed at one of her friends. "You told me you wouldn't until you got serious, and you did!"

One of the other women—a pale, curly-haired brunette—had frozen with her fork halfway to her mouth. "Sadie, this isn't the time—"

"Fuck the time!" Sadie hissed, and she threw what was left of her cocktail into the other woman's face.

After that, things became a blur. A screaming match ensued, another drink was thrown, and the uninvolved women went into crisis mode, attempting to tame things between their friends. Two of them got up and rushed the woman who'd been accused, the brunette, off toward the bathroom, and from the yelling that followed her retreat, Lauren finally gathered that Sadie, the woman in blue, was mad that their friend had slept with Sadie's brother as one of her 'regular one-night-stands', whereas Sadie's brother had, irrevocably, fallen for her head-over-heels. Truly, it sounded like a confrontation that would have happened somehow, some way, eventually—elsewhere if not here. It had been coming... though perhaps the explosion wouldn't have been quite so violent if left to its own devices, Lauren knew.

By the time the women had hurriedly paid their bill and disappeared to let the waiters clean up the spilled alcohol and emotions, a manager was coming around to apologize for the disturbance and offer complimentary desserts. Graciously, Johanna accepted on behalf of all of them.

Chapter 18

David had plans for the night, for Lauren, but when she showed up in the doorway, all that changed. Her face was red in a fashion that suggested she'd been sobbing, and scrubbing the tears away over and over again, but warring with that impression was the garment she wore. It looked like an odd, tight-fitting jacket—hugging her arms and hanging somewhat loose over her breasts. With her in his doorway, naked but for the jacket and those odd, home-made bits of jewelry he'd seen before, the impression was otherworldly, and he froze where he sat in bed before he even thought to put aside his book and approach her. She looked weak where she stood, almost half-hiding behind his doorframe as if she feared entering, but she took steps toward him when he stood and they met in the center of the floor.

When his arms landed on the strange clothing she wore, and he got a closer look upon her pushing her head into his chest and holding to him, he understood what he was seeing. The sleeves were tight to her arms, the fabric running snug across her back and shoulders, and it was rough in texture. Even in the dim light of his room, he saw the metallic shavings running through the thread of the garment, covering the whole of it, and thought that it wasn't unlike a tightly woven fishnet which had been stretched and pulled into some absurd mockery of fashion. When one of her hands came up to grip his t-shirt, over his heart, he saw bits of loose fabric hanging along her wrist, and understood instinctively that he was seeing cinching and finger-holes that would, if taken advantage of, have made it difficult for Lauren to put on the jacket fully, or take it off entirely, without help. Like a straitjacket, it was made to be attached to a person; unlike a straitjacket, it was for the coven's protection instead of Lauren's.

Without even attempting to loosen Lauren's hold on him, David backed the two of them toward the bed and sat down at its edge, letting Lauren lean against him. He gripped her thigh with one hand, feeling the familiar magic rise between them, and murmured assurances into her hair. He wondered if she heard any of them, she was so still. It was as if she was in shock, it occurred to him, but he didn't think that was the fault of the jacket—it hadn't been tied and could easily have been slipped off. No, the jacket was for his benefit—what Lauren was feeling the after-effects of was something else.

When her grip lessened, he gently detached himself and knelt down by the bed, willing himself to hold off on touching her further. He wanted everything she'd come for—he wanted her in bed with him all night, beneath him in pleasure—but that had to wait. She'd worn this jacket for a reason, and he meant to take advantage of it. "Wait here, Lauren, okay? You understand me?"

Her eyes were glassy, tear-rimmed, and he knew she couldn't nod, so he simply stood and hurried out to his kitchen area. The junk drawer held nearly a full roll of masking tape, and he grabbed that and a sharpie. Back in his bedroom, Lauren looked at him oddly, but she didn't fight him when he nudged her further onto the bed and then pushed her to lie down with her arms spread out to her sides. Then, he set to work. He ran the tape from one wrist to the other, straight across her back in one long line. Then, he carefully wrote 'wrist-to-wrist' on the length in sharpie, pulled it up from the jacket, and stuck it to his wall so that it wouldn't get tangled or curl. In the same way, he measured the jacket from top to bottom, where it hit her neck to where it landed at her mid-back, and then measured the lower hem, nothing the little holes that he guessed were used to attach one side of the jacket to the other side when it was worn more formally. There were no buttons, and he wondered if Nell used some little ropes or chains or something magical that he couldn't even imagine to tie the front of the jacket closed over her abdomen and breasts. Instinctively, he knew it was Nell. There were such holes at her neck, he realized, as well, when he went to measure the fabric there, and it was all he could do to keep his hands from trembling when he realized that this garment was more of a straitjacket than he'd imagined. It must have taken a lot for Lauren to put herself into it in order to come to him, even if she had gotten used to it, but it was what they needed. This was the clue they'd needed to find her, and explained in one torturous gaze exactly why they hadn't been able to trace the tattoo. The ink's shape was hidden in its entirety, masked by this oddly made fabric.

They'd been searching for the wrong shape.

When he'd finished with his amateur measuring act, there were eight lengths of masking tape lined up side by side on his wall, each one labeled. Probably more than they'd need, but he wanted to be safe.

The tape and sharpie put away, he sat down beside Lauren and pulled her against him. She was back to where she'd landed originally, sitting at the edge of his bed. The glassy look in her eyes had lessened some, though, and he saw her sights lingering on the lines of tape he'd just put up.

"We're going to find you with this," he said softly. "I swear to god. Just hold on a little longer." He swallowed down all of the questions he wanted to ask her, knowing they'd only lead to her struggling to remain quiet, and instead hugged her to himself for a few seconds more, content to feel the grip of her hands on his t-shirt and sweatpants. He was itching to pull the jacket from her body and lay it aside, but he wasn't sure what would happen if he did. Would she disappear on him? Or, in the worst case, was it possible the jacket would somehow then stay with him, in his bedroom, rather than return with her to wherever the coven was keeping her? He couldn't chance that happening, unlikely as it seemed.

Eventually, when she felt relaxed against him and he could feel the warmth of her magic rather than the tension she'd carried into the room with her, he let himself slide down to the floor in front of her. He nudged her backward so that she lay on her back, and felt her stretch—in anticipation, he hoped. Her knees parted for him without any sign of resistance, and he pulled her body closer so that he could smell her arousal. She was wet for him, as always, and he felt the magic rising to his fingers where they gripped her thighs. When he'd pulled her wide before him, he shifted so that her legs hung over his shoulders, and then he began playing, doing what he'd been thinking of doing to her for days, for all of the time she'd been absent. He had the energy now, and he wanted her.

After days without her, the connection he felt to her body was nothing less than a drug pulling him back in. It had been all he could do to put off their pleasure long enough to attend to business, but now he forgot about her captivity, he forgot about the strange jacket she wore, and he simply let himself enjoy her.

Her pussy jolted at the first slow lick he took across her wet center, and he felt the magic rising through her body, through her skin, soaking them both in her juices as he lapped at her, feeling her shudder beneath him. He imagined the whimpers he'd have heard if he had her there with him, but beyond her silence, it felt real. She pulsed beneath him, and when he felt her first climax coming, he locked his wet lips against her clit and plunged two fingers into her body, literally pumping the orgasm from her as her legs locked and tremored around him with the release of tension and pleasure. He only pulled back when he could feel the orgasm's aftershocks running in little pulses through her wet body and he himself was out of breath, and he let his mouth linger along the inside of her thigh as he pulled back, planting slow kisses along her soaked skin.

When he stood, he took a moment to watch her. Lauren's eyes were closed, and she lay panting on the bed, her hands still gripping his comforter. Her legs were loose and parted, weak from pleasure, and he enjoyed the sight of her. Tonight, he had energy, and he wanted to use every bit of it on her. He stripped off his shirt and sat down beside her, and as he took one of her breasts in his mouth after nudging aside the strangely textured jacket, he began playing his hand along her pelvis and abdomen, letting the magic circle and come to his touch before he moved. He dipped fingers into her pussy, gathering wetness that he traced along her body as he played with her breasts, and when he gathered some more of her juices and then dipped his fingers into her mouth, between her lips, she sucked him in, holding his fingers there. The magic was encasing both of them now, swirling through her skin and heating their every point of contact, and he bit down on her breast until she arched up into him, her mouth sucking his fingers deeper in what he guessed was an effort to keep from biting or screaming.

When he rose up beside her, he was panting and hot, and he could see her trying and failing to catch her breath, so he watched her for another moment before maneuvering out of his sweatpants. He pulled her sideways, positioning her fully on the bed, and then he moved overtop of her to watch her. Her eyes had that pleasure-filled look he'd come to know so well, and he could feel heat collecting in her face and along the whole top of her body, reacting to him—waiting for him.

He dipped his hand back to her pussy and thrust three fingers into her this time, and she arched into his hand. He could feel the pulse of her blood and her warmth there, and in her neck when he lowered his lip and took her skin between his teeth, gently, before he licked along her pulse to taste her sweat and played her with his hand. One of her hands gripped his arm, the one working her lower body, and her other still clenched the blankets beneath them. He moved his lips to her ear, whispered that he loved her, and then he took his hand away and plunged the whole of his dick inside of her in one fast movement, taking her breath away in a moment's act. Her channel was tight and hot, and he closed his eyes at the pleasure of it, holding himself inside of her as her body got used to him. When he opened his eyes, he saw her eyes were still tight shut and her lips were panting, and he could feel both of her hands gripping him, one at his lower back and the other on his arm.

He nudged himself further into her, close to bottoming out, and suddenly she shuddered against him, her mouth open in a scream that he couldn't hear as she climaxed for the second time, pulsing around him. He pulled her lower lip between his and kissed her, wishing he could anchor her to him for the rest of their lives through this kiss, and then he began thrusting again, bottoming out within her body before her climax was done so that he could draw it out. Her pulse and the magic were racing, and he pulled from their kiss to pant into her neck. He could feel her body running hot with magic, pulsing in a mix of pleasure and pain, and he held her to the bed and kept thrusting, pushing both of them until he finally erupted in the climax that he'd been at the edge of ever since he'd touched her.

When he pulled up and leaned away, swallowing his breath as his body came down from the release, he saw she was flushed and smiling, her eyes shining with pleasure as much as with pain, and he let himself relax, rolling to her side and curling around her. He had her back—for now, at least. And when his body recovered from this release, and her body came down from the pleasure, he'd take her again, and then again, and he'd make the most of whatever time they had tonight.

Then, tomorrow, the search would start anew.

Chapter 19

Evie used Johanna's trick of giving the waitress an early tip in order to guarantee privacy, and then she sat back to wait. She'd already texted the private investigator they'd hired to tell her that she'd secured a table in the back of the tavern for their meeting, but she was also five minutes early. The woman had shown up exactly on time at their first meeting—to the minute—and Evie imagined it would be the same today. She spent the spare time perusing the menu and sipping on her beer, with her thoughts occasionally wandering to the night before. Lauren had been shell-shocked by the day, between the time in the park and then the scene at the restaurant, and it had been all Evie could do to keep from giggling through the entire night. After hearing what that bitch and her agent friends had done to Johanna and Nell's coven, it was pretty fantastic to finally be seeing the witch brought low. Adrienne was nice enough, if naïve, but faking any sort of truce-type friendship with Lauren had been a chore from the start. And the fact that the bitch had seemed to be buying into it all—after they'd kidnapped her, of all things—showed just how little backbone and dignity she had. Seeing this plan through to the end, and breaking her down entirely before they rewrote her personality, would open up all kinds of avenues for the coven, and Evie knew that. She was simply anxious to be done.

When Shelley Ross walked in, Evie waved the waitress over immediately. The other woman ordered a beer and a club sandwich, and then passed an envelope to Evie without any further comment.

"We got lucky," Shelley explained as Evie began glancing over the information in front of her, which showed a list of credit card receipts, names, and home addresses. "She used a card. Like you said, Lauren went off the radar completely, presumably soon after this happened and before your coven was expecting her to show herself, so it was just a matter of determining the last night out she had—given what you told me, I'm fairly certain this is the one we're talking about. It's a watering hole known mostly for yuppies and margaritas; fucking bleeds pick-up artists who've got more money and ego than talent. Your girl's credit card was run within two minutes of five other people—two women and three men. The men's names are there, and all of them have home addresses within the same city. My bet's on either Jerry Allen or Stephen Eads. The other guy there, Dubeau, is in his fifties, so unless he's an incredibly good-looking smooth-talker, it seems like the other two are better bets. Both in their late twenties, both single. Oh yeah, Dubeau's married also, and by the size of his credit card receipt, he could have been buying drinks for him and his wife, for all we know. But it's small enough that I still doubt he was working on getting himself or anyone else drunk."

Evie glanced down the listing in her hand, nodding along with Shelley's words. "Any idea what the other two do for a living?" she asked, looking back up to Shelley and closing up the folder.

"Eads is a veterinarian and Allen's employed by an architecture firm. For what it's worth, if you're looking for a guy who date-raped a girl, my money 'd be on the architect. I'm sure there are amazing architects out there, but a guy who likes puppies and other furballs seems like the worse bet..." she trailed off, shrugging, and then offered the waitress a smile in return for her sandwich. Evie signaled for another beer and slipped the folder into her purse.

"No, I agree," she said. "You know what the other guy does, by the way? Dubeau?"

"Some middle-management type. I can text you the name of the firm later since I dug it up, but I think the age range makes him unlikely, and Lauren's bill was small enough that I think she was only paying for herself—hell, unless she's a serious lightweight, I bet she didn't even pay for all of her drinks. You said she was pretty drunk, by her own admission. Looks like both Eads and Allen were buying drinks for more than just themselves, and the timing and age are right."

Evie agreed, personally. Lauren was cute enough, and what little she'd learned about the night included the fact that it had started out as a girls' night out. It was hard to imagine that that somehow would have led to a fifty-something 'middle-management type' taking her home for the evening. Hell, Evie wouldn't even let something like that happen to Sarah, who was quite a bit older and more boring than the younger witch. "You sent the bill already?" Evie asked.

"Figured I'd hold off until I was sure you're good to go," Shelley answered after swallowing a bite of her sandwich. "The retainer you sent lets me know you're good for it."

Evie nodded, unsurprised. Shelley had come to them with the best of references, through one of Johanna's contacts, and she was nothing if not professional.

"Perfect. I'll start looking into these names today—okay if we let you know by, say, the weekend if we need anything else or if you should send the bill on?"

Shelley grinned, flashing a thumbs-up as she chewed her food, and then she leaned forward. "By the way, I've given some thought to what you and Johanna told me. If the offer's there... I think I'd like to take you up on dipping a toe in. Seeing if it's a good fit for you all and me both."

For the first time since the other woman had walked in, Evie let herself offer a wide, unguarded grin. When they'd broached the topic of witchcraft with Shelley, Evie had gotten the impression she wasn't interested, but having her as a part of their group would be fantastic. The idea of exchanging any reliance on Adrienne—though Evie thought Sarah might want to keep her as a pet project, which was fine—was welcome. They already knew Shelley had cruel bones in her after the last job she'd helped them arrange.

Evie glanced over to the waitress and called for another round. Then, she turned back to Shelley. "I'll drink to that. Let's get this last bit of a headache with Lauren wrapped up, finish our work on that, and we'll bring you into the fold. You'll be one of us before you know it.

***

By the time Evie stood outside Jerry Allen's apartment door, she was cautiously optimistic that he'd be the culmination of their plans. She'd gone to see Stephen Eads first, and eliminating the veterinarian had been a fast thing. Even aside from the fact that she felt fairly sure he was gay, the man was shy and diminutive—unless he had a black belt hidden in his closet, which Evie sincerely doubted, Lauren could have taken him down without issue. Maybe not if she'd been drugged, but from the little Lauren had said about the man who'd attacked her, it seemed clear that Lauren had been attracted to him at first, not tricked into accompanying him anywhere, and drugged with nothing more than a few too many margaritas. That wasn't the same thing as roofies, and as Lauren had described it, the man had physically overpowered her. There was no way Stephen Eads could have done that.

And that left Mr. Jerry Allen as suspect number one.

When he opened the door, a waft of smoke hit Evie alongside his cologne, and she nearly took a step back. His lips moved in a hello, but more than that, what she noticed were the way his eyes moved up and down her body. Involuntarily, her fists clenched. This was the kind of smug asshole that she wouldn't have minded taking down for no reason at all. Instead, she forced a smile.

"Mr. Allen?"

"You've found him." He leaned against the doorframe of his apartment, and she got a glimpse beyond him— overly modern furniture that couldn't possibly be comfortable, and décor that spoke more of excess wealth and a desire to show it off than anything close to taste or intelligence.

"I'm here on behalf of the new Montrose Bar on 13th Street. You've heard of it?" she asked, wishing she could work a silent spell to close her nose. The man reeked of cigarette smoke—what the hell had Lauren seen in him, even for a night's time?

"Heard of it. Haven't been there."

"Well, you're in luck! Your name came up in a drawing of local professionals." She handed him an open-amount gift certificate with a reservation already made for the following Friday. Getting the document from the manager had been a pain, and required more spellwork than she would have liked, but it would be worth it if this worked. "You've got a reservation for this Friday at 8 PM, for a party of four to six, so you can come out and see what it has to offer. Help spread the word, at no cost to you," she added. "Consider me the welcome wagon."

Examining the gift certificate, he glanced back up at her. "I've never heard of a gift certificate made out for an exact time and day, lady. And from what I hear, Montrose is already doing pretty well. What do they need me for?"

Fucking pain in the ass. Evie leaned sideways, mirroring his posture and arching her back just a bit, making the most of her tight blouse. "It is doing well, but we want to spread some goodwill and make sure we bring in professionals from across the city to give it a try. If you're not interested, though...." She made as if to take the gift certificate back, but he pulled it inside his apartment and laid it on what she guessed was a table just within the door.

"Hell, why not? I'll be there with bells on."

Chapter 20

Lauren splashed water over her face for a second time and then gazed up into the bathroom mirror. She looked bleary and tired, as groggy and worn-down as she felt. The coffee she'd had just a half-hour before had either failed to help or not yet kicked in, and the truth was that she wanted to go back to bed—as she had since she'd finally rolled out of bed at around ten in the morning. The last few days had caught up with her, it seemed.

Yesterday and into last night, she'd lost track of how many spells she'd cast with the coven. None of them had been all that serious—nothing to really give her pause— but they'd added up, particularly when she'd already been tired from the day out of casting and her first night in a while with David. To sit in the coven's casting circle and help reinforce the wards on the building and vehicles again had itself been tiring—not to mention pointless, in Lauren's opinion. Though Johanna and Nell seemed positive that the agents would have employed another witch to help track Lauren down, and would thus come armed with spells if they did find them, Lauren truly didn't imagine that was the case. And even if David and

Josh did have the help of a witch—though the how and where of that happening seemed absurd, considering how hellbent against witches they'd been even recently—they wouldn't bring a civilian along on a raid. She knew it hadn't even occurred to them to ask for her to accompany them when they'd been hunting her mother's coven and going after the various witches. Warding these buildings against anyone's magic but their own might help the coven somewhere down the road, but it wouldn't matter when it came to David and Josh finding her. They'd be relying on tech, if anything, and the witches had no defenses against that but the shrug she wore everywhere, so far as Lauren could tell.

After those wards had been renewed, things had taken a stranger turn that Lauren didn't particularly understand, but she still didn't feel uneasy over it. Sarah had stopped the circle from ending and insisted that they cast a ward on Adrienne and Lauren specifically—to keep them from being 'misinterpreted' or 'misunderstood'. Johanna had balked, at first, but then Nell had suggested that if Sarah saw it as being so important for their newest members, perhaps they should cast it on all of their number. To that, they'd been able to agree, and so the additional warding spells had begun. Again, Lauren didn't see the point, but she doubted there was anything nefarious hidden in the warding—not if Sarah had proposed it, and not if Johanna and Nell had agreed to have it cast on themselves as well as the rest of them. Whatever Sarah was thinking, Lauren had no quarrel with it, as she trusted her more than any of the other witches in their group anyway.

And to follow all of that up with a night with David, in which they'd lost themselves to the same pleasure they usually did and then fallen into still more of it, even though he'd said he could see how tired she was.... Her body had kept running with the magic all night, even when she'd accidentally gone to answer some question he'd spoken without apparently intending to, and landed back in her own bed. That had even been something of a relief, with her body already weak with pleasure and hot with so much magic.

And now? Now, her limbs felt leaden and tired from all the magic use, and her mind felt groggy, her throat stale with casting. She'd brushed her teeth five times that morning before she'd finally had to admit that the oddly discomfiting taste in her throat came from residual magic being brought up out of her blood and body to such an extent—it was something she'd heard of happening, but not experienced, and she'd been drinking water and juice all day to try to rehydrate herself and get rid of the sort of blank staleness in herself. Nell had told her she'd get used to it—that it was only because she'd used magic so sparingly and for such small needs over the years that it was getting to her now like this, with all this purposeful casting and spellwork—but the truth was that Lauren didn't want to get used to it.

She'd never considered magic unnatural, and she still didn't. But, it had begun to occur to her that using it this much, so often, was extremely unnatural. Not what the human body was built for, at best, and against some unspoken rules of the universe at most. Did she believe in karma? She wasn't sure. But she did believe in what her body told her—and that was, clearly enough, that she was overdoing it.

And now, with Sarah and Adrienne off gallivanting elsewhere for some reason Lauren didn't know, Nell and Johanna expected still more from her.

With a sigh, Lauren dried her face with a paper towel and headed back out toward the circle. Whatever was coming, she might as well get it over with, she supposed. The other women were already settled onto cushions, with the fourth side left open for Lauren. Without meeting the eyes of any of them, she settled down onto the cushion they'd put out for her and crossed her legs, tucking the skirt she wore around her as if it were a small blanket. The shrug tugged at her shoulders, but she didn't bother attempting to adjust it—she was used to the discomfort of it at this point.

"Alright then," Johanna began. "Today is about casting out prior demons. I don't believe Sarah and Adrienne need this so much as the four of us, which is why I've sent them on another errand. Lauren," she added, focusing her eyes directly on her, "this is about you, especially. You're allowing a demon from your past to hold you back—and it's not David Fredericks. This is a demon you are, essentially, denying existence to. Pretending it doesn't exist. But that's no way to embrace your power and move forward. It's no way to be yourself. That's what today is about."

Lauren's mind spun to figure out what the other woman might be talking about, but she was getting nowhere. These witches certainly considered David to be a hurdle and a demon, to them as well as to her, but if that wasn't what they were speaking of.... She felt herself leaning forward to meet Johanna's eye, despite herself. "I don't understand what you mean. Are you... are you talking about Mom?"

A little grimace flitted across Johanna's mouth, and Nell sighed beside her. "We all carry some... familial weight," Johanna said carefully. "Your mother is part of that weight. None of us deny it. But, no, that's not what I'm speaking of. We're going to work our way around the circle. If you haven't realized your demon when we get to you, we'll speak of it then more directly."

By some prior arrangement, Nell reached out and took Lauren's hand, just as she took Johanna's. Johanna in turn took Evie's, and Evie took Lauren's other hand. And then, Nell began speaking.

"I was in seventh grade when some girls at school started bullying me. The normal shit. Pushing me to the side or into lockers when we were in a crowded hallway. Spreading rumors. Stealing little things just to do it and cause my headaches—like my tennis shoes before I put them back in my gym locker, or my soda on another day. It was all subtle enough that teachers could ignore it, and since they were the popular girls and I was the 'weird wicca freak', as those girls so kindly put it, it went on and on and on. My mom told me to try harder to fit in, and bought me more expensive clothes that I didn't like. My so-called friends mostly just backed off because they didn't want to end up targets themselves. And then I got back at them. Little spells here and there. You can imagine all that. It was my last year in the public school system, though, I'll tell you that.

"But those days have been living rent-free in my brain for a long time. Getting back at the girls and principal didn't stop those memories from coming back. When I'm asleep at night, or I see a bunch of popular-looking kids out laughing and giggling, it all comes back. The thing is, it wouldn't have been so bad if the school hadn't allowed it. If the administration hadn't sided with them instead of me, or at least just opened an eye—hell, slitted one eye on one day only—to see a little bit of what was being done to me. Then, it never would have gone as far as it did. It wouldn't have gone as far as this. Because Johanna's right—I've been living with it, and I'm done. It's time to send all of the negative energy of those years back to roost."

Lauren watched as Nell took her hand from Johanna's and dug into the back pocket of her requisite black jeans. She pulled out a folded and creased photo and put it in the center of their circle, where it stared up at them innocently. It was the picture of an old brick school. The buildings had been updated and it looked well taken care of, but it was an old school. The photo had been taken so that the corner of the photo showed the school's welcome sign. 'Welcome to Piers Lindsok Middle School, Home of the Hartfield Hawks.' The picture was nondescript, the school was nondescript, and there were no people in the image to give it any sort of reality beyond the brick and mortar of a structure. Yet, Lauren felt her heart going heavy and solid over whatever was coming.

Nell glanced at her watch. "It's a quarter past five. School's out. Kids are leaving or gone or in small, organized groups that will get out easily. Let's do this. Let's send everything they left to weigh me down back at them."

Nell's hand gripped Lauren's tighter, and as one, the witches closed their eyes. Lauren was no initiate to group spellwork at this point. And whatever the witches had planned, she was in no position to fight. She even sympathized with Nell. Being an outcast was torture—especially when you were young. Willingly, she pooled her energy into Nell's hands, and she felt Evie's magic passing through her as it traveled to the lead witch for this spell. It felt heavy and dark, nothing like the wardings which they'd focused on casting the night before, and when Lauren's hands went hot with the power of whatever Nell was intoning, through unfamiliar syllables that Lauren mostly tried to block out, she wasn't surprised.

It seemed to take ages before Nell's hand relaxed in hers, the heat draining back into their blood naturally and leaving what was only a warm residue of energy as a reminder. Lauren's bones felt groggy, heavy with the energy and the work, but she kept silent. When Nell released her hand, Evie did the same, and Lauren stretched her shoulders, sitting quiet. It was Nell's place to speak first again.

"Let's take twenty minutes," Nell suggested, glancing around the group. Lauren looked to Johanna, expecting an argument, but saw none there. "Coffee, Lauren?" the other witch asked her. Confused, Lauren nodded and then stood up. She followed Johanna over to the coffee set-up at the edge of the room while Evie and Nell pulled their phones from out of nowhere and put their focus into the devices rather than the circle.

With a cup of coffee in her hand, Lauren watched as Johanna prepared her own and waited for her to speak, but the other witch seemed content to remain silent. Unsure whether to be thankful or worried about that, Lauren leaned herself back against the counter and willed her body to accept the caffeine she was dribbling into it. The waiting they were engaged in—whatever they were waiting for—carried its own small sampling of adrenaline, but not enough to lift her from the morass she'd been in that day. When she slid down to sit on the floor and stretched her legs out in front of her, Johanna made no comment, and so Lauren focused on her coffee and let her eyes close, looking for whatever contentment and rest she could get from these few silent moments as she sipped her coffee.

The twenty minutes passed fast.

When Nell raised her arm and waved them back to the circle, Lauren accepted a hand up from Johanna and followed her over to the small circle, where Nell had set her phone down in the center of the cushions. Evie came around to crouch over her corner, and then Nell hit play on the paused news clip on its screen, a 'BREAKING NEWS' banner across the lower rim.

When the screen unpaused, they all saw a reporter standing in front of a mess of firefighters, flames rising high into the air beyond them.

"I'm on Lindsok Avenue, about half a block from what you all know as Piers Lindsok Middle School, which went up in flames loosely fifteen minutes ago. An electronic alarm sent an alert to the fire department, and as far as we know, nobody was actually in the building when it caught fire. You can see behind me that the fire is still burning out of control with firefighters expecting to work well into the night. We've learned that the flames seem to have started in the southwest quadrant of the school, though the cause is still unknown. Based on the original alarm and the school's layout, there's some speculation that a simple electrical fire—perhaps located in the kitchen, which was undergoing some renovations in one area—spread to the area of the drama, woodworking, and art department, where stores of paints and chemicals such as wood thinner might have worked as accelerants to amplify the flames and their spread. Although there are no known injuries or fatalities at this time, I'm sorry to report that the school is expected to be a total loss, with firefighters primarily focused on containment at this time."

Nell silenced her phone and pulled it back to put it in her pocket. She wore a grin, brighter than any Lauren had seen her wear in the past, and it seemed to soak Lauren's own heart in horror.

"We did that?" Lauren whispered. "Your spell, the school, the fire... that was us?"

Nell turned her eyes to her, and met Lauren's gaze without flinching. "And I'm freer for it. Better for it. You heard the reporter. Nobody was hurt."

Lauren swallowed down whatever words might have come, speechless. To be part of the cause of that much destruction.... She didn't know what she'd thought they were doing, but to think they'd done all that was chilling.

Johanna cleared her throat, and seemed to be waiting for Lauren to look up at her. She finally did.

"Alright, then. One hurdle cleared. Now, Nell's wish to clear her hurdle was more direct. The rest of them won't be," Johanna began. "We sent that flame through from here, but the rest of us will be pooling magic to power a spell that we'll then use in the near future. I want to make sure we all understand what this freedom entails. This freedom we're attaining—it's necessary. It's also to bring us forward past hurdles which have, until now, been handicapping us. For my part, however, this is literally a matter of freedom to move forward." She turned to Evie and went on, "Lauren and Nell already know this, but I and Nell were the natural successors to the leadership of the coven that was... dismantled, so recently. We were able to save much of our own supplies and records, but those of other coven members were lost. That's the hurdle I'm aiming to clear with the spell we're about to store power for, and it's a significant one. Nell and I have built a plan which will entail counteracting the wards which have been placed on the old homes of the witches who were in the coven and have since left the sisterhood, in order to gain access to their stores and records." She paused, turning her eyes back to Lauren. "You have a question?"

Lauren hesitated, but since Johanna had obviously seen the question in her face, there seemed to be no point to remaining silent. "Wouldn't the witches' supplies, and any records, have been cleared out already? I mean, the homes must be up for sale... I'd think?"

"They are," Johanna agreed. "But each of us in the coven kept a secret space—a small trunk stored in a wallspace or crawlspace, or a secret room. These spaces were warded by the coven, and Nell and I have already ascertained that the wards are in place. The problem is that the agency which your very own lover works for has managed to place extra security and, in some cases, actual warding around the homes themselves, and we'll need a number of spells in succession, with significant power behind them, to get past those barriers and regain what's the rightful property—intellectual and physical—of the coven."

"I can't," Lauren said simply, shifting in her seat and shaking her head. "I won't help you kill more agents."

Nell laughed aloud, and Lauren's eyes shot to her, but Johanna was the one who spoke. "We're not talking about killing. There are very few security guards in place, per se, versus alarms and wards. And the guards who are in place are not worth the trouble to kill; they're low-level security guards who have little intelligence and no real power against us, and yet their deaths would earn us a great deal of negative attention. No, there are no plans to harm them, Lauren, I promise you. The spells we're talking about are focused on breaking through warding and allowing myself or Nell to become invisible to both human sight and alarms—so that we might go in and retrieve the supplies and records. Nobody will come to any harm. Would you like me to swear on that?"

Lauren was surprised by the offer, but after a moment, she nodded.

Johanna and Nell both grimaced, but Johanna nodded. "Very well. I realize there's still some time to be had before we've built up enough trust that you'll simply believe my intentions. So, let it be." She held out her hand toward Evie, and Evie handed her the small pocket knife she kept on her person. Johanna nicked her arm enough to draw up a line of blood, and then held her hands out toward the center of the circle, palms up, and closed her eyes. Slowly, the other witches all reached out and placed their fingertips against Johanna's fingers, and then she intoned, "On my and this coven's every connection to magicks and the supernatural, I swear the spell we're about to call up upon my direction, and sink our power into, shall not be used to directly injure or physically harm any person in the way of our goals." She cracked an eye open at Lauren. "Satisfactory?"

Lauren nodded, knowing the witch wouldn't endanger her own power or place in a coven for a simple charade.

From there, the four of them took hands, and Lauren only half-listened as her power went out through Evie and Nell, toward Johanna, to power the spells she'd need for her purposes. The witch had placed a pendant of some sort in the circle to collected the stored spells and magic for later use, and Lauren could see it quiver on the ground between them as it absorbed all of the power.

When Nell and Evie finally released her hands, Lauren's arms felt leaden with the magic she'd offered up, but there was no pause this time before Evie began speaking.

"We all have baggage, but mine's more the standard." She pulled out a creased photo with lousy resolution, clearly printed out from social media, and slapped it down into the middle of the circle. It showed a younger version of her, with the arm of a boy around her shoulders. Lauren guessed they must both be teenagers in the picture. "Meet Lee. High school sweetheart—hell, middle school sweetheart since that's when we first got together. We had a big fight right around the time of graduation." She glanced around the circle and added, "I guess it's rare for a witch to have a normal educational background, from what I've heard from all of you, but I did. Practicing magic was kept strictly private, and my family didn't move around. We were just dysfunctional in all the normal fucking ways. I was so normal that I lost my virginity to Lee on prom night. I was in tenth grade and he was in eleventh. Things were fine right after that, but of course we kept sleeping together until we broke up a year later, and I was a dumb teenager. I let him take some pictures of me in the buff. I'd been fine with him taking them, but he spread them around after we broke up— among all his buddies, social media, you name it. Talk about humiliating."

Evie had never put away the bloody pocket knife she'd loaned to Johanna for her oath, and now she placed it at the edge of the picture, and sliced down through the middle of it, leaving a bloody track of torn photo paper and two separate halves. She picked the side of the paper that showed her own smiling face back up, and tucked it into a pocket as she set aside the knife. "This is about him," she concluded. "And I'm not going to kill him," she added suddenly, as if reading Lauren's mind as she looked over at her. "But I am going to humiliate him."

The look on Evie's face was murderous, but Lauren saw no sign of deceit in it—and, of all the witches, Evie had no poker face whatsoever. If she'd been lying, Lauren was confident she could have seen it in the other woman's expression. So, after a few moments of hesitation, Lauren nodded, and she took the other witches' hands so that the process could be undertaken once more. When their hands pulled back, Lauren felt more exhausted than ever—weighted. She understood now that everything they'd been doing had been focusing negative and surreptitious magic, magic bordering on truly black magic, and turning it to dark purposes. Dark spells. She wouldn't call it black magic in thinking about it—they weren't directly harming people, after all—but there was no denying its darkness. Her whole body felt to be tingling with it, warm and hollow, and she examined her hands when they'd been released, as if she'd see some residue of the dark magic there, but they were only her hands, as visibly clean as ever.

When she looked back up, the other three witches were all staring at her. "I don't..." Lauren began, and then she started again, "I didn't have time to think about this. I don't have a hurdle in mind, something holding me back."

"That's because you're in denial," Nell said quietly. "You have been for a while."

Lauren glanced to her, and then she shrugged and looked back to Johanna. "It doesn't make sense to be talking about my mother right now—she's gone, obviously, and there's no revenge to be had. And you said this wasn't about David. So, get to it. What do you think is this hurdle I'm in denial about?"

Nell's hand went to her other back jeans pocket, and came out with a photo that Lauren at first couldn't see, in the way it was angled. But then she dropped it in the center of the circle, so that it glared back up at Lauren with a reality that, it was true, she'd been driving herself to forget about for some time.

The glaringly white grin. The preppy tan. The long limbs and slightly overgrown haircut. The flashy watch on the wrist and the cocky expression. The guy in the picture was the one who'd attacked her, so violently that she'd landed in the hospital and then needed weeks upon weeks to recuperate.

It was Jerry, and just the sight of him froze the air in her lungs.

She looked back up to the women circled around her— to the sympathy in the eyes of Evie, which almost broke her in itself because this was a young woman who'd never shown her any such emotion or kindness, though now her expression held an understanding that was all too honest. To the anger and disgust in Nell's face, turned down to focus on the photo. And to the patient understanding of Johanna's face. These women had dug into her past and found an anchor on her soul and body that she'd fought off over and over again, pretending it—and he—didn't exist, all so that she could try to focus only on David and her future. But here he was, in face and flesh and attitude, staring up at her. She wondered if he'd even thought of her since that night. He'd affected her forever, and she guessed he'd simply moved on.

Some of the leadenness in her limbs had lifted as anger took its place, and she felt herself clenching her hands into fists, her lips steeling into a thin frown. These women were right. David wouldn't have understood it, and she couldn't have explained it to him or even to Adrienne or these women gathered around her, but it was true. This man was a weight on her, and he'd gotten nothing of what he deserved. Now, she could change that.

"Okay," she said quietly. "Tell me what to say."

Chapter 21

David shuffled into the office beside Josh, peering around Barry's shoulders to the computer monitor in front of him. The tech had wanted them to come in for this meeting, and that seemed like a positive development—better than emailing them files upon files that amounted to no news at all, certainly. It had to be.

Or, it better be. Tired as David was after just two more nights of Lauren's nighttime visits, he could have used the rest at home rather than trekking into the office for no reason. Adrenaline could only push him so far.

"Eight hours with the new info means...?" David trailed off, waiting for Barry's fingers to stop skimming the keyboard before him.

"Eight hours means we're almost golden," Barry answered. "Take your seats, gentlemen, and prepare to be impressed."

Thank fucking god. David pulled up a stool on one side of the tech while Josh took one on his other side, and the two of them leaned in. "Am I reading this right?" David asked, his heart nearly in his throat and his exhaustion forgotten. "You've narrowed it down from hundreds of possibilities to five?"

"Kind of," Barry acknowledged, and he lifted his finger to gesture to the various dots spaced around the upper United States as he began explaining. "These five dots are all exact matches—or as exact as we can be with this tech and no visual confirmation, anyway. Since we have five matches even though the parameters are pretty strict, I'm thinking the coven had five of these jackets you saw prepared. Four to serve as decoys, and one for Lauren to wear."

"Or four other prisoners," Josh commented, but Barry only shrugged in response.

"We got any other inked agents missing?"

"No," he admitted. "But that only means they haven't targeted our agency."

"They've seemed pretty focused on us," David said.

"I mean, Josh might be half-right," Barry admitted, leaning back from the keyboard and examining his screen. "These witches are pissed at you. It's possible these aren't decoy jackets so much as jackets that are waiting for other bodies—like yours. But my money's on them being decoys."

David glanced across the tech to Josh. "You didn't see the jacket. No way would that jacket have fit either of us without being torn in two. It was made for Lauren."

"Yeah, but we can't get that exact—not without knowing how stretchy it is, for instance, or the density of the metal. You didn't by chance gauge any of that?" Barry asked, half-seriously, and David shook his head. "Okay, then, so we're mostly dealing with shape and schematic," the tech started again. "I'm not going to sit here and guarantee you that one of these couldn't fit a muscled-up athlete since we don't really have any way of knowing. But, here's why I think they're decoys more than anything." He used two fingers to point to the dots in

Alaska and Idaho. "You see these dots? They're sitting still. Now, we haven't gotten too close because there's a chance that snagging any of these or getting too close could alert the witches who are holding Lauren, and they'd know the jig is up. And if her jacket is one of these other dots, there goes our lead if we don't hit them all at once. But here's the thing. These two dots aren't moving—like, not at all. So, we dig in and discover that this one, the one in Juno, is actually smack-dab in the middle of a post office."

"Like, a U.S. Postal Service post office?" David asked after a beat.

"Yeah, smartass, exactly that," Barry said. "So, my guess is, they sent a jacket to someone up there and it's sitting in a box, waiting to be picked up. Hard to imagine Lauren's being held at a post office, right? And with the jacket not moving...."

"Makes since," Josh allowed. "So, what about the one in Idaho?"

"Also still, but that one's at a farm. Get this, though—the farm belongs to the family of one of those witches you killed in that raid early on. I looked into her, and she's got a sister about Lauren's age. You want my bet? They sent this jacket as a gift, maybe in honor of the dead witch, and suggested she wear it as a special favor or in remembrance, thinking she would. Instead, she leaves it sitting in a closet."

David stared at Barry for a second, and then raised an eyebrow. "That's an awful lot of assumptions. Tell me everything else we're gonna talk about here has more fact than assumption?"

Barry gulped from an energy drink and shrugged. "Yeah, but trust me on this—I fucking dare you to prove me wrong. If you saw how much this girl posts on anti-witchcraft, anti-wicca, anti-supernatural boards, you'd understand where I'm coming from. The bitch is more hard-lined against witches than most of the guys in our agency," he added.

"What about the other three dots?" David pressed.

"Okay, so here's where I think we're on the money," Barry told them, grinning at the screen with no little amount of pride. "We've got three jackets that have been moving around most of the day, but each one in a small space. They might stay still for a while, but we're talking a few hours—like if you were watching a TV or eating a meal, reading a book or whatever. Not like a jacket sitting in a box. And they're all in fairly confined buildings; spots where it'd be easy to keep Lauren hidden if they've taken over a part of the building for themselves or their new coven. We've got a townhouse in Illinois that's in the center of a triplex—so, not many windows, and based on satellite views, it's got a private backyard. Probably not too hard to keep a few women there and not raise suspicions or allow them any easy escape plan if these witches are smart, which we know they are. Option number two, a condominium in Ohio—but there are only a few condos per floor since they're pretty high-end. Not hard to imagine they took over a floor or two to keep privacy, and windows wouldn't matter much if they're high up. Third option, we've got an office building in Indiana. Looks like it's got various sections rented out to different entities, but a lot of mostly satellite operations with primarily remote workers—hard to tell how active the building is in general, and with recent renovations, I'm not even sure we could guess at how much the witches could have taken over through a fake business or shell corps or two if they wanted to seal off a section of the building for themselves. If the specs David gave me are right, though—"

"They are," David cut in.

"...Then, as long as that ink is still on her, and I don't know how it wouldn't be at this point, I guaran-fucking-tee you that Lauren's in one of these three spots."

"So, we plan simultaneous raids on these buildings," Josh said, "and we'll get her back without alerting the coven that we're onto the way they're masking the jacket."

"Right," Barry agreed. "Or all five, you want to be on the ultra-safe side, but I'd say it's pretty much a guarantee that she's in one of these three spots and the coven has other people, witch or otherwise, wearing these jackets that are moving around in the two decoy locations."

"We go in with forces at each location," David decided quietly. "Any luck, we find Lauren and Adrienne at the same time and we take the witches, no lives lost on our side."

After a beat of silence, Josh reached over and cuffed his shoulder. "What's your gut say about which location they'd take Lauren to? You've spent more time with them and studying Nell and Johanna than anyone."

David nodded, swallowing. "I don't like the townhouse—too suburban. Between the office building and the condos... I don't know." He looked between the dots, but finally shook his head. Adrenaline had overtaken every bit of his blood, and warmed his thoughts, but even if it hadn't, he wasn't sure that either option seemed more likely than the other. It was enough to know they'd narrowed it down this far. Hell... it was enough that they'd narrowed it down to five possibilities, let alone two. "I don't know," he repeated. "But you and I, we know them and we know Lauren. We split up. Each of us'll take one of these two spots." He looked to Barry. "Can you scramble teams we'll lead and get another on the other three locations?"

"You got it," Barry agreed, his fingers already going back to his keyboard.

"Thanks, man. Thanks," David said, clapping him on the shoulder.

"Hell, I like Lauren more than you guys," Barry offered over his shoulder as they headed toward the door. "Which one of you wants which location?"

"I'll take the condos since they're closest," David said. "We'll leave in the morning." He met his partner's eyes, and Josh nodded at him. The rest of it didn't need to be said. If he only had to get to Ohio, he could be at the ranch house tonight in case Lauren appeared, whereas Josh ought to leave that evening in order to reach Indiana.

"We'll get her back," Josh said quietly, and turned around to wave his thanks to Barry one more time before they moved out together. Out in the hall, he grabbed David's arm and pulled him to the side of the hall. "Are you up for this? How's your energy?"

"It's Lauren," David replied, shaking him off. With another glance in his partner's eyes, though, he relented, "I'm tired, yeah. But this isn't much of a drive. With a full team? I'll be fine. We'll go back to the house and I'll crash as soon as we get there, after chugging one of El's concoctions. Then, I'll chug some more of them in the morning. I'll be good to go."

Josh stared at him for a moment, but finally set his jaw and nodded. "Let's get back to the house, then. The sooner I get going and you get to bed, the better."

***

Whether because she made some sound to wake him or simply because he sensed her entrance into the air of the suite, David's eyes were open when Lauren came to the door of his room. In the dim light from the lamp on the nightstand, he saw her nude form pausing in the doorframe, landing there for a moment before she really entered. He sat up fully as she reached the bed and crawled up beside hm, to sprawl on her side beside him and almost... almost pose for him, he realized belatedly.

There was something off about her tonight. A stillness, and her eyes seemed somehow darker than usual—heavier, maybe. As if she was wide awake, but wanted to sleep. But when he reached out to touch her, and trailed his hand along her hip, his fingers brushing the round curve of her ass, the magic rose to his touch like it always did, ready and warm, and her lips parted with the same breath of desire he'd become used to seeing on her face. He ran his hand up and down her thigh, feeling the heat of her magic and blood, until her hand landed on his where it rested on her upper thigh. She pressed down, and then her fingers curled around his, pressing them harder into her body, and she closed her eyes and leaned toward him as if she were waiting for something. Sitting beside her and watching her, he reached for a breast and lifted it, cupping it, and her other hand followed his, curling his fingers deeper into the fullness of her breast until he knew she must feel the pain of a bruise forming. He tried to pull away, to loosen his grip on her, and she dug her fingers in—she was using his hand to hurt herself.

He let out a breath. "You want me to be rough with you tonight," he realized aloud.

Her hands pressed even harder into his. That was a yes.

Until now, he'd been sitting beside her somewhat awkwardly, half-turned to where she was reclined on his bed as he played with the heat of her blood and thought about what he wanted to do with her tonight. What he wanted to say. But the way she was acting now had changed anything he might have planned or been expecting. Just like last time she'd walked into his room, her demeanor had changed everything. And whatever this meant... he didn't think he had it in him to say no to her.

Moving over top of her, he lay over her lengthwise, knowing she felt his stiffness through his sweats even as he braced himself above her and mostly kept his weight from her. He rested his hands on her forearms where they lay to each side of her head, as if she'd been expecting him to pull her hands above her head—and he would—and he put his lips near her ear. "We're coming for you, Lauren. Whatever you're going through, whatever's happening, it's going to be over soon. I just need you to hold on a little longer. If you need to tell me something, if there's something you need to say, I've got some reason to believe—" his breath hitched. Her body was straining for his, her naked groin pressed up against him with one of her legs hooked around his leg as if she couldn't wait.

Was she even hearing him? He wondered.

Still, he caught his breath and said again, "Lauren, listen to me first. If there's something you need to tell me, something you need to say before we come for you—we've got some reason to believe that, if you say it at a moment when the magic is at full-blast, when whatever spell you're under has its hands full with channeling magic out of what we're doing, there might be some lag time. Some time when it's busy enough with taking in magic and needs a minute to catch up to the fact that you've said something and take you away from me. A few seconds where you can communicate before disappearing if you do it at just the right moment. When you can barely think," he gasped out against her ear, hoping he'd made sense. He lifted up from her some, and saw that there looked to be awareness in her eyes—she didn't look so hazy and drugged with desire as she sometimes was, overtaken by the spell. He thought she'd understood, and that would have to be good enough.

When he leaned into her this time, it wasn't with the intention of communication—not verbal communication, at least. For whatever reason she wanted it rough, he was willing to oblige. That had been the plan before, to get to a point where she could communicate with him, back before they'd had a solid hope of getting to her tomorrow. But now... the thought of pushing her excited him, and he could feel it exciting her.

He bit down on her earlobe and sucked it between his lips as his hands gripped her forearms. Her nipples were hard buttons of desire against his chest, and she arched against him so that he could feel the blood sparking beneath her skin, rising to the contact. When he moved his lips to her mouth, he took her. He pressed down in a hard kiss and then invaded her mouth with his tongue, stealing her breath and thrusting toward her throat, controlling her as he held her down and she remained arched into him, one of her legs still wrapped around his upper thigh and pulling him hard against him. Only when he felt her struggling for breath did he pull up, back, just to look at her. Now was when he could see some of her thought being overtaken by pleasure, by desire. Her eyes were hooded with a need for more, her gorgeous lips gasping, and in the dim light, he could even ignore the odd jewelry around her neck.

He hadn't taken his hands off her forearms, but now he rolled away abruptly, landing on his feet beside the bed, and shucked off his sweats and underwear. He'd been hard for her from the moment he'd seen her tonight, but the way she was acting with him had drained any tiredness away from him. She was all he wanted, and he had plans for her.

Standing beside her, he pulled her to the edge of the bed and then off, and gently pressed on her shoulders till she was down on her knees before him. Looking down at her, he could see just from the heaving of her chest that she'd wanted this, and he didn't have to prod her to wrap her hands around his shaft and bring him to her lips. As he fisted one hand into her hair and let his other fall to her shoulder, he pulled her into him deeper, and one of her hands went around to his ass so that she could steady herself while the other found his balls and cupped them, her fingers exploring. Her mouth was as hot and wet as he remembered, and the feel of her magic rising to her warmth and his body inside hers was enough to make him tighten his grip on her, and have to hold himself back from exploding in her rightaway. Her tongue was exploring his length, her lips moving along him, and she had to sense what was coming as he finally thrust into her mouth, into her throat, and began a hard, fucking rhythm as he used her, feeling her struggle to keep taking him as the magic egged them both on. Spasms ran along her throat as she gagged and he felt the heat rising between them. Fisting her hair tighter, he pulled her into him again, treasuring the way she was both fighting and embracing him at the same time, both of her hands holding onto his body for purchase.

When he finally pulled away and let her go, his cock throbbing with the need for release, she bent over on the floor gasping, and he had a moment of doubt, but then she looked up at him. Her face was a mess—of tears, sweat, and saliva—but she was smiling. He knelt in front of her and pulled at one edge of the discarded comforter until it reached her face, and he wiped away all of the moisture until it was just her smiling at him, even the tears gone. He guessed they must have come up with the pressure of the gagging. She must not have been wearing any makeup, either, because there were no smudges like he'd seen on her sometimes in the past. Just Lauren, and if he let himself look away from her face, the damnable jewelry. Before anything else, he dipped his lips to her neck and kissed her, nuzzling her skin and grazing it with his teeth until she was gasping, her hands gripping at his shoulders and trying to pull him to do more. He hadn't bit down, and he could feel her trying to goad him into pushing her body, but in some things, he wanted to take his time. He kept kissing her neck, teasing the both of them and knowing that the gentle slowness of it might have frustrated her desires on even the most innocent of nights, until he could sense her whimpering before him, her hands gripping him and begging for more. One of her hands moved down to his cock, and began stroking him, but that was when he finally pulled back.

Grinning at her, at the naked desire on her face, he shifted and slid a few feet away from the bed, staying on the floor and waiting for her to follow him. When she did, landing to sit beside him, he put his hands on her shoulders and pressed her backward onto the floor, and then he nudged her in the side until she got the hint and turned over. For a second, he just admired the view—this gorgeous, petite girl, all desire and curves—spread out for his taking on the floor of his bedroom. He could smell her desire.

She propped her elbows on the hardwood and braced herself half-upward, shifting so that she could glance over her shoulder at him. Smiling, she then inched back slowly until she was on her knees and elbows. He watched as she slowly, purposefully, spread her legs further in a clear invitation, and then he couldn't wait any longer.

From behind her, he reached to her center to make sure she was ready for him. Juices were all but dripping from her, but he slipped two fingers into her, then three, and thrust as he held her body against him, letting her feel the hard length of his cock against her thigh. Her body was running with heat now, her core wet and ready, and he could feel her breathing heavily against him as he gripped one breast and then the other, squeezing and playing with her nipples. He thrust his fingers into her again, and then brought his hand up to her lips. She sucked them into her mouth, tasting herself as he slid the head of his cock up and down her pussy lips, enjoying the wet heat coming off of her.

Before he entered her, he put one of his hands over hers on the floor, intertwining their fingers, and then he leaned into her, pushing aside her hair to kiss the nape of her neck and then the part of the tattoo that circled her shoulder. When he felt her somewhat relaxed under him, resigned to his taking his time... that's when he pushed.

In one deep thrust, he shoved himself into her in a way that took her breath away, and he kept one hand on hers, one wrapped around her chest, holding her body back against him. She'd been soaking wet, but she was also tight, and he felt her gasping for breath as she tried to get used to his size again from this angle. He didn't stop or wait, however. Instead, as soon as he was all the way in, he pulled back and then thrust into her again, enjoying the wet heat of her channel as he took her. He could feel the magic rising between them, slipping beneath her skin in a fluid echo of the smack of his flesh on hers as he fucked her, pressing in harder and deeper as the rhythm built and built between them, until his heart was pounding and he could feel her gasping with the pleasure of having finally fully gotten used to him again.

When she was pushing back against him, meeting him thrust for thrust in an almost violent demand for more, he moved his hand from her breast, lower, tracing the sweat and the curves down to the bundle of nerve endings above where his cock was burying and reburying itself into her gorgeous form. On the next thrust, he landed his fingers at her clit at the same time that his lips sucked at her neck and he shoved all the way inside her, and he felt her explode beneath him. She was shuddering, heat and magic and pleasure rolling across her in the waves of the orgasm as he rubbed circles around her clit and kept licking at her neck, pressing into her, pulling the pleasure from her in one endless shiver of heat and sweat. She was gasping for breath as he kept working her clit and then pulled back once before thrusting back into her violently, exploding inside of her with his own gut-wrenching orgasm even as he milked more pleasure from her spent form, all but collapsed beneath him.

Chapter 22

Lauren closed her eyes and worked to catch her breath, enjoying the way the heat of the magic ran through her blood and the slight, gaping soreness at her center. She'd rolled onto her back, and lay on the hard floor of David's bedroom now. Breathing deep, she could sense him beside her catching his own breath, and she knew that if she reached out her hand, she'd find him sprawled beside her. This was what she'd needed. What she'd wanted. Since that last circle with the witches, she'd been needing the concrete reality of his body against hers, and maybe even more than that, she'd needed the pain. Slight as it was, and as much as it was tied to pleasure, she'd needed it.

There was a guilt circling her, like some sort of monster waiting to pounce from a darkness that she didn't quite understand or care to think about. And she knew where it came from for her, but she couldn't push it away—and that made the guilt worse. It wasn't just guilt over what she'd already done and what she'd contemplated, but guilt over what she was planning. Tomorrow, before any more time was lost, she knew what she'd agreed to do. More than that... what she wanted to do. And the guilt over it was insurmountable. The fact that she was going forward with it anyway wasn't something she quite understood, but perhaps it was like the pleasure and the pain of being with David in some ways. What she wanted to do was like a pain that had been inside of her, and despite how wrong it might be to exorcise it, the pleasure of that was something she needed. Even if it had taken the witches to make her realize that.

David's hand landed on her stomach, resting there, and she put her own hand on top of it, grounding herself in his touch. She could feel the magic rushing to him, warming her body along the way, and treasured the pull of it, as well as the way it responded to him. When he spoke, whispering to her, she didn't at first even open her eyes.

"Do you want more?" he asked for the second time. "I don't know what you're thinking, what you're going through. I can't tell, and I know you can't tell me."

The ache in his voice made it gruff, so that each word sounded like a struggle, and that was what finally made her open her eyes and turn her neck just enough so that she could meet his eyes. Holding his gaze, she pressed his hand into her skin where it was now, over her belly, and she took her other hand and traced the muscles of his other arm, from his shoulder down his bicep and his forearm to his wrist, where she played her nail along his skin until she finally just held his hand where it rested on the ground.

When he didn't make any move, she scooted sideways until the length of her body was touching his, but she was on her back and he was on his side. She could feel his cock against her thigh, still thick, and she reached for it and ran her hand up and down his length, using their own fluids to allow herself to stroke him back to full attention. When she could feel him catching his breath, she squeezed, and then he rolled sideways onto his back.

"God, Lauren, whatever you want. I'm not saying I'm done. Just making sure you're up for more."

She took her hand away, not wanting to waste his next release on the air and her fist, and took his hand and placed it on her breast. She squeezed his fingers around her skin until she knew she was wincing from the pain, and had to look down to make sure that his nails weren't actually drawing blood. But he understood. He had to, because when she took away her hand, he kept gripping her, squeezing as she pressed harder into his hands and along his body, demanding more. More punishment. Even if she couldn't have said it out loud to him, had she been able to, that was what she wanted from him right now.

What she needed to try to scare the guilt she felt back into a corner, and get through the next twenty-four hours.

She wanted him to use her until she couldn't move. Until the ache she felt now in her throat and in her core was everywhere in her body, with magic and heat keeping her going alongside adrenaline. She wanted him to take everything from her and then take some more, and maybe that would even make it so that she couldn't get out of bed tomorrow, and couldn't do what she was planning on doing... and that would be okay, if it was what was meant to be. If him using her, being with her, kept tomorrow from happening, then that was meant to be the outcome of all this.

Maybe he'll get to me in time to stop me.

The thought flitted across her brain, and she shut it away as soon as she recognized its meaning. No. She wanted what was coming. She'd live with the guilt, and no matter how she'd gotten to this point, it was what was meant to happen. All this time, fate had been leading up to her recognizing that, on some level, she was her mother's daughter. She wouldn't truly be Nell or Melania or Johanna or anything like them, not ever... but she wouldn't lie down and be a nothing, either. Not for anyone. She'd be her mother's daughter tomorrow, and she'd survive it, and she'd survive the guilt, and then David would help her recover from it all and this would be behind her. And they'd be together again.

David was sitting up, getting to his feet, and she let him pull her to her feet beside him. The kiss he pushed on her lips made everything else go away. It was searching, demanding—punishing, as sore as her jaw was—and as hard as his hands were on her biceps, holding her against him, it was everything she needed. When he pushed her back toward the bed, she felt her magic boiling between them, and the heat of it took her breath away and renewed the wetness at her center.

He pushed her to sit down on the edge of his bed, and then he moved over to open up the drawer of his nightstand. For a moment, she remembered the handcuffs he'd tried to trap her in his bedroom with, the second night she'd visited, but she knew he'd learned from that experience—unless he was trying to get rid of her now, which she sincerely doubted was the case, that wasn't his aim tonight. When he turned around with what looked like a small jar of lotion, though, she felt herself relax an iota. It wasn't exactly the punishing sort of mind-blowing experience she'd been expecting him to initiate after that kiss, but she imagined it would lead them somewhere more exotic. Forcing a smile onto her face, she scooted back on the bed at his direction and laid back, relaxing into his mattress. He dragged the upper sheet and comforter the rest of the way onto the floor so that they'd just be on the fitted sheet, and then he sat down beside her with his eyes on hers.

"I don't know if this'll be too much," he began, "but I was thinking that it might be the thing to get us a second of communication, so I bought it anyway. If it's too much, I know you'll find a way to tell me."

Lauren's instinct was to laugh—he was holding lotion. But then he held it out, angling it so that she could better read the label, and her breath caught. Warming lotion. As much as the magic already heated her blood and the magic, there was no telling what it would feel like.

It was perfect.

She reached for it, and he let her grip it. Maybe he thought she was going to throw it across the room, but instead she began twisting open the lid, and he grinned above her.

"Hold on," he said as he took it from her. He set it to the side and nudged her into the center of the bed, and then he positioned her on her hands and knees again. When he leaned in beside her, she felt the magic rising to her neck and shivered at his breath on her ear. "First, I want to see my handprint on that ass of yours."

Her breath caught, and she felt herself getting wetter with just the thought of him spanking her. She didn't know why he'd brought out the lotion now if that was his intention, but she had no intention of arguing. No... she just wanted to make her own desires clear. With any of her inhibitions long drowned out by the magic that contact with David had already brought up on this night, she arched her back until she knew she was presenting her ass obscenely to him, her breasts hanging low toward the mattress. She glanced back at him, and saw that his eyes were fired up with the same desire she felt running in her own blood. Swallowing, she looked forward again and closed her eyes, wanting the surprise of the smack. The surprise of the pain. Somehow, he must have read into her mind that she wanted him to punish her, to force the guilt she felt out of her body for at least this night, and he aimed to do so.

She felt him repositioning himself, to the side of her and behind her, and then his hand came down hard on her left ass cheek, making her scream aloud in an echo of the sharp smack of skin. He hit her cheek again, and the stung took her breath away, but the magic was rushing to that spot, heating her....

And then she felt it.

He must have rubbed the lotion into his hand, because the warmth she felt now wasn't just the warmth of skin hitting skin or magic rising to the occasion. It was as if she'd sat against the hood of a car after its engine had just turned off, before realizing it was hot to the touch from running and from the sun, or as if she'd sat down on sun-heated leather and rested herself into the skin without thinking about it. The heat rang in her skin and stayed there, elevating with every moment so that she felt sweat breaking out anew along her back, arms, and thighs.

David's hand came down again on the same cheek, and then again, and again, heating her in a way that felt dangerous, feverish—burning. She was clenching her hands into the sheet, gasping for breath, but kept arching upward, burying her face and her silent screams into the bedding as she kept her ass in the air for him, welcoming every hot hit of his skin against hers. Each smack sounded wet now, with the sweat and the heat and the moisture of this simple lotion, but there was a fire lapping at her. He switched to the other cheek, and she nearly screamed with the new heat of it against the relentless burning in her other cheek. She couldn't imagine how red she was, and wondered if he could see his handprint, or if he only knew from her heavy breaths and fisted hands that the sensations were as intense as anything she'd hoped for. Gasping, she finally collapsed onto the mattress, and that was when his hands began working her back, spreading the torturous lotion up from her ass over the muscles of her ribs and the small of her back, massaging it in. It brought on the heat of a red-hot sunburn, and she could feel the magic swirling beneath it, reacting to his touch and embracing the warming lotion as it seeped into her skin. She had to imagine that even her sweat burned right now, her body felt so incredibly hot, but his murmurs of approval above her grounded her in it, and she lay there shivering beneath his touch without making any attempt to squirm away. Occasionally, he'd slap her ass again, jarring her and making her scream and renewing the devious lotion's presence there were the skin was already insanely sensitive, but she screamed into the mattress when he did it, and only pressed into his grip all the more when he asked if she'd had enough.

She lost track of the spankings, of the ringing of his flesh against hers, and the times he dipped his hands into the lotion to renew its heat and spread more along her back, as high as her shoulders and even down along her upper thighs, just below her ass. The heat was trembling through her body, magic rising to it as if she were sunbathing on hot metal, and all of her focus remained on the pain of it, and on David's hands knowing just what she needed, controlling the magic and her body as he delivered it.

Her hands were cramping from gripping the sheet when his touch left hers for more than a few seconds and she felt the mattress shift beneath them, but she didn't look up. She was still lost in the torturous heat that had overtaken her, and instinctively, she knew he wasn't done with her, but she also didn't need to know what came next. She heard water running in the bathroom, and guessed he must be washing his hands. Then, he was beside her again, and she felt him doing what she'd both hoped he would do and also hoped he wouldn't do. His fingers were there again, at her back entrance. She braced herself, but didn't squirm away, and one of his fingers entered her, cool and slick. She guessed he must have used some other lube, and thanked god for it, but the pressure was still incredible.

Catching her breath, she made herself push back against him, and somehow, unbelievably, his finger went further. Then, even as she tried to get used to him, his other hand came down on the small of her back to hold her there, and she felt him add a second finger. Tears came to her eyes, and she couldn't make herself push into him this time.

"Relax, Lauren. Relax. Relax into it. I've got you. You wanted rough, right? You wanted it hard tonight. I can see it in you. See it in the way you embraced that lotion. And, god, baby, you should see my handprints on your ass. You're so sexy."

He kept murmuring, and Lauren was still so heated, so wet for him, that his fingers became only one more drastic sensation pulling her under the wave of desire that the magic always pushed on her. She sank into his words, focusing on the repetitive murmurings of his voice, and finally she felt her body getting used to him—not to a point of comfort, but to a point where the magic and heat rising to his fingers inside her was more pleasure and easy pressure than pain. When he took his hand away from the small of her back, she didn't complain, and then he began massaging her ass with that hand as he thrust his two fingers in and out of her.

Somehow, ridiculously, the pain was no more than the pleasure, and her body was reacting. Soon, she felt herself moving with him, pushing back against him as whimpers rose out of her throat and he whispered encouragement.

And then she was empty, catching her breath and leaking with desire as she did. She went limp on the mattress, still feeling the heat on her back, her ass, and down her thighs, with the magic simmering beneath her skin. David was shifting around her on the bed, but she blocked him out and tried to focus in on the hot ache that had all but overtaken her. Caught off-guard when he grabbed her by the hips and turned her over on the bed, she almost gasped with the surprise of it, but it was welcome. Her body was begging for him—she could feel it, and she knew he could see it.

"God, you're gorgeous, Lauren," he breathed out, standing by the bedside and looking down at her. His examination was so honest, so complete, she thought she ought to be either closing her legs or blushing, but her body was limp with want, and there was nothing he didn't already know about her. Not really.

He caught her knees and pulled her closer to the edge of the bed, and then he told her to close her eyes. Obediently, she did. His hands trailed up her thighs first, followed by his lips, and then she felt him at her center. At first, she thought he was pressing a finger into her, but then the very stillness of what was inside her made her realize it was some toy. He was turning it, wetting it with her own desire, and she knew what was coming. It was like at the center, but she was ready to welcome the pain and the sting of it this time, and she let him know by pressing forward toward his hand, thrusting her own hips, to be rewarded with his deep chuckle.

She was empty again, but not for long. He pressed her legs further apart, and then the toy was at her back entrance, pressing, and he was telling her again to relax, to trust him, to let him in. She gripped the sheets, her chest going heavy with the pulse of her blood and the fast beating of her heart as he pressed the thing deeper into her. It was bigger than the last one he'd used, and she could feel it filling her, sitting in her like some odd weight. He didn't move it at first, and just when she thought he wouldn't, he began pulling it back and then thrusting it back in, making her gasp with the weight and the force of it. On the third thrust, his other hand came to her pussy, and three fingers filled her, at the same time as the toy, so that she screamed and arched against him.

The orgasm ripped through her like nothing she'd ever felt, and David's fingers curled inside her, hitting her g-spot as he played the toy in her ass and the magic raced to her center, reacting to him and heating her beyond what felt safe. He milked the pleasure from her as she gasped for breath, and when the orgasm finally ran out of her, she heard the wet pop of the toy leaving her and felt his fingers run their wetness down along her thigh, stroking her. But her eyes were closed, lost to the pleasure of it all.

She heard the sound of the sink again, and opened her eyes and looked toward him in what felt like a haze. He was exiting the en-suite bathroom now, drying his hands on a towel, and there was a grin on his face. His dick was hard and long and thick, anxious to have her again, and her mouth salivated at the sight of it. Her jaw still ached from the way he'd used her before, but she didn't think her vagina could take much more.

But then... wasn't that what she'd wanted when she'd come here? To be used? Punished for what she was about to do, what she was allowing herself to fall into? Hadn't she wanted the pain?

Some expression she couldn't name crossed his face, and she realized her own feelings must be showing. She'd come here for escape, though, and if she still had the energy to think of what was coming... no, she'd handle whatever David had in mind, and more, if there was any chance of it clearing her mind. She'd been so close a few minutes back. Her body was still hot and aching from it. Surely, if he took her again, she'd be too exhausted for these thoughts to keep running through her mind. Too exhausted, even, to do anything about them, maybe.

Struck by the urge to keep going, no matter how sore her body might be, she forced a come-hither smile onto her face, met his eyes, and then rolled over. She turned away from him then, inviting him to fill her again. Ignoring the soreness she already felt, she spread her legs again, and propped herself on her elbows so that she could gaze back at David over her shoulder.

There was a look of naked lust on his face, and she saw him swallow hard just before he made some sound low in his throat, which might have been intended as words before they'd been overtaken by desire.

In a moment, he was on top of her, landing hard and lengthwise along her back so that he covered her, knocking the air from her and into the mattress. His arms moved hers above her head, one hand holding her wrist, and then he explored her. She fell into the sensation of his hands and lips—kissing, licking, touching, groping— moving over her as if he'd been starved for her. The weight of him on her skin was both a relief to the heat and a renewal of it, as if their sweat reignited the lotion and began burning along her spine so that she writhed beneath him. His hard cock twitched against her ass and thigh, and she pushed her ass into him, wanting desperately for him to fill her, but he only nibbled at her neck and then circled one hand beneath her to hold and squeeze her breast, tweaking her nipple until it was so painfully hard, he might as well have been pinching it continuously.

When he finally lifted himself off of her, she remained still and waiting, knowing he'd come for her again and wanting the surprise of it. She didn't have long to wait. He nudged at her knees, and she took the hint and lifted, and he put a pillow under her hips and belly, so that there was a cushion there which she lay across. Her pulse sped up at the telling angle of it, desire leaking from her, and then she felt his fingers at her core and spread her legs wider for him, welcoming him. But instead of his cock or his fingers, she felt a round hardness, unfamiliar and ungiving. She moved to look, but he put one hand on the small of her back to hold her there, and she pushed down the urge to squirm away. The thing—a toy, a dildo, it had to be—was bigger than any he'd ever used on her, and it filled her like he did, but in a way that felt... off. Her pussy had already been sore, and whatever this toy was, it filled her like David did, but without the give of his muscle, and without the magic to rush in and ease the ache.

She tried relaxing, and he began rubbing her ass and her back as if to accomplish the same, but she didn't think she'd ever get used to the fullness. More than anything, she wanted to tell him to take it out and fill her himself, especially when he pulled at the toy and thrust it in and out of her channel a few times—it felt both good and wrong at the same time, with not enough give, nowhere near enough warmth, and no way to pull the magic in and ease the ache of it with a headier desire—but she stayed still beneath him, willing herself to accept it, and accept him, as he was asking her to do with his hand on her back. If he wanted to use her in this way, what was the harm? She'd seen his dick. She knew he'd fill her again soon, and then the magic would be back in her core, easing the deep ache she was starting to feel.

He moved behind her, and she expected him to take the toy out, but instead she felt him massaging around her clit, twirling the toy in a way that made her gasp with the pain of its new angling even as pleasure inched her along toward a new climax. She felt her body responding, straining back toward him, and then there was that deep chuckle again. He took his hands off her, and readjusted the pillow beneath her belly, and then his hand was on her lower back, pressing her into a deep arch. She gave in to it even though it tilted the toy within her, making her feel ever fuller, because she knew how round her ass must look to him, and he smacked it hard as if to say he'd noticed just that. The pain of his hand spanking her shifted the toy so that she gasped with the fullness of her pussy pulsing around it, bringing up new sensations as the magic rushed to his fingers at her clit and the heat of her ass. The pain was welcome, and he did it twice more, the sting of the harsh skin-to-skin contact bringing up a new burn that she could fall into. He played with the toy some more, turning it and shifting it in a way that she might have protested at another point, it felt so unnatural, but she could tell from the sounds he was making that he was happy with her, enjoying her, so she made no attempt to pull away from him. More than anything, he was playing with her body and her magic as if they were toys for his pleasure, and she welcomed that. Another hard spank hit her in a way that jolted the dildo inside her body, and she arched with it, screaming some mix of harsh pain and pleasure into the mattress.

Seconds later, she was still gasping for breath when his hands left her clit and the toy, and took a firmer hold of her ass and hips, pulling her higher and back into him on the cushion. Finally, she thought he'd take the toy out and enter her, but instead, she felt a blunt pressure at her back entrance, and her breath stopped in her throat. He couldn't possibly....

The head of his dick was forced into her, and she arched again, crying out and whimpering at the pressure of it as he pressed forward into her, his head feeling like it was splitting her apart as he pushed deeper, harder, pulling her ass back against him. He was grunting with the effort of it, and she clenched the sheets, willing herself to relax, but she couldn't. The magic was rushing in, heating her core, but somehow that only added to the pressure of his shaft moving slowly, inch by excruciating inch, into her ass. She'd never felt anything like it, and then the way he pulled her against him shifted the toy that was still lodged in her pussy, so that she groaned.

She was so full. So painfully full. And he was still pushing forward, forward, pressing into her. His hands were massaging her ass, his voice whispering to her that she was doing great, that she was his, that this would feel good if she gave it time, but she felt like she was being split apart, with the burning magic rising to mix the pleasure with pain in a way that made it hard to think.

He finally stopped, but she could feel him pulsing within her body, throbbing, and she couldn't begin to imagine the way she must look to him right now, with both of her holes filled and her back arched into the mattress, still gasping for breath that couldn't be caught. Tears kept leaking from her eyes in a perverse echo of the moisture she felt still building in her body around the toy tucked deep into her pussy, but the two of them stayed frozen like that, with David buried in her, holding her to him.

He massaged her ass, and then reached beneath her to gently tug at the toy, just enough so that she felt it twist and move in and out of her a fractional amount. It was enough to make her gasp and cry out with the pain of being so incredibly full, though, even as desire leaked from her. But her body spasmed as if in pleasure, and he took it as encouragement, twisting the toy and whispering encouragement to her as he massaged and squeezed her ass harder, deeper, remaining buried inside of her. She could hear the strain of it in his voice, of keeping still, but then he moved.

"Just a little more, baby," he whispered.

She'd only begun to process his words when she felt him moving again, but not away as she'd expected. Instead, he pressed forward, deeper, and she screamed out in both pain and pleasure as his balls hit her skin and he touched something inside her that made a climax rip through her suddenly, without warning.

And then he was moving inside her, thrusting back and forth, fucking her ass with his cock as he grunted with the pain and the effort of it, and her release shook her to her very bones as she cried out, rushing heat along her blood toward every point of contact they had as she shivered and gasped beneath him, sobs being torn from her along with the inescapable sensations of pleasure and pain centered on her core. He kept fucking her, slamming into her and the pressing in and out, so that she felt torn apart with each move as his hands gripped her hips. The toy kept shifting in her pussy, an anchoring weight that she knew he must feel through her inner walls as he pressed into her again and again, harder and harder, until he sped up, and she cried out again as he shoved into her all the way and spasmed within her body, filling her with his seed as mini-climaxes rolled and roiled through her body in a way that left her gasping for breath, crying out for relief from the very pleasure as well as the pain.

When he finally pulled out of her, she went limp, and the removal of the toy from her vagina was barely a blip on her awareness, it was so minor a relief after the pressure of everything together had finally abated. She was spent, utterly, her mind lost to anything but the full ache she felt even as her body processed the new relief of emptiness and the magic still swirling in her blood and at her core, desire leaking from her even as she finally crashed into a tortured sleep.

Chapter 23

Josh passed by the parking garage opening that would be his team's entrance, walking on down the block casually. Not hard when he had a full tray of coffee in his hands. There was a coffee shop at the end of this block, and even in the short few hours his team had been camped around the building in various SUVs, he'd seen a number of pedestrians pass by the garage's entrance multiple times. No matter where you went, even on the outskirts of a city where it seemed there wouldn't be enough pedestrian traffic to demand it, people were addicted to their coffee. His earpiece buzzed, and he tapped his smartwatch to give the go-ahead and answer.

"Josh, it's Barry. You at your computer?"

"Will be in a minute. Coming back from a coffee run. We're still set to have everything in place in two hours?" He'd hoped it would be faster—he'd been ready faster—but scrambling as many agents and plain-clothes cops as they needed to surround the destinations was taking longer than planned. Even in his own location, they were waiting on a few more cops to come in and be ready to watch the entrances to the few shops on the building. For a building that took up a whole block of space, there weren't many, but they also only had one shot at this—if there was one exit they missed, one connecting doorway from the area the coven had set up to where everyone else was, giving them an exit, they could be screwed. And this was the place; he knew it in his gut. Just that morning, the rings had showed up at a pawn shop not three miles down the road, confirming the instincts he'd already been following.

"Uh, yeah," Barry agreed, "I think so. Problem is, I don't know if you're going to get Lauren."

Josh's step faltered, and then he picked up his pace in heading toward the SUV. "You gonna explain?"

"So, we kept satellites tracking all of the jackets so we'd see them if they moved, right? Simple enough. Just set our sights on them and locked in, no biggie. No movement, either. Problem is, we no longer have the jacket at your location."

Josh was at the SUV now, climbing into the passenger seat. He passed the tray of coffee to the agent in the driver's seat, pointed to his earpiece to signal he was talking to someone, and began tugging his laptop from its carry bag. "Explain."

"Right, okay, so, there's a patch at your location. A big one. Sometime last night, Lauren's jacket went into the patch—"

"What the fuck do you mean by a patch?" Josh interrupted him.

"I don't know what else to call it. A box, a space, a location—there's a patch of space in the building that's covered in the same metal as what's in the tattoos. I don't know if ceilings are painted with the metal or what, but there's a whole space that shows as being our material. I don't know if they took the stuff they made the jacket out of and tacked it to the ceiling or what, but it covers a patch of space."

"Okay, so we're talking what, a room? Two rooms?"

"Something like that, yeah, and assuming this is Lauren we were tracking in Indiana, Lauren went into it last night."

"So, what's the problem? We go to the patch and we get Lauren, assuming she's the one in that jacket. It's not like she's invisible and we need the fucking jacket to see her, or like this patch you're talking about is miles wide."

Barry was silent for another few seconds, and then he just said, "I hope it's that simple, man."

"Why wouldn't it be?"

"Because... yesterday she was moving around all day, but since I've come back to the computer and been watching these blips, I'm not seeing any movement at your location. And that got me to thinking about how the tracking is set up. I'm worried that when the jacket was absorbed into the patch of the building we're talking about, the tracking lost the jacket and locked onto the patch instead. I think that's what's happened. It wouldn't have been able to see the jacket through a whole mess of the metal, so the lock pulled out to hold onto the space, this patch we've got on our radar. At least, I'm pretty sure that's what happened. We got an alert when she went in, and turned it off when we saw what had happened... because like you said, it's just a room, easy enough to find someone in. But I think the tracking changed over without anyone noticing."

"Okay," Josh began, processing, "so, not great... we don't know where she is in the building, or for sure that she's there, but she could be? I mean, that's kind of where we were before."

"Yeah, kind of," Barry replied, though he didn't sound confident about it. "She and the jacket might be in that room. They're not anywhere else in the building, but with all of the moving pieces we've got being tracked right now, I'd have to download the program onto some other computer to search the wider area for the jacket, and that's gonna take time."

Time that they didn't have any guarantee of. And there was a decent chance she was simply in that room. If she hadn't moved... that might mean an injury, not that she'd left. Or, hell, maybe it wasn't Lauren at all and she was at David's location.

"Alright," he breathed out. "Keep things moving, but do what you can to get that process started. At least for now, the plan stays the same. But thanks for the heads-up."

"Sorry, man. I guess we should have kept eyes on this location once she went into that space, but it didn't seem to make sense to keep manpower on this all night when we had the tracking in place."

"No, I get it."

There was a pause, and then Barry added, "You want me to tell David?"

"Hell, let's hope we don't even have to. Keep it between us for now. Push comes to shove, I'll tell him."

"Thanks. Good luck."

The line cut out, and Josh took a deep breath and then a sip of his coffee, which had been set in the cup holder beside him. The driver gave him a questioning look, and Josh nodded at him. "We're still a go. Some technical questions about the tracking working is all. I still think we're in the right place, so keep your eyes open."

Because Josh did think this was the place. For one thing, even beyond the rings having turned up, the building was entirely too large to have only the few businesses advertised and no signs for available leases. For another, the plain-clothes cop they'd sent into the parking garage had clocked two different security system cameras, and two entrances to office space—one of which looked to be new, as if that part of the building had been separated off fairly recently and a new entrance built.

Based on plans and the building owners, that was indeed the case, with recent renovations having been finished up only weeks ago. A consulting company had supposedly taken up residency, but aside from a name on a lease, there was no sign the company existed—no business license, no advertising, no website, no number that could be found. And when the property manager had described the woman who'd signed the lease and then paid an incredible amount of money not only for the renovations, but simply so that the building's owner would allow it and put up with the annoyance of it... well, the description he'd given sounded an awful lot like Johanna Wilkins.

Two hours went by fast, and with all of the teams signaling their readiness, Josh led a team of fourteen agents into the parking garage. With two agents left to guard the door, the rest of them entered the office space believed to have been rented and renovated by the coven. It went as planned, with no persons to be seen, and they moved fast. Inside, they were greeted with a staircase and a doorway leading farther into that level, and the teams split there. Josh headed into the doorway, five other agents at his back. Almost immediately, he knew they were in the right place.

The space was open-concept and smelled of recently burned herbs. A quick survey showed a large, empty sectional and what looked like a small casting circle, recently abandoned. Smoke still rose from something that had been burned in its center. Josh held up a hand to split the team in two once again—there were two small halls off of this space.

When he opened the door down one hall, he got lucky. A beam of energy shot by him, not six inches from his ear; if he'd entered dead-center in the doorway, he would have been hit in the head and killed instantly.

As Johanna readied herself to re-aim and shoot another beam at him, he fired. His shot didn't miss. It took her in the head and knocked her backwards into a wall of shelving. From somewhere on the other hall, he heard a shriek, and then demands for someone to freeze, but he was already checking Johanna Wilkins for a pulse and surveying the room. She was dead, and when he looked around, he saw that none of the agents with him had been harmed. That was more than he could have hoped for, remembering the first raid they'd tried on this coven. The room was empty other than Johanna, and he headed back to the open space to intercept the others. It was too much to hope for that Nell would have been intercepted without him hearing shots, and his had been the only gun fired, but they'd found someone.

Sure enough, he found two agents holding the arms of a woman in her early thirties. She'd already been restrained with zip-ties, and her eyes were wide and scared. "You killed Johanna," she whispered upon seeing the blood that was quite literally on his hands from having checked the woman's pulse.

"And she killed some of my friends," he replied evenly. "But you haven't. I've never seen you before. So, how about we start off on a good foot and you tell me where I can find the rest of this coven, as well as the two women you kidnapped."

The woman swallowed, her expression saddening. "I didn't know they were going to do that—kidnap anyone," she said. "You have to believe me." Before Josh could think what to bother replying to that, she went on, "You're Lauren's friend, aren't you? Josh... something. She told me about you. Said you took care of her when she needed to go to the hospital."

"That would be me, yeah. Josh Devlin." Josh took a step closer to the woman, giving her a closer look. She seemed resigned, unsurprised. In unassuming jeans and a t-shirt, she could have been taken for anything other than a witch. Appearances meant little, but just from the way she spoke, he was inclined to think she'd been telling the truth about not knowing about the planned kidnapping. "The coven you got yourself involved in here has been responsible for a number of lost lives—federal agents' lives as well as those of civilians," he added. "And whether or not you were involved in the kidnapping, you've been an accessory after the fact. If you want to help yourself, tell me where I can find Lauren and Adrienne." He nodded to the agents who held her arms, and when they took a step back, he moved in, took one of her arms, and ushered her over to the couch, where he sat her down and stared at her. "What's your name?"

"Sarah Antzen. You might not believe me, but I just met Nell and Johanna recently. At first, I thought they were good people. And then the kidnapping happened, but... well, it was the first time I'd felt like a part of a family in a long time. That's no excuse, but—"

"Is Nell upstairs, Sarah?" he asked, cutting her off. They didn't have time for her to ramble an apology, and he wasn't in any mood to hear it. "And what about Lauren and Adrienne, and the woman who helped with the kidnapping? What's the rest of our team finding upstairs?"

Sarah shrugged, seeming to sink into herself before him. "The only one upstairs is Adrienne. Lauren went out with Nell and Evie—that's the other woman you're asking about—earlier."

Barry was right. That damned patch fucked us.

Josh wanted to throw something, but he settled for crouching down before the other woman and pressing, "Where?"

She shook her head. "I don't know. The guy who attacked Lauren, before you took her to the hospital— they tracked him down. Found out where he'll be tonight somehow. They're going to intercept him. I don't... I don't know where. I'd tell you if I did."

Josh was already turning away from her, his stomach churning with what that might mean, when the woman called him back.

"Josh—Agent Devlin. Adrienne's... she needs help. You can't take her back to her husband."

He stopped, looking back to her. That wasn't any sort of request he might have expected from a kidnapper. "That's not happening," he agreed. "I've met the guy. She's got multiple places to stay so that she doesn't have to depend on him ever again, I promise."

Relief flickered across her face. "I need to tell you something else." She glanced to the other agents, who'd approached as Josh had begun moving away. "I'd rather just tell you," she added.

One of the other agents stepped forward. "Sir, don't forget she's a witch. You listen to her n' get too close—"

"I know, Richards," Josh said simply. He gazed at Sarah for a minute, weighing the odds that she'd have a spell she could affect him with if he got up close, but which she couldn't use from where she sat now and wouldn't already have used against them. "You know throwing a spell my way will make things a lot worse for you right now?" he asked her. When she nodded, he moved in and crouched before her again, closer than he'd been before so that nobody else would hear their conversation.

"Adrienne tried to commit suicide this morning," the woman whispered. "That's how... bad things are. She found out Johanna was blackmailing Lauren into cooperating, threatening Adrienne's safety if Lauren didn't. She was trying to save Lauren from... from the coven, I guess. From what they're asking her to do. Adrienne thought it was the only option, and she's blaming herself for things going so far. I stopped her in time, but if anything happens to Lauren.... I know Lauren's the one who's your friend, but Adrienne's her friend. Whatever happens, she's in a bad place," Sarah added. "And she might need a hospital. I think she's okay for now, but... I was going to get Lauren to take care of her when she gets back. I don't have much experience with healing, but Johanna didn't want to take her to a hospital unless we were going to leave her there for good. And that would have landed her back with Raul," she added after a beat.

Processing what he'd been told, Josh finally nodded and stood. As he walked away, Sarah called after him that she'd planned on packing up and finding a way for the three of them to get away from Johanna and Nell, that that was actually the reason she'd finally sold their rings, but he didn't bother turning to reply. There wasn't time.

He caught up with the team clearing upstairs rooms, and they found Adrienne in a small suite on the third floor, curled up in a fetal position on a twin bed with both of her forearms bandaged. When he entered with his gun up, another agent behind him, she rolled up to sit on her butt and her arms wrapped around her chest. Her eyes were wide, taking in him and the agents surrounding him, and a little sound came out of her throat that might have been relief—or despair, it occurred to him.

"I didn't know if you'd be Johanna," she said, and in another second, tears were rolling down her face, but Josh didn't even have time to reply before she kept going. "You have to find Lauren. They're going somewhere called the Montrose Bar. You have to get to her first, Josh. Please."

One of the other agents was already passing by him, moving in to check on the bandages which were red with blood in more than one spot. What the woman in front of him had just said made it clear what her priorities were, though, and she was as safe as he could make her in the moment, so he stepped back out into the hall even as he was pulling out his phone. A search for Montrose Bar pulled up ten bars and restaurants, none of them anywhere near where he was; only one of them was anywhere near a location that meant anything to him, in fact. An upscale fusion bar and restaurant by that name was located just five miles from Lauren's old apartment. "That's gotta be it," he muttered, dialing David.

"You still at the condos?" he asked when his partner picked up.

"Yeah, but—"

"Stop and listen," Josh cut him off. "We took Johanna Wilkins down already, and I'm with Adrienne. Lauren's with Nell and another witch—probably the one we saw in the ambulance—headed to find the guy who raped her in her apartment. I don't know how they set it up, so don't ask, but they're headed to the Montrose Bar on 13th Street, near her old address. I'll send the address to your phone; it's about five miles from Lauren's old apartment. You and the guys with you are a helluva lot closer than me or any of our other teams right now."

There was a brief pause filled only with some muted cursing on the other end, and then David came back on the line. "I'm leaving. I'll be there in an hour."

"I'll have Barry send reinforcements. You up for this?"

By the time Josh stopped speaking, he'd realized David was off the line, and a glance at his watch told him there was no way he himself could get there in time to do anyone any good, even going thirty over the limit the whole way. Shooting off a detailed text to Barry after he got David the address, he followed those messages up by texting the other team leaders before he slipped his phone back into his pocket and headed back into the room. For safety's sake, Barry would begin sending recon teams to every other Montrose Bar they could find, but none of them were close enough for Josh to make a run at one. Besides that, he felt it in his gut that David was headed to the correct location, and that meant he might as well be where he was.

The agent was rebandaging Adrienne's arms, crouched in front of where she sat on the edge of the twin bed. The discarded bandages were on the floor, showing more red than he was comfortable thinking about. The woman hadn't been crying for help that morning—she'd legitimately tried to take her own life; she'd cut lengthwise up the veins on both her forearms, with one cut being a lot deeper than the other from the looks of it, and the witch he'd met downstairs must have found her quickly and done some real work at triage. More than she'd implied downstairs, at least. Now, though, Adrienne's eyes were red from crying, and there were circles beneath them that suggested she hadn't slept well in at least a few nights, if not more.

"Adrienne?" he asked gently. "Mind if I sit here?"

It took her a moment, but she nodded—slowly, in a way that told him she might be in shock. He sat silently beside her while the agent finished up wrapping her arms in fresh bandages, and then instructed her to see a doctor when she could because she needed some stitches. The agent glanced to him meaningfully, and Josh nodded. The woman would be going to a hospital as soon as possible, whether she wanted to or not.

That done, the agent, whose name Josh couldn't quite put his finger on, saluted and headed out the door with a promise that he'd help search and clear the rest of the building. Josh didn't bother to tell him there was nobody else to be found—he felt pretty sure the man already knew that, just like the whole team was aware that their focus was to turn toward collecting evidence on the coven once it was safe to do so.

"Did they find Lauren? Is David with her? She... needs to be found," Adrienne said, stumbling over words. Her hands were clenched in her lap, and Josh noticed she'd bitten her nails down to the quick. He couldn't remember what they'd looked like when he'd last seen the woman, but when she moved to bring one of her hands to her lips, Josh reached out and took it, and put it back on her knee, with his hand over it.

"He's on his way to her," Josh replied. Promises flashed through his mind, along with all of the things he'd like to be able to tell her, but he kept his mouth shut. He hoped David would get there in time, but there was no point in sitting here and making false promises that they couldn't guarantee.

"Lauren's the healer," Adrienne said quietly, breaking the silence. "Sarah said it made sense to have her do the healing when she got back; she said if she took me to a hospital, she'd have to leave me there, and they'd have called Raul.... She found me pretty fast. Didn't leave me anything sharp enough to finish with."

For a second, Josh didn't know what to say. This brown-eyed woman wasn't the same one he'd met at the center, in those brief minutes between finding the women on the roof and then putting them into the ambulance. "You didn't seem like the type to give up when I met you before," he finally commented, though it felt like the wrong thing.

"No," she said flatly. "I'm not. And that's not what this is."

"Really?" he asked before he could stop himself. "Killing yourself's not giving up?"

Her eyes darted up to his, and he saw some anger in them for the first time—it was the first emotion he'd gotten a glimpse of, cutting through the blankness and despair on her face. "You don't understand. They've been using me against her. Making Lauren do things she'd never do, only because she's worried about me. And if I'd left here, I'd have had nowhere to go but back to Raul. Or to my family, who would have called Raul. You think this choice was easy? I was doing what I could to try to keep them from taking Lauren out today, but I was too late. I thought I'd be dead, and she'd back out, and then you and David would come for her and..." Adrienne trailed off, the anger having left her voice. Tears were soaking her sweater now, wetting the new bandages already. "I didn't know what else to do," she finally said. "I wish I'd thought of using the jacket sooner. I guess that's how you found us?"

"That was your idea?"

"I... yeah. But I should have thought of it sooner. Before things got so bad. Now—"

"You thought of it. That's how we got here. That's what counts," Josh cut her off. He knew what she'd been about to say. That it was too late. But they didn't know that yet, and he'd be damned if he'd let her think that way when she was already this wrecked over what was happening.

He picked up her right arm from where it lay in her lap, turning it so that he could better see the bandages. No red was leaking through now—he guessed that was a good sign, especially since this had been the more deeply injured arm. It looked like he'd be taking another woman to the hospital, though. "Listen, I've got a message for you. From Paul and Christopher. You up for that?"

The names seemed to jar something in her, and her lip twitched in what might have been the ghost of a smile. "Yeah. You've seen them? They're good?"

"Worried about you. They made me promise to tell you, the second we found you, that they're renovating their house. They're going to have a place for you there if you want it. So, you don't have to go back to Raul. Hell, I don't think any of us who've met him would let you. And you'd be welcome at our place, too, if you and Lauren want to stick together for a while. You've got options, and whatever you need—outside of family, outside of Raul. Lots of support. Okay?"

The tears had slowed at the mention of Christopher and Paul, but a sob escaped her now as if some dam had been broken, and she buried her face in her hands, nodding. "That's... that's a lot. Thanks."

Josh waited, trying to give her time to collect herself. She finally wiped her eyes on her sleeves and returned her hands to where they'd rested in her lap. They clutched at her jeans, and he noticed she was trembling now. Shock, he thought again. He pulled a quilt from the base of the bed and wrapped it around her, snugging it tight against her shoulders and then putting the ends gently in her hands.

"I'm gonna take you to the hospital in a minute—my car, no ambulance," he promised, and that did garner him a half-smile, though Adrienne still hadn't really met his eyes since her first plea that they find Lauren, and then that brief glimpse of anger he'd gotten. "But first... is there anything else you can tell me? You knowing the name of the Montrose Bar is huge—we know where that is. We found it. David's on his way. But if there's anything else you can tell me... anything at all, it couldn't hurt."

Adrienne nodded, her eyes still down and on her hands. "I heard Johanna and Nell talking. They thought I was listening to some earbuds, but I'd turned the sound off. That's how I learned the bar's name. They found a way to get the guy there—Jerry? I think that was his name? I saw his license, his picture, but that's all I remember. I don't remember his last name or know what they're planning, but... I think they want Lauren to hurt him. She's... not herself. Not right now." Adrienne paused, and Josh was about to retract the question when she let out a sudden sob and kept going, "I found out it's because of me. They've been... they've been telling her they'll hurt me if she doesn't cooperate. That's why..." she trailed off, holding up her wrists. "I didn't know what else to do. You have to tell her I'm okay, and get her to stop whatever's happening. It'll change her. Hurting him, I mean, will change her. I know that's what they want. Nell's so cruel, so mean, and Evie's the same. They want to hurt Lauren, and they've been using me to get her to... to get her to..."

"It's alright." Josh put his arm around Adrienne's shoulders and pulled her sideways into him, and then he repeated the mantra again, telling the woman she'd be alright as she sobbed and he brushed at her hair with his fingers. There wasn't much more he could say. The coven had already worked hard to tear this woman beside him apart, and whether or not they'd done the same to Lauren already, or taken her beyond some point of no return, was still in question. For now, he didn't even really care to know what they'd already made Lauren do. It was bad enough to have brought Adrienne to this point, and with no way of being sure they could stop whatever next step the witches had envisioned, he didn't see much point in hearing the details any sooner than necessary.

Chapter 24

On his second circuit of the block around the restaurant, David spotted Nell. It was all he could manage to keep his foot to the gas and avoid slowing down, but he did it. She was sitting in a neutral-colored Kia, parked half-a-block down from the restaurant, and her eyes were glued to mini-binoculars she had focused on the Montrose. He was willing to bet a paycheck that she hadn't seen him cruising by—thank god he was driving a team SUV.

The men he'd brought with him had been dropped off at various points—two agents two blocks away so that they could walk in on foot, and two near the parking garage so that they could come in without attracting attention just as easily. The agent in his passenger's side seat, a guy by the name of Cotman, took David's cue and wrote down the license plate of Nell's vehicle before he began texting the others. All of them were in plain clothes. By the time David parked a block off from the restaurant, putting Nell's car smack between him and the Montrose with only a gas station and convenience store between them, they'd heard from two of the agents that Evie was sitting alone at the bar of the restaurant, drink in hand. She had her eye on a table of men and women in casual office attire who were sitting near the window, but there was no sign of Lauren.

"Nell Everett's among the leads," David said as they stalked by the side of the convenience store, keeping close enough to the wall to stay out of her sightline and still avoid attracting undue attention from passerby. This was a downtown area, and the amount of pedestrian traffic was disturbing—if a firefight or, knowing the witches, an energy fight ensued, there were sure to be not just casualties, but witnesses who'd have to be debriefed and dealt with. Given the headache involved in one and the heartache involved in the other, he was too tired to consider which would be worse.

"Bitch is bold, I'll give her that, sitting there with binocs in plain sight. Somebody could have called the cops on her at any time."

"I'm sure she used a glamor spell. She's not dumb," David warned him, pausing to catch the other man's eye and make sure his point got across. "We were looking for her and still missed her on the first pass around the restaurant, so she and that vehicle aren't clean. At the very least, there's a glamor on it."

The other man nodded, grimacing, and David took that for being enough. Every agent on the operation had experience with witches—Barry had seen to it—so David would just have to trust that this would be the only reminder the man needed.

"You want to take the driver's side or the passenger's side?" Cotman asked quietly, palming his gun.

"I want my gun to her head," David answered. Adrenaline had kicked in, and the exhaustion he'd felt on the drive and over the course of the day no longer felt like it was weighing on him. He didn't feel energetic, but he was aware enough to know that he only wanted his own body to be first in the line of fire—both receiving it and giving it, should it come to it.

Their last obstacle to take cover behind was an SUV parked at the gas pump, and they paused there to tell the guy who owned the vehicle to either get inside and get gone or take cover in the store. With a quick count, they then speed-walked to the Kia as if they were trying to escape from some cold air that didn't exist. At the back of the vehicle, they parted, with David going to the driver's side and Cotman going to the passenger's side. Nell had her window down, and she was a second too slow in flinching from the movement before David got to her, gun-first.

"Shouldn't you be passed out in bed?" she hissed, her hands frozen on the binoculars as her eyes shot from David back to Cotman.

David moved to position himself by the rearview mirror, where she couldn't hit him hard with the door if she opened it. "You're going to drop the binoculars and put your hands out the window. Then, Nell Everett, I'm going to cuff you, and you're going to lead me to Lauren." He glanced to Cotman across the car from him, and the man nodded. Nell had had both windows of the Kia down, and he had a clean shot if he needed to take it. He'd already moved his gun beyond the plane of the window, too, proving his training. Even if Nell had warded the vehicle, a shot from that gun would still get to her since it was inside the domain of the car.

Nell's eyes flashed, but then her shoulders slumped ever so slightly. "Okay," she agreed.

He hadn't expected it to be this easy, and that was what made him hesitate, but the witch did nothing but drop her binoculars and put her wrists out the window, as he'd instructed her. She held nothing, and her hands were cupped innocently.

The cuffs he'd brought were covered in warding—once he had them on her, she'd find it impossible to cast against them. With one more glance to Cotman, he took one hand off of his gun and retrieved the cuffs from his belt, and then he holstered his gun. Nell had remained still through it all, defeated. It didn't track with what he knew of her, but they couldn't shoot her for no reason. Plus, they still needed her to take them to Lauren. He opened the cuffs and reached for her wrists, thinking to himself that he'd make sure the cuffs were extra tight on her bare skin, and that was when she moved.

Before he could get the cuffs on her, she'd darted both of her hands forward to his, and she gripped his hands and wrists as if they were about to start twirling each other around in some game. Instantly, the energy was sapped from him. He felt his body loosening, his muscles falling limp, and the gunshot that sounded barely reached his mind. Falling to the ground beside the driver's side door, he was focused only on catching his breath and avoiding going completely limp. He blinked, slow, and managed to look down. There was blood on his hands, along his wrists, but it wasn't his.

He heard radios going off—his and Cotman's both, and another on top of it—and he tried to sit up straighter, but couldn't manage it. His body stayed anchored against the SUV's tire and side panel, too weak to move, and he focused for another minute on breathing.

Two agents landed at each side of him—the ones he'd let out a few blocks away—and he glimpsed Cotman behind them directing passerby to keep on moving. "Strength-letting spell," one of the agents muttered. David couldn't tell him that he'd had none to spare to begin with; he'd been hiding how weak he was all day. The man pulled antiseptic wipes from a pocket in his cargo pants and carefully, without touching David's skin, began cleaning his hands and wrists. There'd been a low-grade weight on him, like a thin layer of fabric, where Nell had gripped him. He hadn't even noticed it until it was leaving him, disappearing with the slight smell of alcohol piercing the air.

"Nell's... dead?" he asked, having to pause for breath between words.

"Yeah. Sorry," Cotman said, glancing backward at him.

"We knew... it might... be that," David managed. One of the agents beside him moved to press a bottle of water to his mouth, but David shook his head. "Back of... the SUV. Cooler."

The man moved fast and without question, to his credit, and brought back one of each of the containers David had had stored there—one container of the cream they kept for energy burns, and one canister of the strength-giving concoction El had been making for him. "Red one," he grunted. The agent who'd been cleaning him up took the red canister and opened it up, and pressed it to David's mouth when David nodded for it. He sipped at it, and then gulped. When it was empty, he asked for another, and when he drank the second one down, he didn't have to pause to catch his breath between gulps.

The other men's radios had been squawking, and Cotman had already headed across the street, but David's mind had been too fogged to attend to the chatter that the two men remaining with him were clearly trying to keep from his notice. They'd turned the volume on their radios down, their focus on him, and it had been all he'd really been capable of to stay awake and drink down what he needed.

"Help me up," he demanded.

"You sure, Fredricks? We—"

"Help. Me. Up."

Each of the men gripped one of his hands and pulled him up, though he let his back slide up the door of the

SUV. He felt Nell's blood soaking into the back of his button-up, but ignored it in favor of the support. Standing, leaning on the car, he staggered to the back of the SUV. "What's happening?" he asked, even as he twisted open one of the three remaining red canisters.

The two men looked at each other, and then the senior one spoke. "Two of our guys followed Evie into the bathroom. They got her, but not before she got them. We've got two men down, officially. The other two are searching for your girl; they recruited a cop who was dining inside to guard the restroom door, but it's just got bodies in it. Bar's on the first story of a building with apartments above it—it's gonna take some time to clear the place."

David swallowed the rest of the concoction in the canister, praying for it to do more good than the other two had, and then reached for the other. He thought he could walk now. He thought he could probably even shoot. But he wasn't sure if he could aim, and he definitely couldn't fight or climb stairs.

And where the fuck was Lauren? If Evie and Nell were down... what the fuck was keeping her from coming out of the woodwork and being seen by the agents and plain-clothes cops they had all over the area?

"You're still in charge, sir, unless you say otherwise," one of the agents said.

David nodded, moving through options in his head. "One of you stay here until we can get some cops here to guard Nell's body. Her spell's gotta still be working in our favor—whatever she had keeping folks from noticing her sitting here with the binocs, it's gotta be the reason we don't have her dead body attracting a crowd. The other one of you, go inside Montrose's and keep your eyes split—one eye on that table we caught Evie watching, assuming they're still there—"

"I haven't seen a mass exodus from the place," one of the agents commented. "Gabins and Jucha had their guns on silent, so what went down in the bathroom went down quiet. Far as the customers know, I think it's just an out-of-service bathroom right now."

"Okay," David said, "that's another thing in our favor. Let's keep it that way. Eyes split on that table Evie was watching and the fucking bathroom. I'm gonna case the buildings on both sides in case they had Lauren walled up nearby. More agents get here, we'll keep spreading out and upward into the apartments. From what Josh says, these bodies mean we have the coven down. This is a search-and-rescue mission now."

The two of them nodded at him, and David didn't wait any longer to see how they'd split duties. He tried jogging across the street, but realized fast that it was too much. Unless he wanted to pass out from exhaustion, he had to go slower. His boots felt weighted with lead, his muscles so heavy that his clothes might have been made of iron, and his brain was fogged. He'd put on a show back at the SUV, wanting to keep himself in charge of the operation, but he was fading. He just had to find Lauren before that happened.

The business to the right of the restaurant was a cramped furniture store. Even the way he felt, it was quick work to look through the aisles and then check the mostly empty storage area. Nobody was there but the owner who'd let him in upon seeing his badge.

Outside, he passed by the restaurant with barely a glance inside—aside from a few agents and cops who could be seen standing suspiciously straight, in front of the restroom and near the entrance, nothing looked out of place. Two people were missing from the table Evie had been watching earlier, though David wouldn't have recognized them off the street. He only hoped they weren't extra bodies in the bathroom that he just hadn't heard about yet. Continuing on, he was about to pass by the alley on the left side of the restaurant and move into the market on the other side, but he heard something. A scuffling. It was enough to stop him, and make him turn.

From where he stood at the mouth of the alley, he mostly saw wet concrete and old dumpsters. Some lights hung a few stories up, from the fire escapes attached to the buildings encasing the alley and it's dead-end, but most of the alley was in shadow. It took him a minute to figure out the shape he saw poking up beyond the dumpster sitting against the bar wall. It was a head. He took his gun out, and moved toward the dumpster. He wouldn't call out yet. Couldn't call out yet. If Lauren was here, in danger, he didn't want to surprise her without knowing the lay of the land.

Before he moved around the dumpster, he reached to his belt and silenced his radio—he'd been on enough ops to know that they chimed with noise at the worst moments, and that would be any minute now.

Counting to three, evening his breath, he willed his lungs to take in enough air from breathing deeply that he wouldn't be panting, but they were too weak. He was too weak. What had felt like lead lining his muscles and body had become concrete, dragging on his every breath and move. He didn't have any energy left.

Using will more than muscle, he leaned one shoulder against the dumpster and inched around it, half-leaning on the metal structure as he moved. And he still wasn't prepared for what he saw. He sank to a knee with the sight of it, nearly dropping his gun.

On the other side of the dumpster, where she'd been hidden from the street, Lauren had a man up against the wall of the bar. She wasn't touching him directly, but her hands were outstretched. From the side, her arms looked steady, and now that there was no structure blocking him from her, he could hear whispered words coming from her lips even though he couldn't make out any meaning. Her fingers twitched, and the man pressed against the wall groaned audibly. David turned his eyes to him, and wished he hadn't.

The man's lips were tight together—unnaturally so. Something was gluing them together, keeping them shut so that he couldn't speak or yell. His nostrils were flaring and his eyes were wide with pain. His skin showed the pressure he was under; around his cheeks, his neck, and his outstretched arms where they stretched below his short-sleeved shirt, David could see the skin being pressed away from Lauren as if the man were stuck in a wind tunnel, the pressure of hurricane-speed winds holding him pressed to the wall. Lauren said some word louder, twitched a finger, and David saw a baseball-sized indent appear in the man's shirt around his solar plexus, as if he'd been punched by air. Proving the sight, the man jolted, and David thought he would have doubled over if the wind had allowed him to.

Tearing his eyes away from the horrific sight of Lauren and this man, who David could see was struggling to breathe through the pressure, he saw beyond them to a doorway into the restaurant, and a figure lying on the ground at its foot, half-propped against the wall of the alley.

"Lauren." The name came out choaked, half-strangled, but she heard it.

Her face whirled back to him, her arms dropping a fraction of an inch, and David noticed that the pressure on the man was released accordingly. Pain still showed on his face, pressure still pressing him to the brick wall, but his chest looked like it could rise a little easier. Lauren stared at David, her eyes wide, and now he could see that tears were streaking down her cheeks, silent and fast. She wore the metallic jacket he'd seen her in previously, the jacket that had led them to her, but her shirt collar came up over the neckline, and it was wet with moisture that must have leaked from her eyes. She'd been crying for a while.

"Lauren," he said again. "Let him go."

One of her fingers twitched, and a groan came from the man, but David kept his eyes on her, pleading with her.

"He's the one who hurt me," she whispered. "And they're going to kill Adrienne if I—"

"Josh has her, baby," David breathed out, fast. His own lungs ached with exhaustion. He'd never known what it felt like to be too tired to breathe, not until now. He went down to his other knee and let himself rest in a sitting position, his ass on his bootheels. "She's fine."

Lauren's eyes swept over him, up and down. "Are you—"

"I'm fine. Let him go."

Lauren's face turned back to the man against the wall. His face was red now. Tears leaked from his eyes to match Lauren's, and from the angle of one of his ankles, David thought it might be broken. "He deserves this," she said quietly.

Fucking hell. David couldn't even imagine what they'd done to get Lauren to this point, to make her think like this. To make her do this. "Baby, I've got zero energy. I need you. I need you to let him go. Let's take care of the lady over there. Then get out of here. Come with me."

"The woman he was with is fine," Lauren said, her voice a little harder. She took a step closer to the man against the wall, and the pressure strengthened so that he whimpered. Something in him cracked—audibly. "Jerry, you remember me, right?" The man couldn't nod, but David was fairly sure from the look in his eyes that he remembered her now, if he hadn't before. "You hurt me. You sent me to the hospital. You made it so I'll never—"

she cut herself off there, with a sob, and David saw the wind against the man heighten yet again. He was struggling to breathe now.

"Lauren."

Another sob broke from her throat. "He deserves this, David! You know he does. How many other girls has he done that to, you think? He—"

"Lauren, I don't give a fuck about him," David said, willing more strength into his voice. God, he was tired. He said her name again, and then again. Something was happening when he said it, he could tell. He just had to bring her back to herself. "I don't give a fuck about him," he said again. "I give a fuck about you. What happens to you if you do this? If you cross this line? You're not Nell or Johanna. You're not like your mother. You're my Lauren. My Lauren," he repeated, staring at the back of her head.

He moved to get himself back to his feet, but couldn't do it. He ended up just leaning over, till he was on his hands and knees, and from there, he dragged himself across the few feet between them. She was wearing loose, boot-cut jeans, and he inched his hand over to the hem of one foot, and touched her. Beneath his hand, she was real. Breathing and warm and alive. And he could hear her voice, which he'd been missing all this time. Catching his breath, panting for it, he rested his hand around her ankle, beneath her jeans, feeling her skin tremble beneath his touch. Magic rose beneath his fingers, finding him from beneath her skin and swirling there. He could feel her whole body tremoring, stuck between him and whatever purpose had brought her into the alley to begin with.

"Come on back to me, baby. Lauren. Come on back to me."

A second passed, and then a minute, and then something gave in her. He felt it give.

One moment, she was standing braced in the alley with her feet apart, her arms outstretched to torture the asshole who'd tortured her. In the next moment, she was trembling in David's arms, both of them lying on the wet ground of the alley. Her whole body was cold and shaking. Distantly, he heard the man against the wall whimpering from where he'd fallen with a thump to the alley floor.

With Lauren in David's arms, his own energy and will were sapped—he'd done what he'd come to do, and part of him wondered if this was it. If he was dying here in this alley after having finally found her again. He found he didn't have the energy to concern himself with that, after all they'd been through and with the concrete feeling of his bones. He'd used himself up in bringing her back to herself.

"Lauren," he whispered. There was more to say, but he couldn't be heard over her sobs, so he didn't try.

Minutes passed, and he wanted to laugh at the fact that he could feel so distant now, when he finally had what he wanted. Instead, he just held onto her, the last of his energy going into simply holding onto her, holding her to him, as she shook and sobbed and murmured things he couldn't quite make out into his chest. When her body started to still against him, calming, it was a relief, and he thought he might just go ahead and let go, and fall asleep, and with any luck, he'd wake up later on.

When she seemed to freeze in his arms, he didn't have the energy to open his eyes and really look at her, but the one clear thought in his mind was that the coven was gone. The man who'd hurt her was still whimpering in the distance, and he heard nothing else. He trusted she was safe. That was enough.

"Energy-letting?" Lauren whispered against his chest, and he didn't answer her.

But then she was murmuring again, her hands finding his face, his neck, his wrists and hands, touching whatever skin she could reach. An unnatural warmth was in her skin, the magic there between them, but he only felt it distantly. And then she brought out some smoothed stones from somewhere on her person, and began laying those against his skin, pressing them into him hard, and it was as if energy seeped from them. He heard her whispering words he didn't understand, and saying something about the energy she was giving him having been his to begin with. When the stones were put aside, her hands and fingers took their place, trembling against him and nearly vibrating with some energy coming up from within her. Soon, his skin was warming to her touch, to the magic under her skin, with the magic shivering between them as it had in the past, and second by second, he felt himself being pulled back together from the inside out, his muscles gaining strength from whatever energy Lauren was passing to him. She was weak against him, shaking, and he knew at least some of it was coming from her.

"That's enough," he told her, when his breath was caught and he thought he'd able to sit up of his own power. She kept going, the energy dribbling into him until he felt he could not only sit up and talk, but stand and walk, and then he caught her hands and held them tight, some of those stones still in her grip from when she'd tried to keep willing her own energy into him. She stilled in his arms, and then sobs broke out.

"I'm sorry," she gasped. "I'm sorry, I'm sorry, I'm sorry, I'm sorry, I'm sorry...."

David held her, listening to her. He could see now that the woman near the door looked to be breathing and unharmed. The man against the alley wall was in shock, but didn't look to have sustained any life-threatening. Holding Lauren tighter against him, letting her cry, he focused his eyes on the man and stared at him until the man finally met his eyes. "What she's done to you, what she did to you tonight, you're not going to talk about it. You're going to consider it payback, and leave it be. You're going to tell the hospital that the woman who did this to you was a redhead named Nell Everett. I'll show you her picture so you can describe her. And you're going to say that after she did this, you blacked out. You understand me?"

Jerkily, the man nodded, and after another few seconds had passed, David pulled Lauren to her feet. "Let's get rid of whatever was used to seal his lips shut, and then let's get the fuck home."

Chapter 25

Lauren woke up slowly, and she let herself keep her eyes closed at first. Against her back, she felt David's chest rising and falling, the heat of her magic warming both of them at its old, comfortable, normal rate, humming between them and beneath her skin. He was awake. She could tell from the cadence of his breath against her neck, and also the movement of his hands. He was trying to keep them still, she felt sure, but they moved slowly back and forth over her belly and thighs, almost unconsciously. He'd been touching her like this for the last few days, since they'd settled in and gotten back to being themselves together, getting used to each other in a natural setting for what felt like the first time. Wherever they were, whatever they were doing, his hands found her, as if he was still convincing himself she was back, and real. It was the same for her—she craved his touch in the same way, and if his hands never stopped playing on her skin when he was nearby, it would be too soon.

Today was the day they'd officially be moving her things down here to his suite, and then, tomorrow, they'd go get Adrienne's things from Raul's storage unit and make Lauren's old bedroom hers. For now, Adrienne would be staying in the ranch house. She and Lauren had embraced upon being reunited, and held one another's hands for hours afterward, with Lauren sandwiched between David and Adrienne on the couch upstairs. The agents had made it clear that Adrienne was welcome to remain for as long as she wanted, and there'd been no real discussion after that. Eventually, the plan was for her to move in with Christopher and Paul, but until she and Lauren got past everything that had happened, and Christopher and Paul were done with their renovations, this was the ideal solution. Plus, in the meanwhile, El and Lauren would help Adrienne play out her magic just a bit more—there was no real reason for her to give it up, and both Lauren and Adrienne were anxious to meet the woman who'd helped David move past the energy drain of Lauren's visits, regaining enough strength to come after Lauren. The fact that El was Christopher's sister was only icing on the cake.

Giving in to the pressure of morning, and thinking not a little bit of the way David's hands felt on her, the hard length of him pressed into her thigh from behind, Lauren finally opened her eyes and shifted sideways, so that she could look up into his face. As she'd known they would be, his eyes were wide and aware. He'd been getting stronger with every hour since they'd come back to the house, between El's remaining concoctions and being able to rest as much as he needed without Lauren's visits sapping his strength. And Lauren had cast a few of her own spells, as well, to help him along, though he'd insisted she ought to reserve her strength for her own recovery.

On some level, it was true. Her mind was still fogged from the impressions of the coven and the twists her mind had taken at their direction. She'd come so close to falling into a path of dark magic, fed by vengeance and anger.

The thought of what she'd done—not to mention what she'd almost done—still left her feeling sick if she let herself focus on it for any time at all, but the way David looked at her helped. He was looking at her like that now. With such tenderness that, on some level, the expression on his face was itself enough to prove that she wasn't all bad. He'd hated witches all his adult life until after he'd met her. If she'd truly gone bad, and become what the agents had at first thought her to be, she knew in her gut that he wouldn't still love her.

But he did.

"Good morning," he said to her quietly, brushing his lips over her brow and letting his hands roam along her skin more freely. "I was wondering when you'd open your eyes. Your magic's been awake for a while."

"Because of you," she acknowledged. "I could have slept all day." Sighing in satisfaction, she shifted beside him as he moved one arm to cushion her head on his bicep, so that his arm wrapped down against her and allowed his hand to cup her ass through the mini-shorts she'd put on after they'd made love last night.

"We can go back to sleep, if you want," he said, teasing his lips along her earlobe. He sucked it between his teeth, and she lost her breath a little, like she always did when he played with her like this. "Or we could get a shower. I've got some ideas about how I'd like to christen my shower. Among other things."

She grinned against his shoulder. A shower sounded awfully good. Among other things.

THE END

Other HellBound Books Titles
Available at: www.hellboundbookspublishing.com

Spells in Waiting

For as long as she can remember, Lauren Merriweather has fought to separate herself from her mother - by focusing on school and developing her healing powers. Like her mother, she's a natural-born witch, but unlike her mother, Lauren is not a killer driven by hatred.

But, when a fight with her rampaging mother drives Lauren to seek relief in alcohol and mindless flirting, her world is twisted violently out of her control.

Lauren's attraction to David is as immediate as it is undeniable - to the extent that she forgets about the spells that have, until now, kept her from getting close to a man. But, David Fredricks is the government operative investigating her mother for murder, and he and his partner have determined that Lauren is their best lead.

As far as David is concerned, Lauren and her mother are both witches, and that makes them little better than monsters. Lauren's allure doesn't change the fact that her mother is a vicious serial killer, and he's prepared to do whatever it takes to stop her.

An interrogation goes too far, and Lauren finds herself bound to David in a way that neither of them could ever have imagined - and her very survival depends on her trusting the same people who stole her identity.

Spells in Therapy

In Spells in Waiting, Lauren Merriweather's life became entangled with the government agents who eventually became her protectors. And when her ability to cast spells and work the magic she'd grown into was all but lost, it was one of those agents - David Fredricks - whom she could no longer resist. With weakened magic, dangerous spells, and irresistible chemistry pulling her in different directions, even a large victory could only count for so much. Spells in Therapy picks up right where Spells in Waiting ended.With the remaining coven members hunting her, Lauren has had little choice but to embrace what safety she can find with David and his partner, Josh Devlin. Life is less than ideal, but it's safe enough - and compared to the terror she faced in the recent past, 'safe enough' isn't something to be taken for granted. That is, until Josh and David are pulled into a case involving couples who simply vanish… and Lauren is the one who may be the key to help the agents find their answers.Despite the lingering danger of the coven hanging over them, David and Lauren present themselves as bait in the guise of a troubled couple. As they find out soon enough, however, getting answers is not the hard part...Surviving the answers and their aftermath will threaten not just their relationship, but their lives.

The Toilet Zone: Number Two
"Restroom reading at its most terrifying!"

Imagine, if you will, you're traveling through the unknown, hellbound, with no roadmap or stars to guide you. The light fades as you descend into a shadow realm where supernatural terrors make their lair and evil lurks at every turn. Here, dead things don't always stay dead, for this is a world where things that shouldn't be… are, and things that should be are not.

In this world, it takes between 2,500 and 4,000 reading words to pay a visit to the smallest, but terrifyingly necessary, room, and stories are written precisely to chill the bones as you wait for nature to make its call.

You open up the book, and one of the 32 tales skulking within its hellish pages chooses you…

It's too late to turn back now.
You are about to set foot into another dimension, so best watch out for that signpost up ahead...
You've just crossed over into... The Toilet Zone

Madam Gray's Creepshow

A veritable smorgasbord of twenty-three deliciously terrifying treats, each one simmered to blood-curdling perfection and seasoned with just the perfect amount of gallows humor.

From murder and madness to monsters and the downright macabre, the stories awaiting you within in this superlative anthology push the boundaries of horror to the next level... and way, way beyond!

Featuring stories by: Juliana Amir, Ross Baxter, Norris Black, Matt Bliss, Scot Carpenter, Max Carrey, Josh Darling, James Dorr, Gerri R. Gray, Chisto Healy, Carlton Herzog, Scott McGregor, J Louis Messina, Drew Nicks, Cooper O'Connor, Brett O'Reilly, Lisa Pais, Frederick Pangbourne, Clark Roberts, Rob Santana, Kelli A. Wilkins, and Scott Bryan Wilson.

Michaela Cane

A HellBound Books LLC
Publication

http://www.hellboundbookspublishing.com

Printed in the United States of America